BLOOD OF A GLADIATOR

Leonidas the Gladiator Mysteries, Book 1

ASHLEY GARDNER

JA/AG Publishing

Blood of a Gladiator

Cover design by Kim Killion

CHAPTER 1

Rome, AD 62

The roar from thousands of throats in the Circus Gai rose like a bulwark. I closed my eyes and leaned into the noise, as if the strength of the sound would hold up my exhausted body.

LEE-O-NI-DAS! LEE-O-NI-DAS!

They chanted my name as sand burned my bare feet, my skin not cooled by its rivers of sweat. Equally sodden was the loincloth that hung from my hips and the padded arm guard that reached from shoulder to wrist. My chest, back, and thighs were bared to the December sun, my head covered with a bronze helmet that trapped the heat. The grill of the helmet's eyeholes allowed me a slice of the arena and no more.

But I could hear, and the cries of the men and women who'd come to the Saturnalian games grew wilder by the moment.

In the embrace of my left arm was a gladiator, a *provacatur* called Regulus, the *secundus palus* of our *ludus*. I was *primus*. "Regulus" was no more his real name than "Leonidas the Spartan" was mine, and I counted Regulus a friend.

The point of my *secutor* rested on Regulus's throat. I waited, eyes closed, chest burning, for the signal that would either save Regulus's life or tell me to drive the sword home. I smelled blood—from the animals hunted earlier in the day, the humans who'd been executed for their crimes, to the gladiators in the last fights of the afternoon, some wounded, a few dead.

The crowd did not urge me to make the kill—*iugula!* Nor did they scream for mercy—*mitte!* They were simply shouting, bellowing their cheers for Leonidas, the greatest gladiator in the Empire.

In the box of the *princeps*, the curly-haired, lyre-playing, actor-in-training, mother-killing Nero basked in the entertainment. As he'd sponsored the games today, he would be the one to decide what should be done with Regulus.

"Do it!" Regulus's voice came from the level of my knees. "Kill me now. Before he chooses."

Regulus wanted to die. He'd told me this last night, at the meal given in the gladiators' honor. I'd eaten token pieces of meat, barely able to stomach them—I usually existed on lentils, barley, and the best greens money could buy. But those who attended the *cena libera* to watch our last supper wanted to see us eat flesh, like the beasts we were supposed to be.

Regulus had taken me aside after the meal. "This is my last fight, my friend." His brown eyes had held an emptiness I sometimes saw in my own. "If I draw you, I won't be easy on you, but I ask you to make the kill clean. Let me go with honor."

He was tired of the life. I understood. Choosing the day of his death would let him go in some kind of peace.

I'd nodded in agreement, hating the reluctance in my heart. Now, I should honor Regulus's request, but as my sword hovered at his throat, my hand shook and would not obey.

No more death. The words trickled through my head, as though whispered by someone outside me. A god perhaps, or the spirit of one of the creatures dead this day. I was finished with killing, finished with watching men I'd grown close to die on the sand.

Regulus was my only friend left. The others had either joined their ancestors, like Xerxes, who'd been closer than a brother, or were struggling to survive in some far corner of the empire. I barely knew the *tiros*, the raw young gladiators who gazed at me with both admiration and the determination to topple me.

One quick, smooth thrust would end Regulus's life. His blood would gush over my hand and splatter my bare feet, and Regulus would be gone, his body an empty shell.

"Now!" Regulus commanded. "Hurry, you bastard."

A faint sound came on my right. Half-blind in the helmet, I had to turn my entire head to find the source, but it was only the bulky figure of the referee in a plain tunic stepping up to us.

The man cleared his throat. "Caesar has made his decision."

I could not stop my glance at the box, but the *princeps* made no signal, only watched. I couldn't see him well at this distance, but I swore the man's face held a smile.

The referee pitched his voice to be heard through the noise. "His command is for *you* to decide, Leonidas. Kill Regulus or show him mercy for a good fight."

Rage washed over me. I was no murderer—I killed because I was ordered to. I was a weapon, pointed at another gladiator in the ring for entertainment, or at brigands when I was hired out for guard duty.

Regulus wanted me to make the kill. Nero, with his bloodthirsty reputation, probably did too.

No more death.

Regulus let out a breath of relief. "Make it quick, old friend."

The tip of my blade remained unmoving on his skin. I should want to help Regulus die as he wished, to free him from this life.

Then he'd be gone, added to a long line of men I'd known, liked, admired, fought with, drank with, celebrated with. Another loss after so much already.

"Leonidas?" Regulus sounded worried. "What are you waiting for?"

It would be so easy. One push, and Regulus would drop at my feet, dead. At rest with the gods.

I would remain, alone, undefeated, lying in my cell to stare at the ceiling and the crude erotic sketches Xerxes had made there as a joke.

I withdrew my sword from Regulus's throat. I held it high while the spectators screamed their anticipation of whatever it was I'd do.

I hauled Regulus to his feet. He was bleeding from stabs I'd landed on his gut and shoulders, but none were lethal. I too bled from his sword cuts on my chest, thighs, and stomach, but the wounds wouldn't kill me if they didn't take sick. We had the best *medicus* in the world to make sure they didn't.

"What are you doing?" Regulus bellowed at me, his cry lost in the din of the crowd.

"Making you a champion."

I took hold of Regulus's left fist and raised his hand high. I pulled off my helmet and turned us slowly around, forcing Regulus to move, displaying myself—the *primus palus*, the champion—and Regulus, my equal in the fight.

I spared him, I was telling them, because he'd fought valiantly and lost only by ill luck.

"You prick," Regulus snarled. "You bloody *prick*. I'll kill you for this."

His rage cut through the delirious screams of approval, but I didn't waver. Regulus might hate me, and he might kill me, but he'd be alive to do it.

The crowd wasn't finished, but I was. Still holding Regulus by the wrist, I started for the edge of the arena, and the opening to the cells. This was the last game of the day, and we'd have our wounds tended before returning to our *ludus* not far from here. There we'd celebrate victories and make toasts to the dead.

Regulus froze in sudden shock, pulling me to a halt next to him. “Hades.”

Three men strode toward us, two in tunics with cloaks, one in a toga. I didn’t recognize them—they hadn’t come to watch us train or negotiate our price for the games. The threesome proceeded solemnly, one toga-less man carrying an object on a square wooden platform.

I waited, wiping sweat from my shaved head, my heart hammering.

I’d seen a procession like this only twice before. First, the day I’d survived my virgin match, young and terrified, surprised to find myself alive at the end of it. The veteran I’d lost to had been honored thus. He’d beaten me by a slim chance, and my life had been spared because I’d fought skillfully and valiantly. The gladiator, who’d been about thirty summers, had wept when he’d beheld those heading for him.

The second time, the man they’d come for had been half-dead of his wounds, but still standing. He’d been carried from the ring, leaving me to become *primus palus* in his stead.

“I don’t believe it.” Regulus glared at the men and then me. “Why didn’t you kill me, you *stupid bastard*?”

I didn’t bother to speculate that the procession might be for Regulus. I knew it was not. They came for me.

They reached us, none of the three looking happy with their task. The lead man in the toga, whoever he was—senator, praetor—turned and faced the crowd. The one next to him, his tunic and cloak showing him to be of the Equestrian, or middle class, began a loud oration while the togaed man remained silent —a highborn gentleman would never waste his voice on the populous of Rome.

I paid little attention to the words that flowed around me, standard phrases praising the gods and the *princeps*.

At the end of the speech, the man who carried the platform lifted what was on it and held it out to me.

The crowd’s approval rose to blot out all other sound. The

noise snaked into my head, kicking up the pain already there. Regulus cursed again, long and hard, his hatred of me clear.

Paralyzed, I stared at the wooden sword, offered hilt first.

The *rudis*, in the shape of a gladiator's short sword. A reward for a life spent in the games. I recognized the letters of my own name carved into the blade, the only word I could read. The *rudis* meant release.

Freedom.

I couldn't move. The man with the sword glared at me impatiently, his distaste evident. He didn't like gladiators, his stance proclaimed, and he didn't want to touch one.

Many believed the blood of a gladiator cured illness. People had crowded today to the place where the dead fighters had been carried, jamming forward to dip cloths or even bare fingers into the gladiators' still-flowing blood. They'd take it home and store it for when it was needed.

This man didn't want anything to do with my blood, or me. But at last he had to shake my bronze sword from my hand, and shove the wooden one into my grip.

Regulus wrenched himself from me, not gently. The sting of his rage was a distant pain, receding behind the buzzing in my head.

I lifted my arm, the wooden sword strangely light after the heavy weapons I'd wielded this day. I heard my name pouring from the crowd, shouts of joy.

I should share the joy, but at the moment my arm ached and my fingers were lifeless. I turned in a circle, holding aloft the symbol of my freedom, without any sense that the freedom was real.

Nothing was real but the hot sand and my friend's hatred. The noise rolled on, but the heat and blinding light from the arena floor blotted out all but the bite of wood against my palm.

I DIDN'T REGAIN AWARENESS UNTIL I TRIED TO RETIRE TO MY cell in the *ludus* that night. I'd been tended to and bandaged by Nonus Marcianus, the talented *medicus* who kept the gladiators alive to fight another day. After that came wine in great quantities, bestowed upon us by our *lanista* to celebrate the survivors and my new-won freedom.

I drank and drank until I brought up the wine again, disgusting sweet grapes gone to death in the corner of the training grounds. My hand stayed around the sword as I vomited, I clenching the thing as though my freedom would evaporate if I let it go.

Once I was finished being sick, I decided I'd sleep first and then visit Lucia, on whose narrow pallet in the Subura I forgot about death, life, and pretty much everything else. I'd rest until I could better navigate the streets of Rome.

Regulus was in my cell, lying on my bed. He didn't bother to get up.

"Mine now, my friend," he said to the ceiling, eyeing Xerxes's drawings.

"Then where do I sleep?" My tongue was heavy, drink dulling my wits.

"No one cares." Regulus slung his arm over his eyes. "You don't belong here anymore. Go away, Leonidas."

I felt a presence behind me and turned to the hard bulk of Aemilianus, our *lanista*.

"Stay if you want." Aemil's scarred face, as usual, held little emotion. "I can use you to train the others."

"No." My answer was instant. "No more death."

Aemil simply looked at me. As *lanista*, he had to herd forty gladiators through training every day and keep them confined and out of trouble. If anyone wanted to hire us as fighters in the games, or for exhibitions, or as bodyguards, they went to Aemilianus. A former gladiator himself, he knew exactly how to tame us, and one of those ways was to rein in his own emotions.

"You'll be back," he predicted.

"No." I set my body stubbornly, at least as much as my drunken swaying allowed.

Regulus, on the pallet, lifted his arm. "He means, idiot, you either stay and work for him or get out. I'm *primus palus* now. I don't want you here, so go."

"I'm sorry." My tongue, not gifted at the best of times, could not explain why I'd spared him. But Regulus was alive. He had a chance. I didn't regret the decision.

"Hercules strike you down." Regulus slumped back to the bed, arm shielding his face again. "I hope he does."

Aemil continued to watch me from his mismatched Gallic eyes, one blue, one green-brown. "Are you staying?"

I shook my head. Regretted the shake, as the world spun.

"The gate is open for you." Aemil gave me a nod, a dismissal. "Godspeed, Leonidas."

I'd lived in this *ludus* for seven years, well beyond the sentence given to me for a crime everyone believed I'd committed. A life in the games was an almost certain death. Only the gods had assured it hadn't happened to me.

I stumbled out of the line of cells to the gate, the sword's wooden hilt driving slivers into my hand. I still couldn't release the thing.

The guard at the gate, a man I'd known for years, said goodbye to me as I walked out. The gate creaked closed behind me, the only noise in the silence.

Graffiti on the wall outside showed a crudely sketched figure with too-long legs and an optimistic phallus, my sword raised while I destroyed a *retiarius*. The letters beneath the figure spelled my name in crooked capitals.

The click of the gate held finality. Leonidas "The Spartan," was no longer a gladiator, adored by crowds in the arena.

I was free, homeless, and alone in the Roman night.

I WENT TO LUCIA. SHE LIVED IN A HOUSE WITH SEVEN OTHER ladies in the Subura, run by a lean woman called Floriana. They were used to me there, coming and going when I pleased, with Aemil's blessing.

Lucia had a soft body, a wide smile, and eyes that could be kind. Her hair was dyed red, which made it brittle, but some customers liked a woman to resemble the barbarians of the north.

I was tired, drunk, and bewildered. I said nothing at all, only took Lucia to her cubicle and drove into her like a man drowning.

I woke alone, with my hand fast around the wooden sword. I hadn't let it go, even when I'd coupled with Lucia on the low bed, using the thing as a brace on the floor.

Lucia was gone. Sunlight stabbed into my eyes from a crack in the wall—no windows for Lucia. My hand ached but I could not make myself open it and set the *rudis* aside.

"Leonidas."

The voice belonged to Floriana, scratchy and thin, like the rest of her. Very black hair curled around her sharp face.

"Bring me breakfast," I said. My head ached like fury, and I wasn't happy to be alone. Lucia usually stayed with me until I was ready to leave.

"Do you have the coin for it?" Floriana demanded. "And for Lucia?"

I rolled over. I wore nothing, but Floriana, who had seen any number of males with all sorts of bodies, didn't blink.

"Coin?" I asked muzzily.

Floriana folded her arms. "You're a freedman. Means your masters don't fund your meals and your women anymore. I need paying."

She had a point, one I hadn't given a thought to. Aemil had paid Floriana handsomely for me to march to Lucia whenever I wished. I always chose Lucia, she with her quick smile and skilled hands. I pretended to myself that she liked me, and I knew I liked her.

Now I'd have to pay Floriana and buy my own breakfast, but I hadn't the least idea what it would cost or where I'd get the money.

I lay back down and put a hand over my eyes. The sun was merciless and my head throbbed. "I'll find the coin."

The smooth end of a stick poked me in the ribs. I growled and lunged for it, but Floriana danced away.

"Out, Leonidas. I need the bed."

I sat up. Out where? I dimly remembered Regulus stealing my cell last night. Now Floriana was turning me out of this one.

So this was freedom. Nothing to eat, nowhere to sleep, and no money to buy even my basic needs.

Aemil had offered a solution to me. Remain at the *ludus*, train others to kill, fight a few exhibition matches to show off my prowess. That was what former gladiators did, Aemil among them. Perhaps one day I'd start my own *ludus*.

No more death.

I growled at Floriana. Any number of men, gladiators included, shrank from that growl, but not Floriana. She knew me too well.

Smothering a grunt of pain, I heaved myself from the bed. I towered over Floriana, filling the cell, but she never flinched.

"Man outside wants to speak to you," she said as I reached for my tunic. "Wants to hire you, perhaps. If he does, first person you pay with what he gives you is me."

I gave her a nod, finding this only fair. I couldn't imagine who waited for me, and I didn't much care. I wanted only to sleep and not wake for several days. I'd done that before, after horrific matches. When Xerxes had died, I'd not emerged for almost a month.

It was not easy to don my tunic while I still held the sword, but even now I could not make myself release it. My hand was cramped, locked around the wooden hilt.

I managed to slide on the tunic, the sword tearing the fabric. Floriana watched me with great amusement. I gave her another growl as I ducked out of the cell, nearly banging my head on the low lintel.

The house was quiet as I strode down its middle passage, making for the square of too-bright sunshine that awaited me at the end.

I emerged from the doorway into December coolness and the glare of light on pavement. The sun was well up, and even the high buildings that lined the street provided no shade.

A small man in a fine tunic waited outside. He had a neat, slim face, trimmed hair, and wore shoes rather than sandals, well-made pieces of leather that fit his feet exactly.

"Leonidas the Spartan." The greeting held a touch of derision.

I gave him a curt nod.

"The gods have smiled upon you," the man went on in the same tone. "Freedom and a benefactor. How fortunate you are."

"Benefactor ..." I said in confusion. I had no benefactor that I knew of.

"The person responsible for your freedom. He has followed your career, noting every victory, and decided you deserved to walk away from the games a champion. I have been sent to tell you that." The man eyed me with some disparagement.

"Who is he? Who are *you*?"

"I am called Hesiodos. You need to remember that name because I can give you no other."

Hesiodos carried the slightly pompous sneer many Greeks did—Rome was still rustic backwater to a man from mighty Athens.

Hesiodos wore the garb of a freedman, but I guessed he'd begun life as slave. His contemptuous regard told me he didn't want me making comparisons between us. We were both freedmen now, but I was *infamis*, the lowest of the low. All gladiators were, current and former.

When I said nothing, he continued, "What I mean is, I am forbidden to give you your benefactor's name."

I'd find this odd if I could think more clearly. Most Romans who assisted others wanted the fact shouted far and wide, so all would admire their generosity. The recipients of their charity would be obligated to the benefactor for life.

But perhaps the man—or woman—might not want it known that they'd raised a gladiator from his bondage. We were animals fighting for the pleasure of others. No pride in rescuing one. If it were a woman, she would definitely keep it a secret. Hesiodos had said "he," but he'd just admitted he was hiding the benefactor's identity.

I gave Hesiodos another nod to show I understood then jerked my thumb at the door behind me. "I owe Floriana a sestertius. Pay her, if you will."

Hesiodos didn't move. "You misunderstand. This person has not bestowed a legacy upon you. You will have to work for your pay, as any other freedman in this city. Your benefactor has provided you freedom, a place to live, and a slave to serve your needs."

This benefactor sounded less and less reasonable. "What place? And I don't need a slave."

"Your benefactor seems to think you do. Someone to keep an eye on you and report to me." He flicked his fingers toward a corner of a wall across the street.

A bundle of clothes that had crouched in a sliver of shade made its way across to us, stepping carefully in the damp street. It was a woman, swathed and cloaked like a patrician matron, but her plain palla and sandals told me she was a slave.

"This is Cassia," Hesiodos said. "She will not belong to you—she too is in debt to your benefactor. She will look after you, and provide you anything you need."

The woman reached us. Instead of bowing her head and cowering behind Hesiodos, she moved a fold of her palla and looked directly at me.

Brown eyes regarded me from the face of a young woman I would guess not far past her twentieth year.

I saw in those eyes, beneath the fear of being handed to a gladiator, a determination that blazed forth more potently than any I'd beheld in the brutal fighters I'd faced in the arena.

CHAPTER 2

I couldn't see much of Cassia other than the eyes that skewered me and a tendril of very black hair that leaked from beneath the cloth. She had a round face and light brown skin of the peoples of the eastern shores of the Mare Nostrum, but beyond that I could tell nothing about her.

Hesiodos observed this meeting without expression. "Cassia will lead the way to your lodgings. Settle in and wait for instructions."

"Instructions." I jerked my head to him. "For what?"

Hesiodos gave me an indifferent shrug. "Time will tell. Good day. Cassia knows how to send word to me."

Without a nod, gesture, or any other farewell, he turned on his well-fitted heel and walked away, quickly swallowed by the crowd of a Roman morning. My hand tightened around the *rudis* as I watched him go.

I looked at Cassia. Cassia looked at me.

Around us, Rome surged. Men and women, slave and free, strode the streets to the markets for vegetables and fish, and to the bakeries to take their grain to be made into bread.

The stream of humanity was too busy to push us aside and so

flowed around us as though we were two boulders on the pavement. Water trickled along edges of the street, Rome's fountains overflowing to drain to the sewers and the river.

I'd never had a slave before. The *ludus* used slaves to clean up after us and fetch and carry, but they belonged to Aemil, not the gladiators. Rumor had it that we practiced killing on unfortunate slaves, but that rumor was false. We were trained to fight other killers, to put on a show to please the multitude. The slaves were there to change our bedding and bring us food.

Cassia wasn't at all the sort of slave I was used to. The man at the *ludus* who'd cleaned my cell ducked his head as he dragged out my slop pail and did his best to remain invisible. The women at Floriana's were trained to please men bodily and made an art of enticement.

Cassia simply stared at me with the imperious gaze of a patrician's wife and made no move to do anything.

One of us should make a start, or we'd stand there all day. It was the end of the year, Saturnalia finishing yesterday, and the wind was sharp.

"Where are the lodgings?" I asked her abruptly.

Cassia parted her lips, revealing even teeth. "It is above a wine shop, at the base of the Quirinal." Her voice was young and soft, but with a cool patience, as though she was used to explaining the obvious to her inferiors.

The base of the Quirinal sounded promising, though not palatial. I'd visited villas and massive houses at the tops of Rome's hills, expected to perform for my supper—which could mean fighting another gladiator, or displaying my scars, or simply telling tales of my past bouts.

I wondered what sort of rooms my new benefactor could provide. If he'd obtained my freedom, he must have paid a handsome sum to take me from my contract with Aemil. That meant a wealthy man or, as I'd speculated, woman.

Cassia remained unmoving so I made a brief gesture with the sword in my sore hand. "Lead me."

Cassia studied me for another moment before she started off along the narrow street.

She wasn't used to walking, I could see. She stepped carefully in her sandals, moving warily from stone to stone, shying from the rivulets of water on the road's edges.

What sort of slave was uncomfortable with the pavement of Rome? Slaves hurried all around us to get breakfasts or run errands for their masters who lived in the houses, from the grand stand-alone *domii* to the meager rooms in the insulae. I strode along without hesitation in my thick-soled sandals.

I guessed, as we went along, that Cassia was used to riding in a litter. She might have been a highborn woman's slave—dress-maker or hairdresser or some such. I'd seen litters carried about by strapping men, the personal maids of the ladies crouched in a corner inside with their mistresses.

Or else Cassia was unused to Rome itself. Possibly both were true.

"Where do you come from?" I asked.

She glanced over her shoulder then resumed walking with her uncertain pace. "Campania."

Not the answer I expected. Campania was south of Rome, containing the seaside towns of Herculaneum and Baiae. Wealthy patricians built vast villas there, growing olives and grapes for expensive wines. Cassia, as I'd observed, had the complexion of a woman from Antioch or Cyprus. Her Roman Latin was perfect and unaccented—better than mine. I reasoned that she must have been born and raised in Campania, but her parents or grandparents had hailed from the eastern end of the sea.

We left the Subura, skirting the Forum of Augustus and the great wall he'd constructed to shield his grand space from the rest of Rome, and turned up the Vicus Longinus.

From here Cassia took a smaller street, this one filled with shops whose awnings were propped open. The vendors sold anything from oranges and lemons to fresh-pressed oil to the baskets to carry the comestibles in. We passed a *popina* doling out bread and pottage, and my stomach growled, accustomed to being filled soon after I woke.

I halted. "Is there food at our lodgings?"

Cassia realized after a few steps I wasn't following and turned back. "No, nothing to eat there."

"Then we should buy it." I waved vaguely at the vegetable seller whose counter was piled with fresh greens from the farms open to winter sunshine. "You can prepare me breakfast. And have some yourself," I added. It was not my way to starve a servant.

"Oh." Cassia paused in confusion. "I don't cook."

I blinked at her. "No?"

"No."

We regarded each other a few moments. I noted that her nose wasn't perfectly straight.

"Maybe you didn't cook for your mistress," I ventured. "But you belong to me now. I need meals, not my hair dressed." I touched my head, close-shaved to keep me from bothering with vermin or having my hair grabbed in a bout.

I had thought to make her laugh, but she studied me in all seriousness. "I mean I don't know how to cook. Or dress hair."

My puzzlement grew. "Never mind. We can eat what the *popina* sells."

Cassia glanced, mystified, at the eating shop, with its customers leaning on the stone counter, the man behind it ladling out grainy soup from copper bowls sunk into that counter, kept hot by pots of burning wood beneath them.

"Do you have coin?" I prompted. "To buy us something?"

Her brow furrowed. "Any coin is in our lodgings. And there is not much of it."

I was growing impatient with this single-minded personage. I'd taken my meals outside the *ludus* plenty of times when I'd done guarding jobs. I'd preferred to eat at the *ludus*, because our food was much better, but I sometimes had no choice.

"Then we will go to our rooms, and decide what to do. You can sweep up and set the table, or whatever it is a person does in a house."

"I don't know much about cleaning either."

I foresaw a future where I took out the slop buckets and fetched water while this swathed creature reclined on a dining couch, munching grapes while she observed my labors.

"I thought you were *my* servant," I said. "What sort of slave are you, if you can't cook, clean, or fetch and carry?"

A courtesan, was the answer. One to keep the gladiator tamed while his benefactor decided what to do with my obligation to him.

Cassia lifted her chin. "I am a scribe."

Her answer surprised me to silence. A scribe? The gods must be laughing at me. Leonidas, the champion of the empire, left alone on the streets with no money and no food, and the only one sent to assist him was an unworldly scribe.

My hand throbbed where it clutched the sword. Cassia had turned away and continued along the quiet street as I stared in disbelief.

"A scribe?" The words scraped out of me as I strode after her. "Why do I need a *scribe*?"

Cassia halted at a plain door next to a shop whose customers lined up to take away amphoras of wine. She opened the door to reveal a stone staircase that rose into shadows.

She began to ascend, but I put my hand on her shoulder and drew her back, not wanting her to walk alone into who knew what kind of rooms with who knew what kind of person waiting. Rome was not a safe place.

Cassia skittered from my touch like a bug from a boot, eyes enormous. While she hugged the wall, trying to catch her breath, I went past her and climbed the stairs.

Above I found a single, L-shaped room that stretched from the front of the building to the back, with a stone pallet built into a wall under a window. The shorter end of the L opened onto the roof of the wine shop below, wooden shutters leaning against the wall to close off the balcony in the evening.

The room held a table and two rough-hewn stools. A shelf, empty, had been fastened to one wall, but looked as though it would tumble down from any heavy tread on the stairs. That was all.

Cassia entered behind me, her footsteps light. From somewhere within the folds of her robes, she retrieved a wax tablet, the kind with wooden covers that folded in two, protecting the wax inside.

She removed a stylus that had been tucked inside the tablet and made a notation. As I could read no words, I had no idea what it said.

"A scribe does more than write letters." Cassia's voice was faint, but she spoke as one bent on explaining. "I can keep records, read and negotiate contracts, balance books and make sure all moneys owed are paid as well as all moneys owed to you."

I had no money at all. Unlike some fighters, I had not stashed away my portion of prize winnings or fees earned from guarding to buy my freedom. My price was so high I'd known there was no point. I used the winnings to enjoy myself instead, staving off boredom until I had to fight for my life once more.

"No moneys are owed to me," I said.

Cassia studied her tablet. "Your benefactor requests that you seek employment in order to feed yourself and pay the rent on this apartment. What little coin has been left for meals will only last the day, if that."

A very odd sort of benefactor then.

I was growing weary, first from the excess of drinking and debauchery last night, and then from finding my circumstances so changed. I needed to lie on my back for a time, to think, to sleep. I suppressed a yawn.

"Who *is* our benefactor?" I asked.

"I don't know." When I took a step toward her, Cassia raised a hand in alarm. "I truly do not. Hesiodos would not tell me."

I continued past her and peered through the opening to the roof. Our view showed me the narrow street as it spilled down the hill into the main thoroughfare beyond.

"So I am to live here, find my own employment, pay the rent, and wait for instruction?"

"Yes." Cassia sounded relieved I'd grasped it all.

It was strange, but by no means the most strange thing people had hired me to do.

I supposed I could walk out the door, tramp through the streets of Rome, and turn my back on this benefactor. I was a freedman now ... I looked at the wooden sword adhered to my hand.

Or was I?

"Was my freedom registered?" One had to go to the Forum Romanum when one freed a slave, to have it officially recorded that the slave was free.

"Hesiodos said so."

Cassia began to unwind her palla. Out came more things as she unwrapped herself—a small leather case, a few scrolls, a bottle of ink and a pen. She laid them out in a neat row on the table.

"Do you have dinner and wine in there too?" I asked her.

Cassia folded her palla and hung it from a peg near the door without bothering to answer. She opened the case on the table, lifted a small piece of papyrus from it, and held it up to read. "This declares the man known as Leonidas the Spartan, gladiator, is a freedman of Rome." She glanced at me over the paper. "You are not from Sparta," she observed. "Or anywhere Greek."

"I don't know where I come from. Aemil thought up that name."

"What is your real name?" Cassia asked with the first glimmer of curiosity I'd seen in her.

"I forgot that long ago. I'm Leonidas now." I yawned again, this time not suppressing it. "I will sleep." I moved toward the stone pallet, reflecting I had no blankets or mattress, but I'd slept on worse.

"With the *rudis*?"

I stared down at the sword, my fingers stiff around the hilt. I tried to open my hand, but could not.

"It seems so."

Cassia walked to me, footfalls soft. "Give it to me, and I will put it somewhere safe."

I swallowed. "I can't."

For the first time, the fear left her. "Why not?"

I raised my hand, the sword coming with it. "I try, but I cannot let go. I slept with it last night, and my hand is now too cramped to open."

"Hmm." She peered at my swollen knuckles, dark from the sun and crossed with scars and fresh scabs from yesterday's fight.

Cassia reached out a tentative finger and touched my hand. She did it rapidly, a quick brush, as though expecting a jolt to knock her across the room.

When I did nothing but stand in place, she touched me again, less hesitantly. "I will unbend your fingers."

I did not think she could. My strength would overwhelm hers without effort, and if I could not force my hand open, I doubted she'd be able to.

Cassia rested her hand over mine, but instead of pulling at my fingers, she rubbed.

The softness of her touch surprised me. I'd never had anyone touch me like this—I'd been massaged by massive men digging soreness out of my muscles, or women bringing me to a cockstand, but never a light caress that tingled warmth across my skin.

Slowly, slowly, my fingers relaxed, and then they loosened. My thumb unlocked, and with it, my death grip on the sword.

As soon as my hand went slack, Cassia slid the hilt out of my grasp.

Ice cold fear hit me. I started to lunge for the sword, but Cassia had already turned away, and I brushed empty air.

"I will put it here." Cassia laid the sword on the hanging shelf. "You can reach it at any time."

She was humoring me, but I experienced a profound sense of relief. The *rudis* was where I could touch it, and remind myself what it meant.

Cassia came back to me, her hands clasped over her long linen stolla. "What ..." The word trailed off, and she swallowed. "What do you wish from me?"

She whispered the question, and I heard, through my haze, her fear return. Fear that went to the bone. I knew such fear, had experienced it myself.

I took the final steps to the pallet and nearly fell onto it. I turned my head so I could look at her with a single open eye. "Do you want dinner?" It was well past time for breakfast.

Cassia had gone wan, but she gave me a faint nod.

"Fetch it from the *popina* we passed," I ordered. "Bring me bread if there is any."

Cassia remained frozen in place, her very dark hair falling in curls about her face. She was pretty, in a way, in spite of her crooked nose and thin lips.

That was the last thought I had before oblivion took me.

I DREAMED. REGULUS FOUGHT ME, RAGE IN HIS EYES. MY sword and arm guard were gone, and his blade jabbed and jabbed at me until I bled from a hundred holes.

His sword rose, ready to dive straight into my eye.

I roared up to meet him, grabbing the descending arm in a merciless grip ...

And found myself looking into the terrified brown eyes of Cassia.

CHAPTER 3

I released Cassia in an instant. In another second, I'd have broken her wrist.

"Dreaming," I said as I sat up, catching my breath. "Never reach for me when I'm asleep. Floriana uses a stick."

"Floriana?"

"Woman of the house where I slept last night." I gestured vaguely, reminding Cassia of where she'd met me this morning.

If it was still *this* morning. The sun slanted into the room, partially blocked by buildings around us. I had no idea of the time or if this was even the same day.

"It is the tenth hour." Cassia remained very still, out of my reach. "You've slept a long time. I brought food for you."

I rolled up from the pallet, my tunic musty. I needed to bathe. I was also hungry. "Bread?" I recalled asking her to fetch that.

Cassia had backed away when I'd risen, and now she moved to the table. I stumbled after her in bare feet, too hungry to bother with sandals.

The table was now lengthwise near the open door to the

makeshift balcony. One stool rested on the side of the table, and the other had been tucked into the corner.

Covered bowls and several baskets had been neatly placed on the table, along with an eating bowl and a spoon. I lifted the cloth from one basket and found a loaf of the round Roman bread we consumed daily. The other basket held olives, plump and shining.

The covered bowls contained lentil stew and another stew with meat in it. The smallest pot held a smelly, fishy concoction called garum.

I immediately dished out the lentils and tore off a hunk of bread, sitting down to enjoy my feast. A handful of olives went into my mouth. I didn't touch the meat dish or the garum.

"Are you not eating?" I asked once I'd swallowed a few spoonfuls.

Cassia had perched on the stool in the corner, hands in her lap. "You will allow me to eat?"

"Why would I not allow you to eat?" I said around my next mouthful. "If you eat, you stay alive. Besides, you carried all this back. You must be hungry."

Cassia rose and slid her stool inch by inch closer to the table. She removed a smaller eating bowl and spoon from a sack that had been behind the table and carefully set the bowl in the exact center of her side.

As I continued to inhale the lentil soup, which was decent if not the best I'd ever had, she delicately ladled out a portion of the meat stew.

"Eat all of that if you like," I said.

The ladle hesitated. "There is enough for both of us."

I shook my head. "I don't eat much meat. I'll have this." I lifted my bowl to my mouth, drained the liquid, and spooned in more of the lentils.

Neither of us touched the garum.

"Eat that too," I said, pointing to it. "I won't."

Cassia dipped a minuscule portion of bread into her meat soup. "No, thank you. I dislike garum."

Most Romans loved the stuff and ate it by the bucketful. I was considered odd for not doing so.

"I don't like it either." I tore off a huge hunk of bread. "It's disgusting."

Something glinted in Cassia's gaze. "I rather loathe it, in fact."

"I more than loathe it. I think it should be buried in a field and then the field burned."

We both eyed the pot.

"I bought it because I thought you'd eat like a Roman." She studied the innocent round-lidded pot for a moment. "What shall we do with it?"

"Throw it into a sewer," I grunted. "No one will notice."

A tiny smile touched Cassia's mouth, transforming her from frightened rabbit to human being. "It shall be done."

I pictured it—in the dark of the night, a heavily cloaked woman tiptoeing through the cart-laden streets with the pot of garum under her arm, furtively glancing about before she shoved it through a hole in the pavement to the sewers beneath us. For the first time in a long while, I wanted to laugh.

"How did you pay for all this?" I asked. "I thought we had little money."

Cassia pushed aside her half-eaten stew and opened a tablet, revealing rows of scratches in the wax. "The landlord of the tavern and also the baker gave the food to me with the understanding that we will pay for a ten-night's worth of meals at the end of these coming ten days. Next time, we will pay ahead and have whatever we wish until our credit comes to an end."

"Pay with what?" Any time I'd been out on my own and hungry, I'd bought bread or a salad with the few coins in my belt pouch. If I had no coins, I simply stayed hungry until I returned to the *ludus*.

"The money you will make as a guard, or teaching others to fight, or whatever it is you do."

"No one has hired me," I pointed out.

"Not yet."

I lifted my bowl and spooned the remainder of the lentils into my mouth. I chewed noisily and swallowed, then wiped out the bowl with the last of the bread. "Aemil always made arrangements with people and then told me to go do the job."

"Because you were a slave. Now you're a freedman. You find your own work."

I hadn't the least idea how. "Should I stand in the street until someone asks me to do something? I think they will mostly tell me, loudly, to get out of the way."

Cassia took up her stylus. "I admit to you, I do not know much about the ways of the city. I lived in my mistress's villa, which was far out in the country, and went into Neapolis only occasionally. A lovely city. Nothing like Rome. Neapolis is a very old town, settled by Greeks long ago. Like Herculaneum."

I'd been to both places when hired out for games, but I remembered nothing remarkable about either.

"I could ask Aemil." I did not want to go back to the *ludus*, my hand out, when I'd snarled at Aemil that I'd never return. He'd informed me with confidence that I would.

Cassia must have seen my reluctance, because she said quickly, "I will find out."

I studied her, a neat young woman with her hair combed into a tidy coil, her fingernails clean and pared. I'd already dropped broth onto my tunic while hers was spotless. I could not imagine this dainty morsel striding out finding work for a gladiator.

"How?"

"The family I worked for had many connections in Rome. Those people would come to Campania, or, rarely we would travel here. I know the slaves and freedmen and freedwomen who work in their houses. If a patrician needs a bodyguard, he will send a slave out to the Forum to look about and employ one for him. I will go to the Forum and see who I find there. I am bound to recognize someone, and if their masters do not need your services, they might point me to one who does."

I supposed her reasoning logical. I'd never had to think about such things before. I'd only *done* for so long, that I knew nothing else.

"In the morning, then." I flexed my empty hand and glanced quickly at the wooden sword on the shelf, as though reassuring myself it was still there.

She shook her head. "This afternoon. Those left still looking to hire a guard will be growing worried and won't wish to return home until they've fulfilled their commission. I will likely be able to fetch a better fee than if I wait until morning."

More things I'd not thought of. "Be in before dark. The streets of Rome at night are not safe."

Cassia shivered, but her determination to do as she outlined did not dim.

With the darkness would come cold. We'd want blankets.

"You will need a place to sleep," I observed.

I cast my gaze along the empty floor, wondering where that would be. When Cassia didn't answer, I lifted my head.

She watched me, the trepidation in her eyes, which had subsided over the meal, returning.

She expected me to order her to sleep with me, I realized. Or at least pleasure me until I was tired of it, when she'd curl up on the floor until I wanted her again. She expected it, and I could clearly see the thought terrified her.

The women I'd known in my short life had wanted only one thing from me. Some enjoyed it, some didn't, but they all wanted a gladiator, or the coin for pleasuring one. Others, like Floriana, wanted not only the money for me employing Lucia's services, but for the status of having such a famous gladiator prefer her house.

If I touched Cassia, she might fall to the floor in a swoon. Or perhaps die altogether.

Cassia belonged to the sort of people removed from the rest of us, who knew about words, and writing, and the mysteries inside books. This was not a woman trained to sate the primal needs of a fighting man, and I understood that.

"There is room for another bed there." I pointed at the wall near the door, which would be shielded from the window by the table. "We will find one tomorrow. We'll just have to be cold tonight."

"I brought blankets," Cassia said in a faint voice, motioning to a pile in the shadows.

Of course she had. I would need to find work quickly so we could pay for all this.

"I don't need you in my bed," I said bluntly, trying to put her at ease. "I have Lucia."

Her brows quirked. "Lucia?"

"She is one of Floriana's women." I rose, glancing around for my sandals which I found placed neatly by the front door. "I will go to her. You can sleep on my pallet and use the blankets."

Now Cassia stared at me in shock. She'd probably slept on the floor her entire life, even if scribes in large houses enjoyed slightly better accommodations than other slaves.

Before she could object, argue, explain, or ask more questions, I stepped into my sandals and left.

Floriana was still expecting me to pay her. I would have Cassia make a note of it.

Floriana did not want to let me in. She was more interested in coin than in talk of a benefactor, but Lucia came to my aid, and at last, after some heated argument between the two of them, Floriana admitted me.

Lucia was not beautiful, but she had a sturdiness about her, a ready laugh, and skill at putting me at ease. I never spoke much with her—no pouring out the secrets of my life and my world.

Most of the time, I didn't want to talk about my days at all, which were either tedious or deadly. I preferred to listen to Lucia's funny stories about men who came to Floriana's, and the women who did as well, in heavy disguise. Couldn't let it get about that a senator's wife had a favorite at Floriana's in the Subura.

I had new topics for conversation tonight—my new-won freedom, Cassia—but I said little beyond the bare facts. Lucia tried to pry out of me who my benefactor was, but as I didn't know, I couldn't enlighten her. I assumed Floriana had told her to find out that information. Lucia cared little about such things.

I was too tired to do much of anything with Lucia except enjoy sleeping in her warmth. I felt her try to wake me up a time or two as I drowsed, before she gave up.

I slept.

In my dreams I pictured Cassia, curled up alone on my pallet, snuggled into the blankets she'd procured. She was vulnerable in the apartment by herself. The door at the bottom of the stairs had a bolt, yes, but any good thief could force it.

I should not have left her there alone. In my dreams I saw a thief armed with a cudgel bursting into our rooms, delighted to find Cassia ready for his taking. Cassia jerked out of sleep, screaming my name, as the man advanced on her.

I started up in alarm to find myself still in Lucia's bed, in daylight. Sunshine poured through the same crack in the wall, and I rolled over, sore and irritated.

Lucia was once more gone. I reached for my tunic and pulled it on, deciding I'd visit a bathhouse. The public baths were the cheapest but a long walk from Floriana's. The nearby, smaller baths charged fees I could not pay today. I'd always strode in to any bathhouse I liked, but now Aemil wouldn't send a slave hurrying behind me to pay. I might persuade them to let me in so they could say I favored them, but I wasn't certain of my welcome. I was *primus palus* no longer.

Voices came to me, agitated and rushed, as I tied on my

sandals. It was not unusual for Floriana to have trouble with a disgruntled customer or a vigile who tried to procure services in exchange for keeping their building safe from fire.

I'd thrown more than one belligerent man out of Floriana's house. Some seemed to think that Floriana's ladies could be treated like unwanted curs. One look at me lumbering at them taught these gentlemen to flee.

I stepped out of Lucia's cubicle to find her hurrying toward me, face strained. Black tears from the cosmetics she adorned herself with trickled down her cheeks, and the red ochre on her lips stained the corners of her mouth.

"Leonidas, thank the gods. It's Floriana. She's powerfully ill."

Floriana, though reedy, was the most robust of women. However, anyone could eat tainted food and have a bad night, even die from it, and fevers could take one suddenly.

Lucia grabbed my hand and dragged me deeper into the house. The women, groggy and hungover, huddled outside the room at the far end of the corridor, their worry filling me with disquiet.

When Lucia flung back the curtain that hid Floriana's sleeping chamber, I recoiled from the stench that flowed out. I had to swallow bile before I could peer inside.

Floriana's cell contained a small square window set high on the wall. The shutter was closed, and I reached above her bed to pull it open.

The window looked out to the back of the building behind this one, but enough morning sunlight trickled in to reveal Floriana lying on her pallet, her knees drawn to her chest. A black, many-curled wig perched on a peg above her bed, and Floriana's own hair, gray and thin, straggled across her scalp.

She wheezed feebly, her mouth working as she tried to gulp air. Her lips were purple, with a touch of foam in their corners.

I straightened abruptly, nearly ramming into the women who crowded behind me.

"She's been poisoned," I snapped. "Lucia, stay with her. Keep her warm and try to get her to vomit."

I turned on my heel and pushed my way through the ladies, who scattered from me like a flock of birds.

"Where are you going?" Lucia demanded.

"To fetch a medic."

I knew only one who could save Floriana's life. I plunged out into the bright Roman daylight, marching resolutely for the Tiber.

CHAPTER 4

It was not easy to navigate the thronged streets between the Subura and the bridges that crossed the river. Not only did I have to push through the crowd, but as often happened when I walked through Rome, I drew a band of followers. All recognized a gladiator, and most recognized me in particular.

I might now be, by law, just another nobody, but I was still Leonidas, the man thousands of people had cheered for until their throats were hoarse. I'd been their champion.

Now they followed me, calling my name, asking me to scratch my letters onto their souvenirs—cups, pictures, an oil lamp with a crude statue of a fighting gladiator on it.

I evaded them as best I could, but even my snarls to get out of my way were received with delight. They wanted me to be the ferocious fighter they saw in the games.

I didn't have time for the attention today. Floriana was dying, and the only man who could save her would be at the *ludus*, patching up the gladiators who'd survived the Saturnalian games.

I avoided the imperial fora and the crowds there, skirted the Theatre of Marcellus, and crossed the Campus Flaminius to the

Tiber. I headed north to the Pons Agrippae, taking it over the river to the Transtiberium and so to Aemil's *ludus*.

The *ludus* consisted of a large rectangular open area for training, surrounded on four sides by a two-floored building that housed the gladiators, trainers, slaves, and equipment.

Did I feel a throb of fondness when I looked upon the gate, a wistfulness that I would not be exercising, dining, and bedding down with my fellow gladiators?

I had no idea what I felt, and I was not a man to examine his emotions. At the moment, I was too worried about Floriana to be nostalgic.

The gate guard straightened as I came toward him, followed by a few of my devotees. He stared at me in surprise then shouted to a boy who raked the practice ring to run for Aemil.

"No," I yelled after him. "I want Marcianus."

The guard opened the gate, closing it quickly as the devotees who'd followed me surged forward. He'd done this for me many a day.

"Did you come to be a trainer?" the guard asked. He liked me, possibly because I'd often tipped him to let me in or out after curfew.

I didn't bother to answer. Aemil headed for me in his loping trot, the sun glinting on his close-cropped, light-brown hair. He moved swiftly for a man who'd retired from his fighting days ten years ago. Ruthless, he'd been. A gladiator drawing Aemil as an opponent made his peace with the gods beforehand.

"Only a day." Aemil peered at me smugly. He was a Gaul, captured in battle as a child, but now as Roman in attitude as any consul. "Only a day, and you rush back home."

"I've come for Marcianus. A woman is ill. I need him."

"Woman?" He scowled. "What woman?"

"Floriana." I was too hurried to explain, but Aemil knew.

"You want to waste Nonus Marcianus on a whore?" Aemil's eyes widened in incredulity. "He's busy."

Gladiators were more valuable, he meant. We commanded a

high price, while prostitutes could be found on every street for an *as*.

Aemil had no intention of sending for Marcianus, I could see. He'd only come to crow that I'd returned to beg him for employment.

Fortunately, the boy I'd called out to had heard me and was now trotting from the cells, with the lanky *medicus* behind him.

Nonus Marcianus had gained a reputation for being able to save even the most injured gladiator, alternately cajoling and cursing said gladiator to hold still and let him work. Aemil valued the man, because he couldn't afford to lose many fighters. The idea that all gladiators battled to the death in every match was a myth. A *lanista* put years, dedication, and money into training a gladiator for the games. Aemil could ask any price he wanted for us, because he had Marcianus to keep us whole as long as possible.

Marcianus had brown hair and a nose too large for his face. He appeared amiable and even simple, but he was the most capable man I knew.

"You seem to be whole." Marcianus looked me up and down when he reached me. "Why the commotion?"

I hastily explained, words tumbling. Aemil's sour expression deepened. "She's already dead then." He dismissed Floriana with a wave. "No one survives poison."

"Not necessarily," Marcianus said. "Let me get my things."

Aemil planted himself in front of the *medicus*. "You're working on *my* men. The whore is beyond saving."

"I've set all the bones I need to and closed the worst of the wounds. I have a few moments to spare. I fear the poor lady does not."

Aemil was large and fearsome. Marcianus, who'd begun life in an Equestrian family, was small-boned and pale from sitting indoors peering at books. However, it was Aemil who grunted and backed down.

"Go on," he grumbled. "I know you'll have your way."

Marcianus immediately left us and disappeared into the cells. He returned in a moment carrying a cloth sack. "We should run."

Without waiting for my answer, he jogged past me to the gate and out.

By the time we reached the Subura, interested passersby had gathered around Floriana's house. I pressed through, clearing a path for Marcianus.

A few vigiles lurked on the street, looking on in case the crowd turned into a mob. Vigiles worked mostly at night, watching out for fires, but part of their job was to keep order at any time. A man I recognized as an urban cohort, who performed the same function during the daylight hours, hovered on the opposite side of the gathering, eyeing the vigiles in mistrust.

Neither the vigiles or the urban cohort would even look at the Praetorian Guard who'd stopped to watch. The Praetorian must have been passing on another errand, because those elite fighting men kept themselves to the Palatine or their training field in the Campus Martius.

Lucia hurried out to meet me, parting the onlookers to tug me inside. Marcianus slipped in behind me.

"Has she died?" Marcianus asked in clipped tones.

"No, but she's powerful sick." Anguish rang in Lucia's voice. The other ladies hovered, fearful. Floriana wasn't always a kind mistress, but if she died, the women would be out on the streets.

Marcianus made his way to the small room at the end of the hall. I heard a whispered groan as Floriana struggled to live.

I pulled Lucia to my side. "Leave him to it."

Marcianus could make healing concoctions I'd never heard of and knew how to stitch wounds with fine thread so that they closed and mended. Some believed he used magic to assist him, but Marcianus believed in little but what his own experience told him. I had faith in his skill.

He knelt by Floriana's pallet, never minding the filth pooled there. I do not know what he assessed, but he reached quickly into his bag and instructed that someone bring him a mortar and pestle.

The youngest lady in the house, Marcia, peeled from the group to obey. Marcianus never snapped, never commanded. He simply asked in his reasonable voice, and others hurried to do as he wished.

"Leonidas," he said in the same quiet tone.

I knew what he meant. "Out," I said sternly to the hovering women. He needed room to work.

Marcia hurried back with the mortar and pestle. Marcianus dropped something white and hard into the pot and told Marcia to begin grinding. The other women lingered, either from concern or curiosity, but I mercilessly herded them down the hall and out of the house.

Lucia hung on to me as we emerged into the sunshine. Her brown eyes were filled with fear under her henna-dyed hair.

"If she dies ..." Her words held agitation.

"I'll look after you."

Annoyance drifted over Lucia's worry. "How? I am fond of you, Leonidas, but you are a moneyless freedman."

"I have a benefactor now," I reminded her.

"One who has given you no means to sustain yourself. What sort of benefactor is that?"

I couldn't answer. I did not understand my situation, but for now it was enough that I did not have to sleep in the streets.

"You will have a place to stay, in any case," I promised.

"You had better ask your slave if she is willing to wait on a woman like me. She sounds hoity-toity."

I thought about how cleverly Cassia had made certain there was plenty of food, drink, and warm blankets for sleeping when I hadn't enough money to cover the costs. For a woman who'd lived a sheltered life, Cassia had coerced the hard-bitten shopkeepers of Rome to do what she wished.

I wasn't certain what she'd make of Lucia. But Cassia belonged to me, and should obey my wishes ... shouldn't she?

I had no idea what to do with a slave. I wasn't the commanding sort, and Cassia so far had not waited for instructions from me.

The hordes outside the brothel hadn't thinned. It was the third hour on this winter day, the sun well up, and the streets were full. Onlookers created a jam on the road, which led from the Esquiline Hill to the heart of the city. Those who needed to pass shouted and cursed. Others stopped to ask what had happened and lingered in curiosity. Romans ever sought entertainment.

The vigiles and the cohort tried to get people to move on, but with little success against the thick-bodied costermongers and determined matrons who watched from behind folds of embroidered pallas.

The Praetorian Guard looked on with disdain at the vigiles' efforts and made no move to help. He caught my eye, frowned a moment, as though wondering what a gladiator was doing here, then his gaze slid past me.

I spied another figure in the crowd. A small woman, nearly hidden in her plain cloak, peered around the crush to see what I'd gotten myself into.

I wondered how Cassia had known to come here, but news of a commotion and possible poisoning would travel quickly. She might have been out and followed the crowd, or overheard people speaking of it in the wine shop beneath us—she'd known I'd gone to Floriana's and could easily ask the way.

Cassia made no move to approach me, simply watched, dark eyes taking in everything.

Time at last dispersed the throng. As the hour passed, with no word from inside the house, the spectators grew bored or realized they had better finish with whatever task they'd been sent on, and began to drift away. Lucia ducked inside, I unable to stop her. The other ladies sat in the shade by the wall, arms around knees, heads back, dozing. The day warmed, though it was a far cry from the heavy heat of summer.

By the time Marcianus emerged, only a handful of people remained, including the cohort and the Praetorian. The vigiles had given up and gone home, their night shift long finished.

"She will live," Marcianus announced to me. The ladies, sighing with relief, climbed to their feet and trickled back inside, ready for sleep.

Marcia had followed Marcianus out, carrying his bag and watching him with a sort of reverence.

"She will need care," Marcianus told her. Marcia's carefully curled black hair hung lank, her face creased with weariness, but she nodded fervently, eager to help. "She must drink the concoction I mixed and eat nothing more until I see her again tomorrow."

Marcia listened to his instructions attentively. I didn't think Marcia was more than sixteen summers, but she was brighter than most.

Marcianus turned to me. "Floriana ate the leaves of rhubarb, from what I can tell. The stems have medicinal use, but the leaves are deadly poisonous. Thankfully, it's a slow poison, which was why I could save her." He frowned at Marcia. "Did she not know? Some make a salad of any green they can find."

Marcia shook her head. "We had no salad yesterday. Or any rhubarb in the house either. We all ate the same—lentils and bread."

"Are you certain? She could have nipped out and bought some for herself."

"Fairly certain. I can find out." Marcia ducked swiftly inside.

Cassia moved nearer to us. She had a tablet open and made quick, precise marks in it. Marcianus noted her, his gaze growing curious.

"This is Cassia," I said. "She works for me now."

Cassia adjusted her palla to cover most of her face and bowed her head in deferential greeting. She studied Marcianus as he blinked in surprise at my announcement, then she began speaking to him. In Greek.

Marcianus's surprise turned to astonishment, then delight. He answered her, and the two began a conversation, both behaving with cordiality, but what they said, I had no idea.

Marcia returned, breathless and flushed. "No salad of any kind. As I said, lentils and bread."

Cassia made a note. "What time did the symptoms occur?" she asked Marcia.

Marcia stared at her and addressed her answer to Marcianus. "We found her like that this morning, in the first hour. Lucia was shouting."

Marcianus nodded, and Cassia's stylus moved across the wax.

"May I see your notes?" Marcianus asked, and Cassia handed him the tablet. He glanced over the scratches in approval. "Very succinct."

"Thank you." Cassia took the tablet as he held it out to her. "I find it helpful to keep a record of events."

Marcia and I exchanged a baffled glance.

"If anything changes, send for me," Marcianus said to Marcia. "My house is near the fountain of the three fishes on the Aventine."

"Yes, sir."

Marcianus had a way of commanding instant respect. His presence wasn't powerful or dominating, but men and women alike fell all over themselves to do what he asked.

He began to walk away, but Cassia called after him, "Your fee, sir?"

Marcianus turned back with a start. He quickly assessed the house with its weary, mussed ladies, me still in the tunic of a slave, Cassia and her plain draperies, stylus hovering.

"One *as*," he said. "Payable whenever it can be done."

Cassia's stylus moved. Marcia slid back into the house with

the last of the ladies. Marcianus gave us a gesture of farewell and strode down the street.

The spectacle over, the lingerers went about their business, ready for the next entertainment they might stumble upon.

"He has much kindness," Cassia observed as we watched Marcianus go, his lanky body jerking, until he faded into the crowd.

"I would be dead three times over if not for him." He'd patched up wounds Aemil had been certain would kill me.

"Astute as well. He knows they can't pay much but would be insulted to receive charity."

"What were the two of you speaking of?" I asked. "I don't understand Greek."

Cassia flushed. "He asked where I came from and why I am assisting you. About my family and background. He was born in Athens, he said, though his parents were from Rome. He knows that part of the world better than this. He said he studied medicine in Athens and Ephesus." She sounded impressed.

They'd exchanged much information. I hadn't known this about Marcianus, and I still knew little about Cassia.

She tucked away her stylus and tablet and gazed at me with a critical eye. "You will need a barber. And a new tunic."

"Later." Now I wanted to sleep.

"We cannot wait," she said. "You might have a job, but you must present yourself at a patrician's house, and you will need to be shaved and in clean clothes for that."

CHAPTER 5

"Job?" I asked in surprise. Cassia had said she'd begin her search for one last night, but I hadn't thought she'd find one so quickly. "Doing what? For who?"

"A retired senator on the Esquiline. We must hurry, or he will cease admitting clients for the day, and we'll have to wait until morning. As that will be another day of expenses, I suggest we meet with him as quickly as we can."

Cassia's urgency was acute. I'd be happy to sleep the day and night away—I could not run up expenses if I ate and drank nothing.

I complied because I was curious about who she expected me to work for and what I'd be doing.

I led Cassia to a nearby barber's shop and ducked into the tiny interior. Cassia informed me she had further errands, and I watched her go in her uncertain gait, her head bent as she tried to avoid others in her path.

"Leonidas!" The greeting surged at me from the barber, Paulinus, whose voice filled the small room. Several men who occupied a bench outside, awaiting their turn under the razor, also hailed me. The man on a stool being scraped by the barber sent me a grin.

I returned the greetings and took my place on the end of the bench. Because the entire shop's front opened to the street, the bench flowed halfway inside.

"Freedman," Paulinus went on in his ear-splitting voice. He reveled in gossip, and repeated it as loudly and as often as he could. "Why are you in *my* shop? You could have your own *ludus* now."

I shrugged, remaining mute.

"You'll have to go back to the games," Paulinus went on. "Life won't be the same for me if I can't look forward to watching you." He winked. "And winning plenty of money on you."

The other customers laughed their appreciation. They knew me as a regular but were avid followers for my career. "You could teach *us* how to fight," one of the men on the bench suggested. "Charge a sestertius a round to learn what you know."

I flexed my hand, the one still sore from clutching the wooden *rudis*. A few splinters remained in my palm.

I didn't want to speak of it, and in fact, would rather walk away than try to explain I didn't want to train others to kill. I wanted nothing to do with any of it.

But if I jumped up and left, I'd have to explain to Cassia why I hadn't stayed for the shave. I knew she wouldn't understand why I'd jeopardized the chance to make money to pay for what she'd already purchased.

I realized that I'd have to pay Paulinus today. He'd always sent the bill to Aemil.

Paulinus finished with the man on the chair, who rose, cupping his red cheek with one hand. Paulinus wasn't the most gifted barber, but he was quick and cheap.

He invited me to the stool, ahead of the others. The men on the bench waved me on, not minding I cut them out. They never did.

Paulinus sharpened his half-moon shaped razor against his

stone while I seated myself on the small stool. He lifted a dipper from a bucket of water, poured the water over the blade and then into his palm, and smoothed the water onto my face.

Then he began. The process was never pleasant, but my skin was tough. The blade scraped off the day and a half growth of beard, nicking and cutting as it went.

"Now it's Regulus," Paulinus observed. "As *primus palus*, I mean. He's good, but not in your style. Think he'll be defeated? He only ever fell under you."

I remembered the hatred in Regulus's eyes when I'd raised him from the sand, refusing to slay him. He'd wanted to die, and I'd denied him. Hadn't I been obliged to end his life, as a friend? Did my wishes outweigh his?

I'd never had to ponder such things before, and it made my head ache.

"Regulus is a prime fighter," I said, hiding my troubling thoughts. "He will be a good—"

I broke off as Cassia passed the door of the shop. She carried several bundles, and as I watched, a man on the street tried to relieve her of them.

Cassia jerked away, turning on him with the imperiousness of an upper-class slave. The man simply snarled at her and lifted her from her feet.

I was off the stool and out the door, Paulinus giving a startled cry as he snatched the razor from my throat at the last second. I stormed into the street, an animal-like noise leaving my throat, and wrapped a giant hand around the assailant's neck. Cassia, released, skidded on muddy stones and dropped her bundles.

I shook the assailant, a Roman freedman with greasy dark hair and a prominent goiter. He'd gone wide-eyed and limp, like a rabbit caught in a wolf's mouth. He wheezed, trying to breathe.

"You should let him go, Leonidas." Cassia's clear but quiet voice cut to me through the buzz in my head.

Passers-by had halted, and Paulinus and his customers

crowded the doorway of his shop. The street filled, and it was only a matter of time before a cohort or concerned citizen tried to drag us off to a magistrate.

I gave the man a final shake and flung him at the wall across the road. He crashed into it, pushed himself up, and ran. Most in the crowd laughed, men waving fists in appreciation.

Cassia struggled to pick up her packages. I gathered them for her and guided her with a firm hand into Paulinus's shop. He and his customers scuttled back as I sat her on a spare stool.

"This is Cassia," I told them. "She will wait for me."

Paulinus shrugged, waving me back to the chair so he could continue with my half-shaved face. The men watched in puzzlement then slowly returned to the bench, the excitement over.

When Paulinus finished, Cassia calmly asked him the price of the shave, as though she hadn't been accosted by a brute on the street only a short while before. She made a note of Paulinus's answer and serenely told him he'd be paid at the Nones of the coming month.

I followed her out, and we walked along toward the Quirinal.

"Were you hurt?" I asked.

"No." Cassia sent me a quick glance. "Thank you."

"You belong to me." I had to cough—Paulinus's shaves always scraped part of the skin away, leaving me with a rough throat. "That means I take care of you now."

I'd never had a slave of my own, and I wasn't certain how things worked. But Aemil had seen to my needs in all my years of slavery, and I assumed this was the way of it.

Cassia glanced at me with an unreadable expression then put her head down, stepping gingerly from stone to stone. I would have to teach her how to walk on Roman streets.

CASSIA HAD PURCHASED ME SEVERAL TUNICS, WHICH WEREN'T much different from tunics I'd worn as a gladiator, but were of better cloth and a tad longer. Freedmen were prohibited the toga, so I wouldn't have to bother with that, which suited me. Cassia had, however, found a cloak for me, large, dark, and woolen, to wrap up in when the weather grew too cold.

As I stripped out of my dirty tunic and donned a new one, Cassia averted her eyes, as though a man's flesh embarrassed her. Without looking at me, she gathered the old tunic and dropped it into a corner. Everything else, she hung neatly on pegs.

"You will need new sandals," Cassia observed, and I glanced at my old ones. They were well made, only the best for the top gladiators. But I'd worn them all year and the straps were fraying and soiled.

"I hope the job you found pays much," I observed as I took up the cloak. "Or we'll be fleeing the city to avoid being arrested for running up debts."

"It will," Cassia answered with confidence.

Her lack of worry did not reassure me, though I had to admit her skills in bargaining had let us eat well so far.

The sun was up, the day warming, by the time Cassia and I walked along the lower slope of the Quirinal, past the shops where I'd had my shave, and to the Esquiline. A wide fountain at the hill's base drew a crowd of mostly women who filled jugs of cool, flowing water. This was a large fountain with a pillar in the middle and four spouts, each fashioned into a face—the water came out of the mouths.

The women stared at me in blatant interest as we passed. One set her jug on her bared shoulder and trudged up a narrow, steep street. Cassia shifted that direction. The woman glanced once behind her then ignored us.

Shops made up the ground floors of five- and six-storied insulae that lined the lower streets of the Esquiline, the buildings towering above us. As the road bent up the hill, the insulae fell away to be replaced by one- and two-storied homes, the *domii* of the wealthy. Shops were built into these dwellings as well, as owners of the houses saw no reason not to collect extra rent by letting out part of their property.

I'd been to homes on this hill before, invited by the highborn to perform at suppers, or simply to sit while the *dominus's* acquaintances marveled that a dangerous fighting man reposed in the triclinium during a banquet.

Women had brought me to this hill as well, wealthy matrons craving novelty, though I'd rarely accepted an invitation. Aemil liked to crisply declare he wasn't running a brothel and that he'd sell a gladiator who brought scandal to his *ludus*, but some, like Regulus, did sneak away from time to time to be their lovers.

The slave woman with the jug turned a corner and disappeared into a side door of the very house Cassia halted before.

The front door of this *domus* was nearly hidden in a recess between a basket-maker's and a pastry shop, the latter of which poured out a scent of warm honey to those waiting to purchase the delights. The benches that lined the niche before the door of the house were empty. Here the clients would sit, waiting for the *paterfamilias* to see them, but usually the appointments were first thing in the morning. We were late.

The door slave, a young man with lanky hair who lounged on one of the benches, sprang to his feet as I bent my head under the low roof of the entryway.

The door, wood with its large cross beams studded with bronze, a bronze knob in its center, stood open, letting air into the *domus*. We must have been expected, because the door slave scurried inside, beckoning us to follow.

This house was not as large as some of the villas I'd visited, but it was spacious enough. Water quietly trickled into a square basin in the atrium, the basin reflecting the blue sky in the open square above it. Green plants lined the edges of the fountain, and a large gathering of flowers in a vase decorated a lone table on one wall.

The walls had been painted white, in a new style, replacing blocks of red and black that typically outlined scenes of the outdoors or famous battles. The white walls held intricate lacy patterns of gold draped around clusters of figures. They were soldiers, I saw on closer inspection, but sparring and drilling, not slaying enemies.

A shrine stood against one of the longer walls, with small statues and several plaster masks that I assumed were the ancestors of the *paterfamilias*.

The majordomo of the house, a haughty man with black hair carefully combed in his attempt to hide a bald spot, emerged from a shadowy hall beyond the atrium. He was likely a slave, but a lofty one, like Cassia.

"You are late," the majordomo announced.

"My apologies, Celnus." Cassia bowed her head. "An unavoidable delay in the streets, and then we had to make ourselves presentable."

She spoke with deference but far less tension than I'd seen her with the barber and his customers, or Lucia and Floriana's ladies. She'd also relaxed with Marcianus. I realized she considered the medicus and this majordomo as her equals—Marcianus in intellect and the majordomo in social status.

Celnus grunted. "He is waiting. This way."

He turned on his heel and marched into the hall on the other side of the atrium. I started after him, but Cassia hung back.

"You aren't coming with me?" I asked her in some alarm.

"Not my place. I will wait." She glanced out the door at the benches, where the door slave had retreated.

"I need you with me." I dropped my voice to a whisper. "I won't know what to say."

Cassia's brow furrowed. "You've guarded such men before, haven't you?"

"Yes, but Aemil negotiated the post for me. I turned up where he told me to go."

"I see." Cassia's expression didn't change, but I couldn't help feeling I'd sunk in her estimation. "Very well. But only if you order me to."

"Do I have to order it?" I truly didn't know.

"Yes. If they ask. Better hurry."

"All right, then. I order it."

I strode off after the majordomo, relieved to hear her pattering behind me.

Celnus waited rather impatiently for us at a double door at the end of the hall. When I caught up to him, he gave me a disapproving look then opened one of the doors and led us into a green space.

This was the garden of the home, a private area. I was surprised the majordomo brought us here, not to the tablinium where the *dominus* usually met his supplicants. A walkway lined with columns formed a rectangle around green shrubbery and trees, with a long fountain burbling in the exact center of the garden. The walkway was marble, the fountain's floor covered in mosaics of fish and strange sea creatures.

A man in a knee-length tunic belted with a rope at the waist leaned over a dark green plant with shining leaves, and carefully snipped a twig. He dropped the twig into a finely woven basket resting on a bench beside him. While his tunic was plain, it was made of finely woven linen, and his belt held the sheen of silk. I knew this wasn't the gardener.

The majordomo cleared his throat, and the man glanced up.

He stood a head shorter than me, about Cassia's height, and unlike his majordomo, he didn't try to conceal his baldness. Gray hair, neatly trimmed, framed his ears and was cut short on the back of his neck. A former military man, I guessed, considering the wall paintings I'd observed. He had the bearing and the simplicity of dress of a general who'd spent a lifetime on campaign.

His nose was large and beaked in a face that was thin but not pinched, his slenderness from strength, not hunger. Here was a man who'd survived wars and the even more dangerous world of politics under Nero.

"I enjoy tending the gardens." The man's apologetic tone was genuine, as though he was ashamed we'd found him thus. "Plants like a bit of care. Like children."

I stood without speaking, Cassia slightly behind me. The majordomo radiated disapproval that she'd joined us, but I had no intention of speaking to my potential employer without her.

"Decimus Laelius Priscus," the majordomo announced in a strident voice. "Leonidas the Gladiator." His tone turned disdainful, and he didn't bother to mention Cassia.

"Thank you for attending me." Priscus gestured for Celnus to depart. Celnus clearly didn't want to, but he walked away, very slowly. He'd probably lurk in the shadows inside the house, waiting for me to bring out a sword to strike his master down.

"I have watched you in the games." Priscus ran a gaze over me that held keen assessment. "You fight with great skill but never throw away a move. You do not strike before you are certain. Tell me—I am curious. Why did you not kill Regulus in your final match?"

I did not even have to think about the answer. "He is my friend."

"I see. But with him gone, your reputation would have been that of the gods."

I shrugged, the new tunic pulling on my shoulders.

"You had another friend, I recall. Name of Xerxes."

I stiffened. Xerxes had been far closer to me than Regulus. Xerxes would have understood me sparing him and not hated me for it, no matter how much he'd wanted to die.

Xerxes had very much wanted to live. He'd spoken of what he and I would do once we achieved our freedom, the roads we'd travel, the wonders we'd see.

He'd been struck down in a match against another gladiator. I'd killed the man who'd slain him in the next round and was laid low with grief for a long while. Aemil had threatened to sell me for wasting his time.

"Yes." My answer was simple. "I burned offerings for him."

Priscus studied me as I faced him. I didn't look him directly in the eye but kept my gaze on an Egyptian marble pillar to his right.

After a long, silent moment, Priscus gave me a nod. "You'll do. My majordomo is incensed that I am not leaving every detail of hiring you up to him or Kephalos, my scribe, but I like to judge a man for myself. You fight well, but you mourn those who have fallen, and spare others you could easily have killed. That tells me you are a man, not a machine. I need you to accompany me to Ostia Antica. I have valuable cargo to retrieve, and I and the cargo will need much protection."

Not an uncommon request. Romans often had business that took them to Ostia, on the coast, either to meet ships from Egypt and farther east or to take care of problems in their warehouses that hirelings or slaves couldn't manage.

The road to Ostia was dangerous, with brigands waiting to rob a man of all he had. Most travelers went in caravans or hired fighting men like me to protect them. Costly goods equally needed protecting.

I bowed my head to show I understood. Whatever Priscus's reasons for the journey should not concern me. I would accompany him and fight off any who tried to accost him.

"I warn you beforehand, we will be in grave peril." Priscus spoke lightly, his eyes taking on a twinkle. "There are those who will try to relieve me of my life, probably before I even reach the port. If they succeed, my friend, you too will be put to death."

CHAPTER 6

"I hope we live to collect the fee," Cassia said when we reached our apartment once more. "It is quite a large one."

She unwound and neatly hung her palla then took the cloak I'd dumped to a stool and shook it out, smoothing the folds before she hung it on the next peg. I wondered why she'd bother straightening a garment that would only get wet and windblown, but I didn't mention it.

Cassia looked pleased with herself. Once Priscus had gained my word that I would protect him on the way to and from Ostia, he dismissed us cordially and went back to his plants. Celnus had taken us to the atrium, where another man had waited—Kephalos, a scribe originally from Smyrna—who had haggled with Cassia over the price.

I'd listened in fascination as Cassia, who'd barely spoken above a deferential murmur since I'd met her, argued loudly with the scribe about risk to me on the road, the senator's declaration that I would be killed if he was—not by his own people, Priscus had said quickly. But, he claimed, those who had failed to guard him well in the past had been struck down later. The gods, Priscus supposed. The only explanation.

Kephalos the scribe had tried to point out I was nothing but a hired freedman, no longer a prized gladiator and so not worth as much. Cassia had come right back with the fact that Priscus himself had approved of me, and that I'd retired at the head of my *ludus*. She'd clinched the deal by implying that I'd had many other offers, more lucrative than this one, and if Kephalos didn't want to disappoint his master, he should agree to my price.

Fifty *sestertii*. Enough to feed and keep us for many days.

"What other offers did we have?" I asked her now. "How much were they for?"

Cassia looked at me in surprise and then gave me a small smile. "No others. I did not so much state that as let Kephalos believe it."

Thinking through her conversation with the scribe, I realized Cassia had never actually said I'd had other offers. I had to admire her resourcefulness.

"Do you think Priscus lied about the danger?" I asked. "To make me guard him more carefully?"

"I am not certain." Cassia laid out bowls for the meal we'd purchased on the way home. "Decimus Laelius Priscus is from an old patrician family, one of the most respected in Rome. My former mistress spoke highly of him, and that was a feat. She disliked everyone." Cassia winced, and I imagined the mistress had taken that dislike out on her household servants, including her scribes. "Priscus has much money but these days not a lot of power. He's retired and interested in his garden, as we saw. He was a very good friend to the emperor Claudius."

Claudius had been Nero's adoptive father. I was not one for politics, but I knew that not all friends or family of Claudius survived Nero's rise to power. Some had quietly left the city, while others had been arrested for crimes real and imagined, and executed.

"Why is Priscus still alive then?" I watched Cassia ladle out the lentil stew and lay the bread in the middle of the table.

"Who can say? I've heard little about him except that he has vast wealth and spends much time reading and gardening. He did not have a lot of power in the senate, though many friends."

And he had money, I finished silently. A man would be respected for that alone, if only in the hope that some of his wealth would fall to those ingratiating themselves with him.

"Maybe we should have asked for a higher price," I half joked as I seated myself and lifted a spoon.

Cassia rewarded me with a fleeting smile. She quickly lost it and retreated to the other side of the table. This time she didn't wait to be asked to join in the meal, but she did not take her first bite until I'd shoved some stew into my mouth.

"No garum today," I said after I swallowed.

Another brief smile, then Cassia nervously opened her tablet. "A savings."

I noisily ate stew, mopping it up with bread. I found a pebble inside the bread, larger than most, and spit it onto the floor. The grit from grinding mills didn't always come out of the flour before the bread went into the oven.

"I need to pay Floriana for Lucia," I said after the silence had stretched. "I've been to her twice."

I thought to set her at her ease, but she gave me another worried look. "I see."

"Though most nights I only sleep."

Many believed gladiators lived to enjoy sticking themselves into any woman or man available, but we spent the bulk of our time training or recovering from injuries. Carnal relief was an occasional indulgence, not a way of life, and most of us had our favorites for that. When I was younger I hadn't been as discriminate, but as I matured, I kept to the woman I liked. Marcianus had explained to me about catching diseases from being too promiscuous, and I needed to be strong to stay alive in the arena. Also, Aemil would turn out a man too sick to fight.

I don't know if Cassia understood but she bent her head over her tablet and ceased speaking.

I left the apartment after our supper and walked to Floriana's to see how that lady fared. Young Marcia was there to care for her, but Lucia had gone out.

Floriana was better, Marcia told me, though weak. Marcia still didn't understand how Floriana had eaten the rhubarb leaves, because no one had found any remains of them in the house.

I looked into Floriana's cell to see her sleeping, and snoring, and departed. "Tell her I'll pay her when I return from Ostia."

Marcia only nodded and went back to Floriana.

Rome was shutting down for the night, the sun setting. Shops had closed long before, and even the baths were emptying now. At night all would grow pitch dark, and the wise were indoors by then. Shopkeepers would stay awake, awaiting deliveries, which were only allowed at night, and the rest of us would sleep until dawn.

I heard footsteps behind me as I made my way to what was now my home. I tensed as the footfalls matched mine and kept pace with me—this was not someone simply going the same way as I did in the dusk.

I turned a corner and halted, putting myself against a wall. My follower came around the same corner but stopped before he blundered through and sprang my trap.

He was a man, but that was all I could see in the deepening darkness. He wore a cloak, a fold of which was draped over his head, like a priest, but I doubted he was one. A priest had no reason to follow me so stealthily.

With a roar, I charged him. If he were a robber or assassin, I'd make him fight for his spoils.

The man spun to meet me, competent on his feet. I had no weapon, but I knew how to fight without one, my fists and kicks as powerful as any sword blow.

I swung my giant fist, but hit empty air. The man melted back into the shadows, avoiding my attack, and then he fled. I heard his boots click on the stones, the sound dissipating.

I shook out my hand, puzzled. Why follow me and then run?

Maybe he'd thought he'd found an easy mark to rob and then realized I was a fighting man, not a weak target. He hadn't expected me to attack.

I continued on my way down the now-empty street, my back itching as I strode along.

When I entered the apartment, I found the detritus from supper gone, the bowls, which I assumed were ours now, stacked neatly, my stool against the wall. Cassia sat at the table, stifling a yawn as I entered.

"You should sleep," I told her. "You don't have to wait up for me."

I was bone tired, ready to fall on my pallet and not wake until I had to. Cassia rose and took my cloak, again shaking it out and hanging it from its peg. Then she returned to the table, opened her ever-present tablet, and made a note.

"What are you writing now?" I asked irritably.

"The time you came in."

"Why?" I found all this writing baffling. What was the point? Was she making notes to show Hesiodos? And why?

Cassia shrugged. "It might be useful later."

"Go to sleep." I untied my sandals and stepped out of them, shuffling my way to the pallet in the alcove.

Cassia pattered behind me, retrieved the sandals, and placed them against the wall in a neat line.

I started to admonish her for tidying up after me, but then decided that would be senseless. I also had the feeling she tidied not because she believed it her job, but because a shoe out of place annoyed her. Cassia liked a sense of order I didn't understand.

"I will wake you before the first hour," she said as I collapsed onto the bed and settled on my back. "We are to meet the senator at the Porta Trigemina at sunrise."

I rose on my elbows. "We? You cannot come with us."

"I think I had better. The senator spoke of grave danger, which means there is a chance we won't be paid. It is important we retrieve our fee as soon as possible and protect it until we settle our accounts."

Cassia was the most puzzling woman I'd ever met. "I'm the best fighter in Rome—no one will take my payment from me."

"Not by force, no."

My eyes narrowed. "You think Priscus will trick his way out of paying me?"

Cassia shook her head. "He seems an honest man, which is probably why he is in such danger. His slaves, on the other hand, know they have a soft place, and will do all they can to keep his money in their house. I know how to not let them."

"Priscus will pay me in Rome, not Ostia. When I return him safely."

"That remains to be seen. What if he decides to stay in Ostia? Or breaks the journey elsewhere? Or sends you back alone? I ought to be there to collect our payment at the point you are dismissed, or we might never see it."

I sat all the way up, and Cassia stepped back in some alarm. But the set of her chin told me she'd not give in on her point.

"If you come with us to Ostia, I have to protect *you* as well as the senator." I hadn't forgotten the ruffian who'd accosted Cassia outside the barber's and how angry the incident had made me.

"I will be one more servant with the other servants. No one will notice me."

It was true she moved silently through the streets, slipping between people as though she didn't want to touch them. Priscus wouldn't be traveling alone, but have a caravan of his servants to cater to his every need.

I imagined that if I forbade Cassia, which I had a right to do, she'd find a way to follow. I'd never encountered a woman with such a strong will, but maybe scribes were a different breed.

I flopped back down to the blankets. "Wake me before the first hour then."

I arranged the covers around me and turned my face to the

wall, rapidly sinking into sleep. I heard Cassia scurry toward her own pallet, and her footsteps sounded distinctly satisfied.

IN THE MORNING, I JOINED PRISCUS'S PARTY ON THE FAR SIDE of the Aventine at the Porta Trigemina, the triple gate to the Via Ostiensis.

Fog coated the city. The nearby river lent its murk to the mists rolling from the hills and we stood in a haze, the gates a dark bulk in the stone wall. The arches of a nearby aqueduct were lost in the white, like a ghostly ruin.

At the blare of a horn signaling the dawn hour, we proceeded through the gate. We were among the first out, Priscus having the standing to be at the front of the line.

Priscus was mounted on a horse, his seat easy. A cart pulled by a mule carried his baggage. His retinue, including me, followed him, both on foot and on mules. Priscus had seemed confused as to why I'd wanted to bring Cassia, but he didn't begrudge me a servant.

Cassia had been right when she'd claimed she'd be absorbed into the household slaves and ignored—no one looked twice at her bundled in her cloak as we exited the city. Their gazes were on Priscus, an obviously wealthy man, and on me, his gladiator bodyguard.

Priscus led our small caravan, which annoyed me. If he worried so about assassination, he should be surrounded by people, not out in front like the head of a spear.

"Habit," he told me when I pointed this out. "I ride in the lead to keep others from accusing me of being the coward I am."

Priscus found himself amusing, but I strode solidly next to him, keeping a wary eye out.

The Via Ostiensis runs alongside the Tiber to Ostia's large port. The road is the artery from Rome downstream to ships waiting to take people and money to the ends of the empire and beyond. Likewise, goods from the entire world are trundled up the river and this road into Rome, to be unloaded to vast Emporium warehouses.

The Via Ostiensis was lined, like the Via Appia, with tombs and monuments to the dead. No one was buried inside Rome, and so the wealthy sought the closest proximity. Prominent families erected large memorials to their ancestors.

The trouble with the tombs was that they made a good place for brigands to lurk, especially on a foggy morning. Mist rose from the river on our right, met the colder air of the hills, and clung to us like a white shroud. Spaces between the tombs were gray with shadows. Marauders could also wait on top of the tombs behind convenient statues or decorative urns, ready to leap down and rob the unwatchful.

Priscus rode without worry, as though he were in an ambulatory—a covered walkway in a villa, protected and private. I kept alert constantly, peering into each foggy shadow and around every bend, halting our train until I made certain the next stretch of road was safe.

At least Priscus accepted my admonishments to wait with good humor. I'd guarded men in the past who'd snarled at me every step, and I appreciated Priscus's willingness to obey me.

The tombs thinned and ceased after a few miles, and the fog began to burn away, but the open countryside was no safer. Instead of knives coming out of nowhere, I had to worry about arrows shot from clumps of trees or from behind small rises in the land.

The first half of the day passed, thankfully, without incident. Cassia rode quietly on a mule, her palla pulled over her face to keep out the mist and dust. She didn't speak at all.

Priscus, on the other hand, was voluble. Possibly from nervousness, though his body didn't betray any tension.

"A long time since I've journeyed to Ostia," he reflected. "Ten years, I'd say. Gracious, how time passes. My wife owned warehouses there. *She* had the money, not I, at least when we first married. I was flattered that she loved an old warhorse like me." He chuckled. "She left all her wealth to me when she went to her ancestors." Priscus lost his smile and let out a sigh. "But I'd rather have her next to me."

His sadness was genuine. "I am sorry." I knew such sorrow, and Xerxes's widow still held on to it.

"Her death was not unexpected, unfortunately. She'd been ill a long time. Now she's young and healthy again, in the fields of Elysium, if you believe in that sort of thing. I used to be quite a skeptic, but now I want to think of my Porcia happy there. One's outlook changes as one grows old."

He appeared hearty enough to me, riding well without fatiguing.

"Tell me about Leonidas the Gladiator," Priscus said. "*Why* were you a gladiator? The story will pass the time as we go."

I'd prefer to pass the time making sure assassins didn't shoot at him, but I'd learned to not argue too much with those who hired me.

"I was accused of a crime. Murder." I stated it bluntly, no reason to evade the truth. "Locked in the Tullianum for it. I was a citizen, even if I look a bit like a Gaul. They gave me the choice of execution or the games. I chose the games, knowing I was a good fighter. A few days ago, I was given the *rudis*." *And Cassia, and a place to live, by a person unknown to me.*

"That is a very short summation of a life." Priscus eyed me in curiosity. "Did you commit the murder?"

CHAPTER 7

"No." The word was harsh, and I closed my mouth.

Another had done the crime I'd been accused of but I did not know who, and I had been in no position to find out. I'd often wondered if the murderer was still out there or if he'd died in the dangerous world we inhabited.

"Who are your people?" Priscus asked me, his interest continuing.

I shrugged. "I was abandoned as a lad of five. I learned to live on my own."

"Then how do you know you were a citizen?"

"There's a record of my birth." I hadn't seen it, and couldn't have read it if I had, but I'd been told this by the man I'd worked for. He'd had to check before he took me on as his apprentice.

"Hmm." Priscus halted his horse, and I came alert, looking about for whatever had startled him. "We should stop for a time," he said, noting my tension. "The others are growing tired."

I sensed Priscus could have ridden straight on without stopping. Despite his declaration of his aging, he was healthy and strong. I realized he was resting for his retainers' sake, a fact that told me much about him.

I remained next to Priscus as he dismounted and did not let him out of my sight, not even when he left the road to relieve himself. Especially not then. A man is at his most vulnerable when he's giving up his water.

The journey continued in this way—we'd ride for a stretch, then rest while Priscus's servants tended his horse and the mules. When we halted for a meal, the retainers nibbled on bread, and Priscus had his valet serve them watered-down wine.

I did not see much of Cassia, who stayed close to the two female servants of the group. She proved her word that she'd keep herself safe, never straying from the middle of the caravan.

We traversed the twenty miles to Ostia in easy stages and arrived at the port at the twelfth hour, just before the gates closed.

Other men I'd guarded to Ostia put up at inns, sometimes taking over half of one for their party, but Priscus led us to a large apartment block that surrounded a wide green space with fountains. These were not typical insulae, but a two-storied complex that held dwellings as large as a middle-class man's *domus* in Rome. The door guard of one of these units gave a shout when Priscus dismounted, and half a dozen servants streamed from within to collect the horse and mules and escort Priscus inside.

Priscus owned this entire building, I learned—another he'd inherited from his wife. I was offered my own cubicle in the spacious two-floored apartment set aside for his use, but I decided to sleep in front of the door to Priscus's room. Any would-be assassin who broke in, or had been hiding inside already, would need to step over me to reach him.

Priscus ate a simple meal alone and soon turned in for the night. I spread blankets before his large bedroom near the atrium and reclined on them, my back to the door.

Cassia appeared out of the darkness after the slaves extinguished the few lamps. She began to straighten my blankets, pretending she'd come to look after me.

"He is paying much money for the cargo he's retrieving," Cassia said in a low voice as she worked. She leaned close, her breath brushing my ear. "So much that he will not leave the collection of the goods to others. But he won't say what the shipment is, not even to his servants. Celnus and Kephalos don't know. This annoys them, rather."

Gold, spices, silk. Such things could double a man's fortune, but only if he brought them safely to the markets. Priscus was wise not to leave the transport in another's hands—a portion of it might vanish by the time it reached his warehouse in Rome.

Another thought occurred to me. Priscus might be buying items he was not licensed to import, such as spices or cloth meant only for the imperial family.

"Do they know where the goods are coming from?" I asked.

"No, but the suspicion is it's something his son is sending. The son, Decimus, is an aedile in Halicarnassus, and the apple of Priscus's eye."

Young men of patrician families were often sent to the provinces to make their names and begin their careers. The more people they pleased, the higher they could rise. Aediles were the men who organized games and negotiated the price of the gladiators who would fight in them.

"Does Celnus or Kephalos know who's trying to kill him? Is it to stop Priscus from receiving the shipment?"

"No one seems to know," Cassia said. "There have been several attempts in the last days, but Priscus has shrugged them off. Celnus finally convinced him he should hire you to guard him on this journey. That's how I found out about it. One of the servants from a family I know told me that Kephalos, the scribe, had gone to the Forum to search for a bodyguard. So I sought him out. It's curious ... Kephalos was pleased when I approached him. It seems that when he and Celnus convinced Priscus he needed a guard, he immediately thought of you. Or, as Kephalos told me, Priscus said, *That gladiator who just retired. He looks sturdy.*"

This fact was not surprising. Many who'd hired me to bodyguard asked for me by name. Those with much to lose wanted the top gladiators defending them.

"He's told me very little about the attempts on his life." I spoke in irritation. Some men could be too reticent about important things.

"Nothing has happened at home. Only when he goes out. A knife in the street. A falling block from the top of a tall insula. That one nearly killed a woman, but the senator pulled her to safety in time."

"Good." I meant that the attempts had been physical, and not poison, as with Floriana. Much easier for me to grab a knife-wielding assassin and hold him upside down than to puzzle out who had poisoned wine or food, and how and when.

"Priscus's servants like him. He's a reasonable man." Cassia sounded admiring.

So, of course he was marked for death. Men who were monsters were cunning and careful, making them more difficult to eliminate. Kind men were too trusting.

"Priscus has no lictors," I observed. No men whose job it was to carry a bundle of staves, merely symbolic these days, to signal that the man they accompanied had power.

"He says he's not important enough, and finds lictors useless." Cassia's mouth quirked into a smile. "I like him too."

I'd met reasonable and seemingly kind men before, benevolent when all was right in their world. But when things went wrong, they could turn into the monsters I'd mentioned.

Cassia hovered, re-straightening the corner of my blanket. Waiting for me to dismiss her, I realized. I'd have to grow used to that.

"Thank you," I said. "Sleep well."

Cassia shot me an unreadable glance then bowed her head and slipped away. I leaned against Priscus's bedroom door, folded my arms, and pondered all Cassia had told me. When I exhausted that, I turned my thoughts to the change in my own life.

From one breath to the next, I'd become a different man. I could barely remember the youth I'd been before my arrest for murder and condemnation to the games.

I was no longer that lad. But I was also no longer Leonidas the Spartan, champion of the world.

I had no idea who I was now. I stared at the dark entrance to the atrium and hoped I would soon find out.

We stayed in Priscus's large apartment three days waiting for the arrival of his goods. Cassia went out to the port with the other servants every morning to watch for the ship that was bringing them from Antioch. At home, Kephalos and Priscus, with argument on the scribe's part, put together two caskets of gold coins to pay for the shipment.

Cassia had explained to me that the usual way for a man to buy cargo was to commission and pay for it beforehand, in an office. When the order arrived, it would be unloaded and taken to the purchaser's warehouse, or wherever he directed it to go. Cassia was puzzled as to why Priscus hadn't used an agent in the usual way, or had his son take care of the entire transaction, including its payment. Perhaps, she speculated, it was so valuable that the son hadn't had enough funds in Halicarnassus for it. The costliness of this cargo was starting to worry me.

The locked chests stored in the tablinium also made me uneasy—they were a good target for a robber. Then again, the caskets were heavy, so a robber would have to bring much help to tote them away. Of course, if a gang broke into the house and killed all the inhabitants, they could take anything they liked.

Priscus grew more agitated as the days passed. He'd been calm enough when we'd arrived, but when his servants returned each afternoon telling him the ship had not yet appeared, he paced the atrium or the garden outside, or climbed to the second floor to stare from the arched window toward the harbor buildings, bright in the December sunshine.

On the third day, it rained, clouds and mist blotting out the view. The apartment was cold, barely heated by braziers Priscus would not go near.

Priscus turned to me from the upstairs window...I'd been watching to make sure no one sent an arrow through it into his brain.

"Do you think I am mad, Leonidas?"

Not a question one wants to answer if one needs to be paid. Priscus studied me as he waited, brown eyes anxious.

"I have not known you long enough to decide," I said.

Priscus's quick smile did not erase the worry in his eyes. "I never used to be mad, but I'm being driven to it. A great fortune is a burden, my friend. Everyone wants it, will do anything to obtain it."

As I'd never owned more than what I'd won as prize money, which had gone very fast, most of it to Aemil, I could only regard him without expression.

"Having what you need and no more is best," Priscus went on. "An excess of money is cold comfort when those you love are gone."

His wife, he meant. Priscus must have been very fond of her. I wondered if he'd lavished expense on her tomb, praising her with a long inscription.

"You must be curious as to why I've journeyed to Ostia myself to fetch this cargo." Priscus turned to the window, hands behind his trim back. He wore a tunic only, as usual when he was indoors, not much different from mine except for its costly fabric.

He seemed to want an answer, so I said, "Yes."

"I'd give my life for what I'm waiting for, though I'd prefer not to." He made a wry grimace. "Which is why I let Celnus persuade me to hire a guard. I hear your slave drove a hard bargain. Winning against Kephalos is impressive."

I recalled Cassia haggling like the best moneylender with Priscus's scribe.

"She is an unusual servant for a former gladiator," Priscus went on.

"Cassia was given to me." I hesitated. Most men didn't want to know the true thoughts of their bodyguards, but I continued, "I'm not sure exactly what to do with her."

Priscus laughed, the lines around his eyes crinkling. "I am pleased to hear you say so. You are not a brute, which is why I have followed your career so closely. You fight to win but not mercilessly. You use skill, not cruelty."

I gave him another nod. I'd learned to battle without passion. Regulus let himself succumb to anger, which is why I always bested him.

Priscus returned to studying the rainy harbor. He twitched, bouncing on his toes.

I wondered—he was vastly wealthy, he'd followed my career and seemed to know much about me, and was interested in my past.

Was *he* the benefactor who'd given me my freedom? He'd asked for me personally when his majordomo had insisted he hire a bodyguard. A man who believed that a person needed only what satisfied basic requirements might have chosen Cassia because she was good with money, and could help me live decently on very little.

I studied the man, a well-muscled former soldier who had enough kindness to let his less-fit servants rest on a journey he could have easily made without halting. A man who mourned his wife, preferring her to the riches she'd left him when she'd died.

It was very possible Priscus had decided to bestow silent generosity on a gladiator who was destined to fight until he was killed on a day he moved too slowly.

I would have to talk it over with Cassia, but I thought it a good possibility.

IN THE MORNING, THE DOOR SLAVE RAN IN EXCITEDLY TO THE room in which Priscus took his small breakfast of figs and cheese, to announce that the ship had arrived.

Priscus's face changed. While he'd been calm but resolute this morning, his expression flickered with terror before settling into that of a stern general.

"I will go in your place," I said, loosening the short sword Priscus had provided me. "You will be safer here."

"No." The word was abrupt. "If I do not attend, it will go wrong."

"There is too much open space at the harbor," I argued. "At least let me scout. I will send for you if all is clear. "

Priscus turned a hard eye on me, the affable man who'd spoken so familiarly with me gone. "You will do as I say, gladiator."

I had no power here, and he knew it. I bowed my head, but I'd never been submissive. "My fee will be the same whether you live or die."

Priscus's hand shot to the dagger at his side as though he'd strike me down in his breakfast chamber. If I fought him off and injured him, I could be condemned to death with no hope of pardon. I waited, letting fate hang in the balance.

Priscus released the dagger's hilt and deflated. "You are right, Leonidas. It is a terrible risk I take. But I must take it."

"Tell me why." It was no business of mine, except that I might die for this man today.

"I wish I could. The burden is great. But spies are everywhere, and I am sworn to secrecy. I do not mind you guarding my life, but some things are more important than existence."

Priscus strode away from me, squaring his shoulders, and I could only follow.

He declared he would pay for and retrieve his cargo himself, with only me for protection, but I persuaded him to bring a few more servants. It would appear normal for him to have a retinue, plus he'd have witnesses if the deal went sour.

Priscus scowled at me but sharply ordered his valet and his horse's groom—his most loyal men, he said—to join us. The two looked relieved that I'd talked him into bringing them. I convinced Priscus to include three more of his strongest servants, and we all set off toward the harbor, the caskets of coin strapped to a donkey's back.

We hadn't gone half a street when I heard quick footfalls behind us.

A glance back showed me Cassia walking along, a basket on her arm, as though she headed out to do some shopping. I frowned at her, but she ignored me.

"Aren't slaves supposed to be obedient?" I asked Priscus in attempt to lessen his tension.

Priscus sent me a tight smile. "Theoretically. But when you make slaves of conquered peoples, their defiance remains. Even after generations, the spirits of their ancestors fill them. It is not the best system, but without the labor of slaves, Rome ceases to function."

I wondered what Cassia would say to this. She was certainly like no other slave I'd encountered, including myself.

Ostia's harbor spread from the mouth of the Tiber to the sea. The day was fine after yesterday's rain, high clouds forming shadows on the deep blue water.

A building under construction at the harbor mouth sported a tall crane, with several men walking inside a giant treadwheel to raise a large block of stone into the air. A small man with a pouch of scrolls slung over his shoulder watched, hands on hips, as the block moved higher and swung out over the roof, where more men waited to guide the block into place.

Additional cranes worked the wharves, hauling goods into and out of the ships docked there.

The number of vessels roaming the harbor astonished me. The high decks teemed with men, and oars lifted and fell in tight precision, flashing in the sunlight.

I would like to come to this place at my leisure, to gawp at the ships and watch them maneuver. The thought that I was free to do so whenever I wished was a jolt. Freedom was difficult to grow used to.

We took a street lined with tall buildings that blocked our view of the harbor. Colonnades formed shaded walkways, though we kept to the middle of the street with Priscus's horse and the donkey. Ostia did not have the restriction on private vehicles during the day that Rome did, and so we had to move aside for wagons and carriages. Priscus wore his toga with the purple stripe, revealing he was a man of high rank, but he did not insist all give way for him.

He turned his horse abruptly into a side lane, and I was hard-pressed to keep up with him. We hadn't gone far before Priscus dismounted and moved quickly toward a dark doorway.

I dared to step in front of him and put my hand on his chest to stop him from charging inside the building. Ignoring his glare, I told him to stand still and ducked through the doorway myself, quickly stepping out of the block of light to let my eyes adjust to the gloom.

Six men waited in a large, empty room. Its concrete rubble walls were unadorned, touched by sunlight trickling through tiny windows high above. A dove fluttered in one of the window openings, uncertain it wanted to enter this dusty and cold place.

All the men were armed. Swords glinted at sides, knives rested in belts. They were not soldiers—ordinary sailors, I'd have said, except for the man at their head. He had the thickset body and stance of a fighting man.

"You were to come alone." His accent put him from outside Rome.

"My bodyguard insisted it was too dangerous," Priscus said apologetically. He'd entered without waiting for my signal, and he led the casket-laden donkey by its rope. "I have the money. Where is my cargo?"

The man frowned at his bluntness. "We are to take you to it. *Alone*." His scowl took in the men who flanked Priscus, and me.

"I go with him," I said before Priscus could speak.

The lead man peered at me, taking a step forward to squint through the semi-darkness. His eyes widened. "Jupiter. You're Leonidas the Spartan."

"Was." I gripped my sword. "I go with Priscus. He will pay, you will give him the cargo, and we will leave."

The leader did not appear happy, but he shrugged. "Very well," he said to me. "You and Decimus Laelius Priscus. No other."

Priscus nodded. "It shall be done."

He was a fool. These men would murder Priscus once they cornered him alone, taking the money and fleeing. Or they might kidnap him and hold him for high ransom in order to pry even more cash out of him.

Priscus didn't seem bothered by either prospect. He quietly told his retainers to remain behind, then stood and waited for the sailors to lead us out.

They headed for a far door, me directly behind them, then Priscus with the donkey. The lead man fell into step with me, saying nothing.

The small door in the back of the empty warehouse opened to a noisome alley, an excellent place for an ambush and assassination. Neither happened. The sailors hurried toward the daylight at the alley's end, as though they worried about being waylaid here themselves.

We emerged into a much-congested main street. The lead man took a grip on the donkey's bridle and marched us in a clump toward the harbor.

A figure in a cloak with a basket scuttled behind us, melding with the crowd but easily keeping pace. Neither the sailors nor Priscus noted her.

The lead man turned us onto a long dock that reached into the water. This wharf was lined with old wooden buildings that all seemed to be empty, no one in sight. Unused, probably slated to be torn down and replaced.

The sailors expected Priscus to follow them onto this deserted dock with no outlet, with his money, and only me as bodyguard.

I stepped in front of the lead man. "No. You bring the cargo to us now."

As my last word fell, a sharp cry sounded down the dock. From one of the many doorways sprang a man, slim-limbed and dressed in a slave's tunic, running hard at us, knife in hand. Several more men, armed, came after him.

I pushed past the sailors, drawing my sword, and moved to intercept the running man.

"No." A touch on my arm pulled me to a halt. Cassia had appeared next to me, and she held my sword arm with her light fingers, her eyes wide. "No, do not kill him."

CHAPTER 8

The young man tore at us. His eyes were wide, his tunic soiled and tattered. Cassia tried to drag me out of his way, but she could no more move me than she could the construction blocks on the other end of the harbor.

Priscus drew his weapon as the sailors surrounded us. I shoved Cassia toward an empty building and safety, and turned to defend Priscus.

Priscus moved to the donkey and now used his sword to slice through the harness, letting the caskets of gold aurei drop to the ground. He then pushed past me, competently elbowing me in the ribs as I grabbed for him, and he slipped from my grasp.

The sailors surrounded the crazed young man, trying to reach him and disarm him. Priscus shoved his way through, oblivious to danger.

The assailant stilled in confusion when he saw Priscus, then he flung aside his knife and burst into tears. A rope, frayed, dangled from the young man's slim wrist.

Priscus caught the young man and crushed him in a desperate embrace, kissing his hair, his face, tears raining down his cheeks.

"Son," Priscus said hoarsely. "My dearest son."

I stopped in amazement, the events of the past days clicking into place. This was no purchase of expensive goods by a careful patrician—this was a ransom. The precious cargo was Priscus's son, now weeping in his father's arms. Priscus's speech that money meant nothing if one was alone became even more clear now.

I stepped back, my heart pounding, awareness heightening. This wasn't over. It all still could go wrong, Priscus and his son in no way safe.

The men who'd run out behind Priscus's son were more of his captors. They now joined the sailors who'd led us here.

I backed up to Priscus and the young man, who were locked in happy reunion, and pointed my sword at the thick gut of the lead man.

Cassia peered fearfully from the shadow of the doorway I'd pushed her through. None of the sailors noticed her, but they could at any time.

"He's paid you," I told the lead man. "We leave. Now."

Hard faces regarded me, a dozen men honed by their profession, none concerned about fighting an enraged gladiator. There was only one of me, after all.

I would teach them to be afraid.

Fighting in the legions, I'd been told, was brutal but precise, each man doing an exact job so that the group fought as one. Melded into a machine that could mow down an enemy army, no matter how powerful that enemy might be. Thus, Rome conquered the world.

Gladiatorial fighting was entirely different. We fought alone, and we fought to win, with no mercy. We threw precision to the wind if we saw another way to be victorious. This was why freed gladiators made poor soldiers. We embraced the unexpected to survive.

I demonstrated this by kicking the lead man swiftly in the chin with my heel, at the same time spinning to plunge my sword into the man on my right.

The lead man stumbled back, grunting in pain. The second man yelped and dodged, taking a graze against his abdomen. The others rushed me.

I heard Cassia shout, and then the sailors ducked and cursed as rocks pelted them, hurled by Cassia.

Priscus lifted his head from his son. Rage flared in his eyes, the determined anger that had once terrified armies in far-flung lands.

He gently pushed his son toward the street end of the dock. The donkey, free of his burden, was already trotting that way.

"Kill them all, Leonidas," Priscus said, his voice hard as he raised his sword. "Leave their bodies to warn others of what happens when they lay hands on my family."

I couldn't possibly kill them all myself. I'd fend them off and make them pay dearly, but if the sailors surrounded and tackled me together, they could stab me and shove my body into the murky water.

But the command made them pause, and gave me an opening.

I struck, kicked, stabbed, and whirled, my training making me come alive like a mindless killing beast.

I heard again the roar of the crowds, felt the chanting pulse of my name, the hot sand under my feet. *Win, stay alive, and give them a show.* The blood of a gladiator was said to heal, but while it beat inside my body, it gave me strength.

The sailors who gained their feet limped down the dock, others crawled from my wrath as quickly as they could. No more death, I'd vowed. But I could make them remember me.

Two of the wiser grabbed a casket of gold and rushed off, balancing the box between them. The others who could run simply did so. At the end of the dock, they leapt over its edge and out of sight, likely to waiting boats.

I feinted with my sword at the final man, the leader, then when he lifted his sword to defend himself, kicked him hard in the ribs. He folded over, arm across his stomach, gasping for breath.

I cleaned my bloody sword on his tunic and resheathed it. If my blood truly healed, he'd be fine, which was more than he deserved.

"Leave Rome," I advised him. "Your life will be worth nothing now."

Once Priscus, his son safe, reported the kidnapping, these naval men turned pirates would be hunted and not spared. Pirates were feared and hated, and the powerful in Rome would be merciless.

Without waiting for the man's response, I turned and strode from him.

"Leonidas."

The voice was Cassia's. She'd hurried to the remaining casket and was trying in vain to push it along the dock. It screeched an inch, Cassia panting from her effort.

I watched her a moment, dumbfounded. Then I went to her, lifted the heavy box under my arm, took her by the shoulder, and marched her to the street.

"How did you know?" I asked Cassia.

We sat in the garden in the middle of Priscus's apartment block, the sun setting in a pale blue sky.

Priscus was inside with his son, Decimus Laelius the Younger. His father had seen personally to having Decimus bathed, shaved, and dressed in fine clothes. The servants, equally astonished and weeping at Decimus's rescue, hovered around, plying him with food and drink. In fact, many of the residents of the complex had spilled forth to lend their sympathy and offers of help. The young man was exhausted and bruised, with hollows under his eyes, but he tolerated the attention with good cheer.

Cassia and I, the outsiders, were given leave to sit in the

garden with a small meal. The rest of the household quickly forgot about us.

"I didn't know." Cassia adjusted her feet as she sat on a low stool under the portico. "Not until I saw Decimus run to Priscus. I guessed, but I wasn't certain."

"The servants didn't realize his son had been kidnapped?" This surprised me. Servants knew everything that went on in a household.

"Decimus is actually his step-grandson. Priscus adopted Decimus as his son and heir, but he's a grandson of his wife, from her first marriage, the only one of his wife's family left. Priscus and his wife raised Decimus from babyhood, after Decimus's parents were killed by marauders."

Decimus must have been certain he'd share his parents' fate. I leaned my back to the marble-faced column, stretching my legs. My muscles were cramped by the fight—no medicus or massage for me today.

"They knew all that but not that Decimus had been held for ransom?"

"The household is as stunned as you are. Decimus had recently traveled from Halicarnassus to Antioch. Now that there is peace in Parthia, Decimus wants to try to expand the business in eastern cities, with Antioch as their base. As far as the servants knew, Decimus was still there, sending dutiful letters home."

"How did you guess, then?" I'd been taken completely by surprise while Cassia had put together—rapidly—the true purpose of our journey.

She finished the last of her meal, grapes, which she plucked from the stem and chewed, carefully depositing the pits into a small container provided for the purpose.

"I thought about how Priscus was behaving. When a man is concerned about costly goods, fearing ruin if something happens to those goods, he's naturally nervous and worried. But when he's concerned about a *person*, especially one he loves deeply, it is different. His fear is more concentrated, and he will also try to hide it. Roman men, highborn ones in particular, do not like to appear sentimental." Cassia arranged the empty stem neatly on her plate and wiped her fingers on a cloth. "I lived inside a villa my entire life, with a very wealthy and powerful family. I learned much about what people are like and how they truly feel, in spite of what they say to others."

I had a vision of Cassia, very young, her serious eyes watching everything going on about her and noting it down on her tablet.

"Who taught you to write?" I asked on impulse.

Sorrow crossed her face. "My father. He was the secretary and keeper of the household accounts. He taught me everything he knew."

The father was dead, I gathered from her expression. Even I had learned how to understand what a person was feeling.

I wanted to ask her more questions about him, and how she'd ended up in Rome, but I fell silent. There would be time for that later, and I did not want unseen ears in this house hearing our private conversation.

"I do not know who kidnapped the poor lad," Cassia said. "The men who led us to the docks and who were holding him make unlikely pirates. I think they were hired by the kidnapper to convey Decimus from Antioch and collect the money. I wonder what will happen to them when they report to whoever hired them that they only retrieved half the ransom? They didn't count on you being there."

A gleam of satisfaction lit Cassia's eyes. I wasn't certain if the satisfaction came from me rousting the men or the fact that we'd saved one casket of coins.

"They might try to collect the second half," I warned. "Or kidnap the lad again."

Cassia nodded agreement. "If so, we will have to raise our fee. You were hired to protect Priscus while he collected his goods, not fight off pirates and abductors."

"Priscus kept the secret well."

"It is possible the ransom demand stated that if he told anyone, Decimus would be killed. Priscus would not have risked that."

I thought of how Priscus had clasped his son to him and wept, and how abrupt Priscus had grown when any questions I'd asked while we'd waited grew too penetrating.

I'd seen men condemned to death, afraid of what they would face, but I'd rarely witnessed fear for another person. Had only felt it in myself once, and then the fear had been realized all too soon. The greatest friend I'd had in the world had vanished from my life between one heartbeat and the next.

Cassia, I suspected, had felt the same fear and grief. I'd seen its remnants when she'd spoken of her father.

The garden was quiet, the household attending to Decimus and Priscus. I wondered if we'd return immediately to Rome or if Priscus would remain here with his son. Would Priscus want me to stay with him, or dismiss me?

It was odd to not know what I would do from one day to the next. In the *ludus*, I always knew. Aemil had kept us to an unvarying routine.

Cassia must feel the same. If she'd lived as a slave in the same house for her entire life, her day-to-day existence would have been mapped out, her duties and restrictions carved in stone.

We both were forging our way into the unknown, like travelers breaking a trail into the wilderness. No roads, no maps to guide us. I wasn't certain whether to rejoice or panic.

At the moment, the need to sleep washed over me, the usual aftermath of a fight and a good meal. My eyes grew heavy, my limbs warm with fatigue.

I mumbled something to Cassia, rose, and shuffled inside to lie down in the atrium next to the silent fountain. Cassia remained in the garden. As I settled myself, folding my arms for warmth, I saw her turn her face serenely to the moonlit sky and the glitter of tears on her cheeks.

In the morning, Priscus summoned me to him. He and his adopted son took breakfast in a large room off the atrium, with wall paintings framed in red and yellow. Satyrs capered with maidens, and a hunt trailed off along another wall, painted to look as though the animals and their pursuers rushed into a wild landscape.

Priscus and Decimus sat on stools at a table of plain wood in the middle of the room. I'd learned in my years of visiting grand *domii* that eating couches were used only for lavish banquets, where guests would recline to partake in a feast. Everyday meals were eaten around a table, as Cassia and I did in our much smaller space.

Priscus smiled warmly as I entered and awaited his instructions. His son regarded me curiously. Decimus bore signs of exhaustion, plus a nervousness that might never leave him. He had dark hair, thick and wavy, and deep brown eyes. He was perhaps a few years younger than I, but plenty old enough to be in charge of a branch of business far from home.

"I haven't had a chance to thank you, Leonidas," Priscus said. "And to apologize for not being more forthcoming about what I faced."

I bowed my head in deference. "I understand. Cassia explained how dangerous it was."

"She is a bright young woman," Priscus said. "Please thank her for her presence of mind to save the money. I'd have left the coins behind. Not bothered about them at all."

"Which is why Mother put *me* in charge of interests in the eastern sea." Decimus sent his father a fond but exasperated look.

"She was indeed wise. You have done well, Leonidas. You may journey back to Rome. I will remain here for a time—we have things to sort out. Send your Cassia to collect the fee from my scribe at home."

I hesitated. I was happy to be finished with this task and pay the merchants Cassia owed, but uneasiness niggled at me.

"Are you safe here? What about the assassin trying to kill you? Was he trying to stop you from rescuing your son?"

Priscus gave me a gentle smile. "I invented the assassin. A plausible reason, I thought, to hire a former gladiator to protect me. I could not tell anyone the true reason. They only knew I was worried."

I went over the journey in my head, understanding now why Priscus had been indifferent about being in the open. Even so, I'd had the prickle in my shoulder blades that told me of a watcher the entire distance, and I'd definitely been attacked in Rome.

Before I could answer, the young man who tended the door rushed inside.

"Sir," he blurted.

I'd witnessed more than one *dominus* beat a slave who dared interrupt or even enter a room without being summoned, but Priscus only waited for the lad to speak.

"I heard word from the port, sir," the boy went on, eyes wide. "The sailors what held our young man—all dead, sir. Every one of them."

CHAPTER 9

Priscus half-rose at the lad's announcement, and Decimus gaped in shock. "How?" the younger man demanded.

"Don't know," the door slave said. "They were found laid out on the dock, every one of them with their throat cut."

As though they'd been executed, I thought.

Decimus swallowed, color leaving his face. "A few were kind to me."

Priscus sank to his seat, laying a hand on his son's arm. "I counted more than a dozen, in the end. All murdered?"

The door lad nodded. "Seems so."

Priscus turned to me, as though I could explain. "How could so many be killed, on a deserted dock?"

"With twice as many armed men than the sailors," I said. "Well organized. Like soldiers."

"Hmm. I reported the ship to the harbor authorities, but the crew would have been arrested, not simply executed in place." Priscus seemed less perturbed than his son, but he lightly tapped the table, his focus in the distance. "I had thought to linger here for a time, but I believe we should return to Rome. Leonidas, would you be so good as to guard us on the way?"

THE JOURNEY FROM OSTIA, WHICH WE BEGAN THE MORNING after the slave's announcement of the sailors' murders, took less time than the journey down. Priscus wanted to keep a faster pace, with fewer rest stops.

Decimus was clearly not recovered, but he sat his horse competently and never complained. A resilient young man. Priscus's servants doted on him, which was plain as we went along. He barely had to mention he was thirsty before they fell over themselves offering him a wineskin.

We reached Rome and Priscus's large house on the Esquiline a few hours before nightfall. Priscus's scribe, Kephalos, duly handed Cassia a pouch of coins, which disappeared inside her robes.

Cassia's step was lighter as we traversed the streets toward home. We stepped against a wall as a procession came through, the tinny sound of jingling bells brushing the air. A priestess of Isis, with a cobra on her arm walked sedately along, her eyes on the snake, while the crowd melted out of her way.

The first thing Cassia did when we reached the apartment, after removing her cloak and shaking the dust from her shoes, was to pour out the money we'd received and count it.

I rubbed my close-cropped hair, finding it coated with dust. In spite of the December chill, I smelled of sweat and the road.

"I'm for the baths," I told Cassia as she whispered numbers. Her stylus flashed as did the beads of the abacus she seemed to have acquired.

Cassia nodded at me, not taking her attention from her figures. I think this was the happiest I'd seen her since she'd been thrust into my life.

I had to pay a quarter of an *as*, the smallest copper coin, which Cassia had pushed at me before I left, to enter a bathhouse on the Quirinal, not far from our apartment. These were not a huge complex like the baths built by Agrippa or the ones

Nero was currently having constructed. This bathhouse had a modest tepidarium, a larger caldarium, and even bigger frigidarium. I had to pay another *as* to buy a strigil—the one I'd used in the past years was still at the *ludus*, with the rest of my meager belongings I hadn't bothered to collect.

The strigil was cheap and thin, but it would do. I stripped down, paid an attendant to look after my clothes, and went to the small yard to work up a sweat.

Men and women crowded to watch me, curious as to what sort of exercises a gladiator would do. I lifted various weighted stones, which had been carved to be easy to grip. I followed this with kicks and lunges, plus arm swings I'd done to warm my body before sword training. Younger men studied me carefully, and when I quit the yard, began to copy my movements.

I handed my strigil to another attendant, who used it to scrape sweat and sand from my body, then I plunged straight into the cold water without bothering with the hot or tepid. This bathhouse had a room even hotter than the caldarium, where people went for extra sweating to cleanse their bodies, but the heat of that made me too sleepy.

The cold bath, on the other hand reinvigorated me. The water in the large pools was constantly replenished by a fountain flowing out of the wall in the shape of a fish's gaping mouth. The excess overflowed the sides, running down into the drains to the great system of sewers beneath the city.

When I emerged from the bath, I noticed I'd drawn a crowd there too. Pretending to ignore the spindly men who watched me, I dried myself, dressed, and departed.

I'd once used a niche for my clothes instead of paying an attendant to care for them, and an enterprising thief had stolen every stitch, knowing that the used garments of a gladiator would fetch a huge price. My friend Xerxes had rescued me, arriving with a tunic in response to my summons, so I wouldn't have to trudge naked across the cold city. He'd laughed so hard he could barely walk as we'd made our way back to the *ludus*.

I missed Xerxes with an acuteness that jabbed my gut.

As I emerged onto the street, a woman ran straight into me. She was wrapped in a cloak against the chilling wind, and she clutched at me, out of breath. A fold of cloak fell, revealing overly bright red hair.

"Lucia," I said in surprise.

"Leonidas. I've been looking for you for days. You weren't home."

"Had to go to Ostia. Job." Not unusual for me.

Lucia gulped a sob. "Floriana. She's dead."

Dead? I seized Lucia by the arm and pulled her with me down the hill and through the side street to my new abode. I tugged her inside.

"What happened?" I demanded as we climbed the stairs. "I thought Marcianus cured Floriana of the poison."

Marcianus could work miracles. If he said the woman would recover, she should have.

"He did. She was healing." We reached the apartment, which was empty, Cassia nowhere in sight. "She felt well enough to go out again. There was a fog, a heavy one—oh, five days ago. Someone stuck a knife into her. Leonidas, I'm so afraid."

I sat down heavily. The morning we'd left Rome, six days ago, the fog had been dense, opaque, typical. "What happened? Who did this?"

Lucia hadn't bothered with cosmetics today, and her face was blotchy, her eyes red-rimmed where they were usually lined with kohl. "They will kill me next. Where can I hide, Leonidas? You are free now. Take me away from here." Her panic was true.

I grasped her wrist, trying to calm her. "Who are *they*? And why would anyone want to kill you?"

"Whores know secrets." Lucia's lips twisted. "At least, people think they do."

"What secrets?"

Lucia pulled from my hold. "I don't know. But they will think she told me. All the girls have fled. Marcia ran off to find that *medicus* of yours—I don't know what good that will do her. I thought of you, but you weren't *here*."

She began to weep, sobs jerking her body. Lucia folded her arms over her stomach, trembling in her frayed linen gown.

I rose and drew her into my arms. Lucia did not embrace me but leaned against me, as though taking comfort in my strength.

Cassia found us like this, me stroking Lucia's hair and trying to quiet her. Cassia set down the basket of bread and the clay pot that smelled of stew and turned to me inquisitively.

"This is Lucia," I told her.

"Ah." The word was quiet but held understanding.

Lucia jerked from me in alarm. When she saw Cassia she relaxed, as though dismissing her as unthreatening.

"Give Lucia some of the money," I ordered. "She needs to leave Rome. Floriana is dead."

Cassia made no move to obey. "Dead? But ..."

"Stabbed. The morning we left. Lucia is afraid. She must go."

Cassia regarded Lucia dubiously, and Lucia frowned. "Do not stand there gaping at your betters, girl," Lucia snapped. "Do as he says."

She might have been a fly buzzing about the room for all Cassia paid attention. Cassia directed her words to me. "If Floriana is dead, are her women released by her will? Or owned by someone else?"

"Floriana freed all of us a few years ago." Lucia also spoke to me as though I were alone in the room. "She'd been a slave herself but was freed by her husband, or a man she called her husband. Fat lot of good he was. He's somewhere in Etruria. He probably doesn't even know she's dead."

"Someone will inform him," Cassia said. "He'll come to wrap up her business, or send a retainer to do it."

"None of this matters. I need to leave." Lucia turned to Cassia. "Fetch the coin."

Cassia glanced at me for confirmation, and I gave her a nod. "Enough so she can journey ... somewhere."

I had no idea where in the empire Lucia would be safe. If Floriana's murder had been on impulse—a robber chancing upon her in the fog—Lucia might be fine a few miles out of the city. But if Floriana been killed by important men, fearing she and her women knew things they should not, Lucia might be hunted with persistence. I would have to warn Marcianus to hide Marcia.

Cassia went without hurry to a spot near my bed, hunkering down to move one of the stones in the floor. She drew from a recess below it the clinking bag Kephalos had handed her. Lucia watched with interest, as did I. I'd no idea where Cassia had hidden the money.

Cassia carried the bag to the table, scooped out a handful of coins, and carefully lined them up. The inevitable tablet came out, she making marks as she sorted the coins into stacks.

"What are you doing?" Lucia demanded of her. "Are you a moneylender now? Just give them to me."

She lunged at the table, but I caught Lucia's arms in a firm grip. "Let her. She'll know how much you'll need."

Lucia gaped at me but subsided.

"If you need to hide from bad men, I know where you can do so," Cassia said. "It is a distance from here, but you should be safe enough."

"Leonidas can escort me."

Cassia was already shaking her head. "Too many will recognize him and know you are his paramour. Also, you will have to change into a plainer dress. I have one you can wear."

Cassia turned to a large wooden box that had not been in the apartment earlier this afternoon. She rummaged through it and emerged with a simple stolla which she shook out. The plain linen was a sharp contrast to Lucia's worn but garish finery. This was a respectable woman's garb.

Without a qualm, Lucia slid from her gown, her bare flesh covered only by a strip of cloth about her hips. Cassia averted her eyes from Lucia's body but helped her put on the stolla, settling it on her shoulders. A brown cloak came next out of the box, also plain and a bit worn.

Cassia always dressed so neatly I was surprised she'd purchased a threadbare palla, but I saw that it disguised Lucia well. Cassia bound Lucia's dyed red hair into a small knot, easily hidden when Cassia arranged the folds of the palla over Lucia's head.

Cassia stood back to admire her work. Lucia now looked like any other lower-class woman heading out to fetch water or run an errand for her mistress.

"There is a house along the Via Appia, at the base of Mount Albanus, near the lake," Cassia said. "It is called the Domus Ceres. They will take you in, give you sanctuary. Tell them I sent you."

"What sort of house?" Lucia asked in suspicion.

"One that will protect you. You can stay there until it is safe to return to Rome."

"How will I know when that will be?"

"Leonidas will send word." Cassia pulled a few hard rolls from the basket plus a napkin folded around dried figs. She dropped them into a smaller basket and shoved it all at Lucia. "You should hurry."

Lucia sent me an inquiring look, and I nodded in agreement. As much as I would miss being with Lucia, Floriana's death alarmed me more than I'd admitted. Lucia was right to flee.

I walked Lucia down the stairs but did not open the door when we reached the bottom. The fewer people who associated the woman in drab clothing with me, the better.

"Godspeed," I whispered, pressing a brief kiss to her lips. "I will burn an offering for you."

Lucia returned my kiss without heat and glanced behind me up the stairs. "That colorless miss will not please you in bed, I think."

"I won't use her for bed," I said patiently. "She's not for that."

Lucia's expression held skepticism. "Do you trust her to lead me to a good place?"

"Yes." So far, Cassia had not given me reason to doubt her. "If she says this house is safe, I believe her."

"Hmm." Lucia studied me for a time, then her gaze softened and she kissed me with more warmth. "Farewell, Leonidas. I hope to see you again this side of the Stygian."

"I will send for you when it's safe," I promised.

She did not believe me, but that didn't matter. Lucia touched my cheek, then she opened the door and slipped out into the stream of people pushing their way home for the night. I watched the brown cloak bob in the current, then she was gone.

When I reached the top of the stairs, Cassia was setting out our supper. I watched her neat, competent movements as she arranged bowls, spoons, and plates in straight lines, her stool in the exact center of her side of the table.

"You purchased extra clothes." I plunked down on my stool and reached for the bread.

Cassia continued serving the food. She'd bought greens dressed with flecks of fruit, oil, and cheese, along with a stew of lentils and beans and a flask of wine.

"I thought the clothes might be handy." Cassia seated herself and lifted a spoon. "I didn't realize they'd find use so soon."

"The cloak was frayed." I wasn't quite certain how to put my puzzlement into words.

"If I need to move through the streets without drawing attention, an old cloak is better than a fine garment. No one pays attention to a poor woman or a slave from a meager household."

"It is true no one saw you following us in Ostia," I conceded. "Except me."

"You are familiar with me and more observant than most, I am coming to understand."

I shoveled stew into my mouth and washed it down with

wine. This was a smoother vintage than what we'd drunk before—Cassia was putting Priscus's coins to good use.

"I'm a gladiator." I tapped my knuckles to my head. "Nothing in here."

"You are a gladiator who won thirty fights with eight draws and only two losses. I have seen the notices on the streets. You must be a very observant man, and a quick thinker, to do that."

I won because I'd trained unceasingly for my bouts, but it was true I never knew what would happen in the amphitheatre. I had to react to the smallest moves my opponent made—or decide not to react. I let my instincts rule, but instinct wasn't always correct and had to be tempered with experience.

"Winning a match is not the same thing as living everyday life," I said.

"It can be." Cassia traced the glazed pattern on her wine cup. "I'm sorry Lucia had to leave. I know you are fond of her."

I shrugged. I liked Lucia, but I had no illusion about who she was or how many other men she pleasured. "She is not my paramour, as you declared. Will she be truly well in this house you sent her to?"

"Indeed, yes. My mistress stayed there several times when she traveled between Campania and Rome, and I came to know it well. The *domus* is run by priestesses of Ceres, and no man may darken its door. Lucia might have to work for her keep, but they will keep danger away."

Did I see a glint of satisfaction in her eyes when she mentioned Lucia would have to work? I wondered if, when Lucia was told she'd have to scrub floors or haul water, she'd stay. Even Floriana's brothel had employed slaves to do the menial tasks for them.

"Who was your mistress?" I asked in curiosity. Cassia knew much about me—most of my career as a gladiator covered the walls in Rome for all to see—but I knew so little about her.

"Glaucia Rufinus." Cassia waited for my reaction, but I'd never heard of the woman. "Her husband, Gaius Petinus, was a consul some years back, very wealthy. He moved to a villa in Campania after his consulship to raise grapes. The villa is beautiful, with a view of the sea."

"You father was this Petinus's scribe?"

"Scribe, secretary, accountant." As before when she'd spoken of her father, Cassia's voice went sad, and she quickly bent to her food.

"I am sorry." I laid down my spoon and wiped my mouth on the napkin she'd provided. "I had a friend called Xerxes. I never had a brother, but it was like that. He was killed in the games."

Cassia looked up, lips parted. "Oh."

"It was very hard to live after that," I finished.

"Yes." The word was soft. "My life changed when my father died. I never realized how much he protected me."

"They sold you?"

Cassia's eyes flickered. "My mistress did. She had me brought to the slave market here in Rome. Hesiodos purchased me. I thought I would be working for him, assisting him in his scribal duties, but then he said I'd suit you. I still don't understand why."

I imagined Cassia, afraid and alone, standing in the slave market, a sign around her neck proclaiming what she did. They might have let her wear a stolla, or she might have been only in a loincloth, or naked, so those who shopped for a new servant would have a look at what they were getting.

My anger stirred at her former mistress, at the slave traders, and even at her father for dying and leaving her alone.

I drained my wine cup, lifted the flask, and poured more. I filled Cassia's cup as well. I steadied my voice as I answered her, "I don't understand why either."

Cassia lifted her cup, the humiliation of her ordeal fading from her eyes. She was with me now, and safe.

"We will simply have to find out," she said.

I SLEPT HEAVILY THAT NIGHT, OBLIVIOUS TO THE NOISE IN THE streets as wagons and carts delivered goods, including wine to the merchant downstairs. My dreams, what there were of them, flitted through my head like ghosts. Xerxes appeared in one, laughing at me from the Elysium fields and raising his wine glass to me as Cassia had done at supper.

A poke in my side made Xerxes dissolve, his grin fading.

I pried open my eyes to see Cassia at the end of a slim stick. She was learning.

Her thick tail of hair tumbled over her shoulder, a black streak on her pale stolla. Her eyes were wide with worry.

"Hesiodos is here," she said in a hoarse whisper. "He says he's come to take you to the Palatine. Nero has asked to see you."

CHAPTER 10

Hesiodos waited on the street. He gave me an impatient glare when we emerged—I'd had to rise and dress, with no time to run to the barber for a shave.

Cassia was neatly coiffed, sandals tied, her palla expertly draped over her spotless stolla. Hesiodos had made clear, she'd said, that the summons included her.

It wasn't rare for a *princeps* of Rome to command a gladiator to appear before him. Nero took great interest in gladiatorial games and chariot racing, even more so than many ordinary citizens. I'd performed exhibitions with other gladiators in Nero's vast gardens in the past. I hoped he would not ask me to perform this morning, but if he did, I'd have no choice but to obey.

Cassia hid her worry, but it was there. Nero could order her to do anything at all, and she'd have less choice than I. Why Hesiodos insisted Cassia accompany us, I didn't know. Hesiodos gave me a flat stare when I asked and turned his back to lead us onward.

We strode down the Argiletum past the Curia to the Forum Romanum. Here, Hesiodos turned to skirt the long, elegant

Basilica Aemilia, the shops under its porticos doing brisk business while people streamed into and out of the halls inside. Past the Temple of the Vestals, we left the Sacra Via and made our way up the steep ramp to the Palatine.

I was struck by the quiet on the hill. We left behind the shouts and stench of the Roman streets to emerge into open spaces and green gardens.

Since the reign of Augustus, none but the *princeps* could build on the Palatine, and so it had become a vast complex for the ultimate rulers of Rome.

Nero currently occupied the *domii* begun by Tiberius and expanded by Gaius during his brief reign, but Nero had begun construction on a building that would join all the palaces together, with walkways and large rooms full of light and air. Part of the hill had been leveled for the terrace on which the house would be built. *Domus Transitoria*, Marcianus had told me it was called.

Men labored there, some hoisting blocks with cranes similar to the ones we'd seen in Ostia. Others built wooden frameworks that would support concrete vaulted ceilings until they were dried and cured. I glanced their way, my interest quickening. The mundane sight of builders easing blocks to the tops of walls, the sounds of hammering, and the shouts of orders and questions somewhat eased my anxiety.

A stern-faced man met Hesiodos and led us away from the builders and through a gate to a large inner courtyard.

Mosaics under my feet showed beautiful goddesses offering plates of plenty to visitors, as well as warriors of old flexing their muscles. This entryway, lined with expertly carved friezes, gave way to a courtyard, with a large fountain laid out in four arced shapes with statues on each corner.

We moved past this, the spray chilling the air, and under a colonnade to a wide and quiet room with another fountain. Arched walls soared above us, echoing the whisper of sandals on marble as the functionaries hurried about on their duties.

The stern-faced man bade us to wait and disappeared under one of the arches. Hesiodos wandered from us, as though not wanting to be seen with a lowly gladiator and the woman who worked for him.

Cassia studied the mosaics and carved pillars with interest. The tall marble fountain in the middle of the room featured a nymph pouring water from an urn into a bowl. Cassia's nervousness came to me in waves, but in spite of that, she paused in appreciation of the artwork.

The stern man returned, beckoning us without a word. Instead of joining us, Hesiodos hung back, gesturing for us to accompany the palace servant. Cassia and I started after the man, but when I turned to look for Hesiodos, I saw him strolling toward the open courtyard.

Cassia and I exchanged a tense glance as we followed the other man in silence.

We went up a short flight of stairs and out into a peristyle garden, its walkway lined with columns of yellow, gray, and red marble. An open end of the garden overlooked the western ridge of the Palatine, probably with a view of the Circus Maximus, though I could not see from where I stood.

A young man with a head of thick dark curls reposed artfully on a bench between two of the columns, one foot on the seat as he leaned against the pillar behind him. He held a lyre that he softly strummed.

The man who'd led us in turned around without a word and stalked out. I noted guards in the shadows of the walkway, thick-hilted swords at their sides, one posted at the end of the garden near the overlook.

The young man on the bench began to sing.

The song, in Latin, was about a beautiful woman in love with a man, the lovers kept apart. They managed to elude those who forbade them to be together, experiencing one night of happiness before dying tragically. To me, it was a cloying and repetitious tale, but Cassia listened with shining eyes.

The piece ended, and the young man sighed and laid down the lyre. He rose, carefully stretching his limbs before deigning to speak to us.

"You liked it," he said to Cassia with approval.

Cassia instantly sank to her knees, hiding her face on the floor. She, a female slave, should not look upon the highest citizen in the land. I also dropped down, in case the *princeps* lost his temper and ordered one of the guards to decapitate me on the spot. My right knee throbbed as it hit the floor—it hadn't healed all the way from the bout that had gained me my freedom.

"Stand up, my friends," Nero said. His voice was almost musical, smooth and low-pitched. "Within this room, we *are* friends. You liked my song."

I helped Cassia to her feet as Nero waited. She nodded, readjusting the folds of her cloak. "Beautiful. Like Limenius."

"Ah, you understand. You are Greek, Hesiodos tells me. We must not expect the gladiator to think as we do."

I kept my face blank, like the stupid fighting man I was supposed to be.

"Let's have another." Nero resumed his lyre, seated himself, and started to play again.

I made myself not shift in impatience. I'd endured this before—Nero had a need to entertain others before others were allowed to entertain him. Many despised him for this, but not, of course, in his presence.

Cassia enjoyed the song, which was in Greek this time, so I did not understand any of it. I assumed it was good. Cassia did not strike me as a woman who flattered without sincerity.

"Excellent." She applauded softly when Nero finished. He smiled at her, a large, genuine smile, relieved he'd found someone who appreciated his talent.

"Now then, my friends." Nero at last set aside the lyre and rubbed his hands, as though they ached from the playing. "You must be agog to know why I've summoned you. It is simple. You man—Decimus Laelius Priscus—on his way to and cia. Helped rescue his son from kidnappers."

as not surprised the story had reached the Palatine. Pris us had reported the crime, and the sensational tale must be the main topic at suppers all over Rome by now.

Cassia and I nodded in silence, neither of us foolish enough to speak without permission.

"I would like you to continue protecting him," Nero said. "I fear for his life. Such an old man, who has made many enemies in his time."

Priscus seemed robust for his age. However Nero was a few years younger than I, and to him, Priscus must seem ancient.

Cassia had told me that Priscus had been a friend to Claudius. Not all Claudius's followers had supported Nero—Nero had been the man's adopted son, displacing and later killing Claudius's legitimate heir, Britanicus.

Now Nero sounded sympathetic to Priscus, worried about him, which was strange. I knew, though, that personal considerations sometimes outweighed political ones ... sometimes.

"Be diligent," Nero went on. "Nothing must happen to Priscus, nothing at all. I brought you here to emphasize that point. Naturally, I could have simply sent you word."

I'd wondered about that. Nero must want more from us than an audience for his music and a warning he could have given us via messenger.

Nero ran an assessing gaze over me. "I must congratulate you, Leonidas. Freedom from the games is quite an achievement. However, I trust you will demonstrate your talent for me from time to time, when I request it."

I bowed my head and murmured, "Of course, sir."

"*After* you watch over Priscus for me. See that he remains home in the coming days."

I glanced up in concern. "Is there a threat? Even now that his son is safe?"

Nero gave me a look intended to be wise, but he didn't have

the face for it. "Rome is always dangerous. Well I know this." He shuddered delicately. "Let us not speak of it and have more music. Leonidas, please go away. I would like Cassia to remain. She has an ear."

My blood chilled. Cassia had no power, and Nero could do with her what he pleased. He might simply play his lyre for her for several hours, but he also might decide to sate a few appetites on her, and she could do nothing to stop him. His appetites were rumored to be exotic.

I cleared my throat. "I have need of her. Sir."

Nero's carefully plucked brows rose. "I can't think why. Off you go, gladiator. I will send her home when I am finished."

I flashed a glance at Cassia, which she returned without expression. I had to leave her—I had no choice. It burned me inside to go through the door, and I kept my steps slow.

I paused in the lavish room outside the peristyle while the guards closed the doors behind me, shutting Cassia in with the *princeps* of all Rome. I waited until I heard the plucked strings of the lyre and Nero's voice rise in song before I made myself walk away.

I REFUSED TO GO HOME. A SERVANT LED ME FIRMLY OUT OF the *domus*, but I planted myself in the outer courtyard, saying I'd wait for Cassia.

One of the Praetorian Guards broke from wall duty and advanced on me. "Leonidas the Spartan," he announced.

"I am."

The man pulled off his helmet and grinned at me, becoming a human being. "I've seen you win many a game. Won plenty of coin on you, I have to say."

"Good."

My curtness did not put him off. "I am Severus Tullius. You can count me as a friend on the Palatine."

I wondered what he meant, but I did not ask or argue. I gave him a cordial nod, but I was too distracted for conversation.

"I will make certain your slave is returned to you," he said good-naturedly.

"I'll wait." I leaned against a block wall and folded my arms. The blocks were stone, fitted together precisely. The youth I'd once been knew exactly how it had been done.

Tullius could easily drive me off, but he widened his grin. "A good slave is hard to come by. One doesn't like to lose them."

"No."

Tullius seemed to enjoy my laconic answers. He gave me a salute and strolled away to resume his duties, chuckling as he went.

The sun was setting by the time I spied Cassia walking sedately along the outside wall. She hadn't exited by the main gate, which I had been glaring at, but a side door, probably shown out by the servants of the house.

I pushed myself from the wall and strode to her, which earned me a surprised look.

"I thought you'd have gone," Cassia said as we started down the hill. "Or would be rushing to make certain Priscus was well."

"Not until he let you go." I was relieved to see her palla was as neatly placed as ever, her face serene. "What happened?"

"Nothing. He sang me several ballads, and we discussed them. When he grew bored, he rang for a servant who showed me out."

I released a breath. We tramped down the hill, skirting the Forum Romanum and its crowds. We moved past vendors and shops on the way to the base of the Quirinal, but when Cassia wanted to linger to look over wares, I pulled her on.

I did not stop until we climbed up to our small apartment and I shut the door.

After the lofty *domus* of Nero, the apartment felt tiny and closed in, but I preferred it. A small space I could call my own, where I could shut out the world, suited me better than soaring courtyards and vast fountains.

Cassia unwound her cloak and hung it on its peg, adjusting her stolla on her shoulders. "If you are worried that Nero demanded I … service him, he did not." She cleared her throat, uncomfortable. "I believe he was happy to find an audience not impatient with his offering. And he is quite good."

"Is he?" The release of being home, with Cassia safe, on top of the shock of Floriana's death, and Nero's strange request that we look after Priscus, was making me sleepy again. It was a reaction I often had when faced with too many worries. "I thought the pieces long and tedious. The one in Greek I didn't understand at all."

"He is skilled—has been well trained. I believe he'd be much happier as a musician than the *princeps*. The songs are complex and take a schooled ear to understand."

I sat down heavily on a stool and removed my sandals, which were full of grit. I wanted another bath.

"And you have a schooled ear?"

"My mistress sent a tutor to teach me music when I was very young, so that I could play and entertain the family. Made a savings on hiring musicians. The music master not only taught me to play but gave me lessons on music history and theory. Pythagoras and Aristotle and so forth. I found it fascinating."

I felt like a mongrel dog who'd been placed in a kennel with a well-bred hunter or a sleek, exotic cat. I wondered if our benefactor, whoever he might be, had planned this, and was amused by it.

INSTEAD OF BATHING OR SLEEPING, I LED CASSIA TO THE Esquiline Hill to check on Priscus. He was home, Celnus told us when he came outside to speak to us, tending Decimus. Neither father nor son had been out since we'd returned from Ostia.

Celnus refused to let us in, but he agreed with us that Priscus and Decimus should stay indoors and safe. Priscus himself hardly wanted to risk Decimus's life again, Celnus said, and so was keeping his son home with him.

Short of forcing my way in, I had to be satisfied with this. I bade Celnus not to let them stir, or to send for me to guard them if they insisted. Celnus answered with a curl of his lip, but I saw that he was worried enough to do so.

When we reached home again, my fatigue swamped me, and I sought my bed. I noticed, as I laid down again, that my bed had grown more comfortable. I had a warmer blanket, a cushion for my head, and a small table on which to set a cup of wine.

I was heavily asleep when Cassia yelped in fear.

I came off my pallet as an intruder pushed his way past the door and had him by the neck in the matter of a few breaths. He poked a short sword into my ribs, the scratch stinging my skin.

The next instant, he landed against the wall, and the sword was in my hand, aimed at his throat.

CHAPTER 11

"Leave off!" The man cried out in terror. "I'm only doing me job."

"Assassination?" I demanded.

His dark eyes rounded. "Checking for fires."

I came to myself with a start. The young man in my grip wasn't a Thracian gladiator ready to stab me in the heart, or a *provacatur* battling me to the death.

He was one of the vigiles who swarmed Rome at night, on the lookout for fire, which was always a grave danger. They used their power to bully their way into houses as he had apparently bullied his way into mine.

"No fires here," I said in a hard voice. The only flame came from an oil lamp, which Cassia had just lit.

The vigile gulped. "Well, I saw a flare. Thought there could be danger. Made the wine merchant open the door downstairs."

"And you've checked. Found that all is well."

"Yes."

I began to release him then looked him over sharply. "You were at Floriana's. Outside her house, when she was sick."

The young man jolted, his face taking on a greenish tinge. "So? It's on my patch."

A large patch, if it stretched from the Subura to the lower slopes of the Quirinal. I didn't know exactly how the vigiles divided up their duties, so he could be telling the truth, but I remained skeptical.

I shook him. "It was midmorning when I saw you."

"I was on my way home. Interested, wasn't I?"

His voice held defiance, but his terror was real. I couldn't be certain whether that fear came from guilt at Floriana's poisoning and death, or because a large man had him by the throat.

I eased my grip and allowed his feet to touch the floor, but I kept hold of the sword and steered him toward the open door.

"If we have a fear about fire, we'll summon you."

As the vigile teetered on the edge of the stairs, I let him go. He flailed then caught his balance and started downward.

"Wait."

He peered back at me in concern. I handed him the sword, hilt first.

The vigile grabbed it from me. I watched him debate whether to try to go at me with it then decide departing was the wisest course. He clattered down the steps, his boots noisy on the wood, then he was gone. The outer door slammed, and a breeze wafted up the stairs.

I moved a shutter at the balcony and walked out into the cold night. The lane was quiet, no sound but the fast retreating footsteps of the vigile. Wagons clattered by on the Vicus Longinus not far away, but none ventured down this road.

"He didn't see a light." Cassia stepped beside me. "I put it out hours ago."

I nodded grimly. "He came to see what we were doing."

"Out of curiosity?" Cassia let the question hang.

"Maybe." I ran my hand over my head. "Tomorrow, I will visit Priscus again."

I led the way inside and reset the shutters in place.

"Good," Cassia said as I led the way inside and reset the shutter in place. "I worry for him. Priscus is a kind man, for a *paterfamilias*. If not ... perceptive."

"I like him," I said.

"As do I. The servants told me as we journeyed back that no one knows who kidnapped Decimus, including Decimus himself, or why. The thought is that the sailors were out-of-work mercenaries hired to snatch him. If Priscus knows who hired them, he's not saying."

"Is he afraid someone will do it again if he tells?" I settled the final shutter in its slot. Our tiny lamp, in the shape of a woman holding a bowl, flickered in the darkness, the flame glowing on Cassia's face.

"Possibly," she mused. "I wonder why he hasn't taken Decimus off to a country villa to be protected by his own guards. Priscus has little reason to stay in Rome. He has clients who help look after his wife's business interests. I imagine he'd be happier puttering around an estate garden."

If I had my own villa, I would sit in the sunshine every day, or walk along the shaded ambulatory, and learn to garden. I'd bring Cassia, and she could sing her complex ancient ballads beside a trickling fountain.

The vision enticed me. An impossible one for a freedman and a slave who considered extra covers for the beds a luxury.

I took to that bed after relocking the door and murmuring a good-night, seeking dreams of a secluded home, where none would stare at me but the birds.

THE DREAMS DID NOT COME, ONLY DARKNESS. IN THE morning, I woke to a rumbling voice on the stairs. Cassia retreated hurriedly to the balcony as a large man burst through the door. I'd bolted it after the vigile departed, but the wooden bar was flimsy. I would have to replace it.

"Leonidas!"

The shout filled the room. At one time, I'd respond with a hearty, *Regulus!* But his tone held no friendliness. It was early, perhaps the second hour, sunlight scarcely filtering into the narrow street outside.

I rose from my pallet, pulling on my tunic, slipping feet into sandals that had been laid out by my bed.

I said nothing as I walked from the alcove to face him. Regulus had said he'd kill me, and he might have come to do just that.

Regulus was a Latium, a bit shorter than I was. His dark hair was shaved close, his brown eyes hard and intense.

"So this is freedom." Regulus glanced around the narrow room and slice of sunshine from the balcony. "Not much bigger than my cell."

Which had once been mine.

"I don't need a lot of space."

"No, Leonidas was always content with what he had, never wanting more. Ready to die in the games. So was I. Remember?"

His glare pinned me. Regulus and I had been friends, not as close as I had been with Xerxes, but after Xerxes had fallen, I'd found refuge in bantering with Regulus. We'd shared triumphs, drink, stories, laughter.

I saw none of that in the man who faced me, his rage pressed behind a wall of scorn.

"Now *you* are the champion," I said. "Stay alive and gain your freedom."

"Not if freedom means *this*." Regulus swept his gaze over the barren room, the stools at the table, clothes on pegs, the wooden *rudis* on its shelf. "I thought you'd have seventeen women in here. Where are they?"

He glanced under the table as though expecting to find a group of scantily clad dancers hiding there.

"I preferred Lucia. She had to leave Rome."

"Huh." Regulus transferred his gaze to me, his expression too knowing. "After Floriana was gutted. Some say *you* did that, Leonidas."

I eyed him in surprise and alarm. "Why would I kill Floriana?"

"Everyone knows you owed her money and couldn't pay. The arrogant *primus palus*, turned away by a madam. You were in the *lupinarius* when she took sick. When she didn't die, you used a more direct method."

My alarm turned to impatience. "I brought Marcianus to the house to heal her. Why would I do that if I wanted her dead?"

Regulus shrugged. "A blind. You had no way of knowing if Marcianus could save her. You could have hoped the poison too strong or that it had been too long inside her."

"I wasn't in Rome when she was stabbed," I pointed out. "I went to Ostia."

"How will anyone know that? She was killed in the early morning, about eight days ago now, in the fog. Body found when the fog cleared."

The wooden shutter scraped back, and Cassia ducked into the room from the balcony. Regulus started, then gave me a smirk. "You see? I knew the women were somewhere."

If he thought Cassia a promiscuous brothel slave, he'd be disappointed. She looked more like a *domina* with her hair in its tidy knot, her dress modest, baring as little skin as possible.

Cassia opened a large wooden box and withdrew a stack of tablets and several scrolls. She opened the first tablet and scanned through the writing.

"Leonidas left Rome seven mornings ago at the first hour." She pointed to a line of text she'd written then touched a papyrus scroll. "I have the contract between him and a retired senator to escort him to Ostia. Leonidas left this house before the first hour and traveled directly to the gates, where he met the senator. He was not out of my sight or the senator's or his servants' from that hour forward. We returned to Rome four days after that."

Regulus listened with his mouth half open, his dazed expression almost comical. "Who is *she*?" he demanded. "Your council?"

"Cassia. She keeps accounts for me."

"Accounts?" Regulus stared at me in bafflement. "Why did you buy a slave to keep *accounts*? I think you've slipped into madness, my old friend. No wonder you refused to kill me. Your mind has been stolen by the gods. I should feel sorry for you, I suppose."

I didn't want to explain. A tale of an anonymous benefactor who'd procured Cassia for me, and this apartment, but provided no money would sound as mad as Regulus thought me. Let him speculate.

He gave me a smile that hinted of our old camaraderie. "Or are you canny? A woman who keeps tally of expenses as well as warms your bed?"

Regulus pivoted on his heel and stalked to Cassia. He looked her up and down then abruptly hauled her to him, planting his large hand on her breast.

In the next instant, he was hanging in my grip, my wooden sword against his ribs. It was the closest weapon at hand, but if I wielded it hard enough, I could stab him to the bone.

Regulus stared at me in incredulity, then his fury returned. "Go on, Leonidas. Do it. Kill me. As I asked you to." His contempt rang. "In the arena, it would have been merciful. You'd have been praised for the win. Now it will be murder." He pushed his face close to mine. "And for that you'll be executed. Torn to pieces."

The rage inside me wanted to drive the sword home. Regulus might once have been my friend, but I saw that he could be a dangerous enemy. His companionship had hidden the spark of cruelty I spied in him now, one that would spell death for those he fought.

I withdrew the sword and shoved him from me at the same time. "Get out."

Regulus's lip curled. He gave Cassia a leer, then he backed

from me, keeping me in sight before he turned to plunge out the door and down the stairs.

It satisfied me that I'd seen fear in him, the acknowledgment that I could still best him in a fight.

Cassia let out a long breath as I faced her across the table she'd retreated behind, the *rudis* once again imprinting itself on my palm.

This was the second time I'd saved her from being accosted, and I did not regret either event. Cassia was mine, and it was my duty to defend her. She was the entirety of my household, protected by me as its head.

Her fingers shook as she closed the tablets and replaced them and the scrolls in the box. "Perhaps we had better find out what happened to Floriana. In case others think to accuse you."

"You have it written that I did not." I gestured at the box with the *rudis*. I hadn't understood what she'd meant when she'd said she'd keep records, but I admired her efficiency now.

"Yes, but the word of a slave is worth nothing in court. Priscus would have to swear you were with him, but we can't compel him to speak. He's a former senator and a wealthy man, and we have no power to influence him."

Priscus, a man who'd proved to be kind, *might* speak for me, but at the moment he was preoccupied with his son, and he was in danger himself, if Nero was to be believed.

My alarm began to rise again. If Regulus told others of his suspicions, I could well be arrested for Floriana's murder. Why not take the retired gladiator who owed her money and was present when she was poisoned? Easier than hunting for a murderer who might have fled the city days ago.

They'd send me back to the *ludus*, where I'd be fighting for my life once more, or this time, simply executed.

"How can *I* prove who killed Floriana?" I asked. "I wasn't here. Lucia knows, but she has fled." I remembered how afraid she'd been, fearing the killer would be after her too.

"She *might* know." Cassia had taken up her basket and now

wrapped her cloak around her shoulders, preparing to fetch our breakfast. "She could have given Floriana the poison herself, for whatever reason. You sleep soundly, Leonidas. You would not have heard her rise." Her cheeks reddened as she said this, shy about that aspect of life.

I made myself return the *rudis* to its shelf. "I agree she could have poisoned Floriana, but I don't know why she'd want to. Floriana divided the spoils among her women, and protected them."

"There is perhaps no obvious reason," Cassia said. "So we must discover another possible explanation—if one exists. We will find out who killed Floriana and put the information into the hands of someone who can help. Priscus, or Nonus Marcianus, the *medicus*. *He* seems trustworthy and intelligent."

I agreed. Marcianus was a respected citizen, even if he'd descended so far as to treat gladiators. He did so not only because Aemil paid well, but he said he learned much about the body and its ills by so frequently stitching up injured men.

Cassia departed after that, leaving me to stew, and soon brought home bread and cheese, dried grapes and figs. The weather had grown colder with the year's end, and now there was rain. Drops began to patter on the balcony as Cassia returned, and became a deluge as we ate. Cold wind flowed past the shutters to our unheated room.

I finished my meal quickly and prepared to go out, my worry and the cold making me want to move.

"How I can possibly learn what happened on a day I wasn't in Rome?" I asked. I had pulled on a clean tunic while Cassia was shopping, and now I put on boots she had brought home the day before against the rain. I tucked a knife into my belt, one I hadn't been able to reach when Regulus stormed in. That had been a miscalculation.

Cassia was already tidying. "Visit Floriana's house. Ask her neighbors about any odd visitors, or any person who might have threatened her. Find out exactly where she was killed and look for eye witnesses."

"In Rome?" I let out a laugh. "Any who watched the entire thing beginning to end will suddenly turn blind and deaf. They don't want to go to court or be marked for murder themselves."

"Then we must ask subtly."

"I'm a gladiator, not a trained man of law. I don't know how to be subtle."

Cassia gave me one of her assessing looks. "I believe you better at it than you believe. You have to make many decisions in a fight, don't you? I've seen you battle a few times now, even if only brawls, but you don't lash out. You calculate, and attack to win."

Of course I did—that was my training.

"Men of law do the same thing," Cassia said. "Except with words."

"I don't know these words. Unless you mean I should shake witnesses until they tell me what I want to learn."

I half-joked, but Cassia considered my suggestion before dismissing it. "I suppose not—a person would say anything until you ceased. Make conversation with people, as though you are merely gossiping. Remember everything anyone says and tell me exactly."

She had to be mad, but she regarded me in all seriousness.

I refused the cloak Cassia suggested I take. It would hamper me, and the rain would wash my body until I was able to go to the baths.

I left Cassia sorting through her tablets and clumped down the stairs into the street. I'd do as she said and visit Floriana's and then check on Priscus again. I hoped his house had better door bolts than mine.

The rain had lessened, but it came down hard enough to keep most people inside or scurrying from building to building. The roads flowed like rivers, the curved pavement encouraging the water along to gutters that would drain into the sewers beneath our feet.

I walked across the streets on stones that stuck up for this purpose, having to join a line of pedestrians to do so. There weren't many crossings, and we all had to file along one behind the other.

The Subura was as busy as ever, those who lived here not having the luxury of waiting out the rain. They worked or they starved.

The door to Floriana's *lupinarius* was open. I ducked inside, glad for the rain to cease drumming on my head, and waited for my eyes to adjust to the dimness.

The air held mustiness. The shutters had been closed, retaining an odor of burned oil and unemptied slops.

I heard a noise in the back of the house. Not from an animal or trapped bird—a person had made that sound, a thump of a fist on a wall.

Cautiously I made my way down the hall, my fingers around the knife I'd tucked into the pouch on my belt. I sprang silently into the end room, Floriana's, knife ready to strike.

A man inside, small with dark curling hair touched with gray, a toga wrapped carelessly around his frame, turned with a jerk, and then screamed.

CHAPTER 12

I lowered the knife and stared at the man without recognition.

He adjusted his toga and peered past me, as though calculating whether he could get around me and out the door. In his left hand, the one half-tangled in the toga, he held a string with a lead weight tied to it. A tiny thing, nothing one could use as a weapon.

"Who are you?" I demanded.

"I could say, who are *you,* young man?" He looked me up and down with no recognition in return. "You are the intruder, sir."

"I am Leonidas." I saw no reason to lie. "I was a ... friend to Floriana."

"One of her customers, you mean." In spite of his fear, his eyes took on a knowing twinkle. "Former customer, that is. The poor woman was brutally murdered."

"I know. I am trying to discover who struck her down."

I could imagine Cassia's disappointment at my frankness, but I'd warned her I was not subtle.

The man raised thick brows that seemed to perch on the edge of his forehead. "Are you? Well, good luck to you. Probably a robbery. No one is safe on the streets at night, or in a morning fog."

I gestured at the lead weight in his hand. "That is a plumb bob."

His surprise grew. "It is indeed. Are you a builder? You look more like a gladiator."

"You don't attend the games?"

He shuddered. "Too gruesome for me. I know it shows my lack of courage, but I invent excuses when my friends press me to go. I prefer buildings. Dangerous in their own way, but when handled correctly, perfectly peaceful."

I agreed. "Are you measuring these walls?"

"I am. I'm an *architectus*. Gnaeus Gallus. Perhaps you've heard of me?" He watched me hopefully.

"No."

Gallus's face fell. "Ah, well. I try for fame, but I am no Vitruvius. Maybe if I worked on great public buildings instead of former *lupinari* in the Subura, I might make my name. But it is the brickwork and concrete beneath the marble that render the buildings sound."

"I know." I ran my hand along the bricks that showed under the flaking wall paintings. "I once worked for a master builder."

Gallus eyed me doubtfully. "As a quarryman? You appear to be strong enough."

"As an apprentice." So long ago, the days almost forgotten in the blur of training, sleeping, fighting, staying alive.

I recalled my master's sonorous voice as he explained about lifting bolts and the precise fitting of blocks, how the Greeks had built the Parthenon steps in a slight curve so that the entire edifice appeared straight to the eye. How to design walls with a lip on top to hold a wooden ceiling mold so the corridor could be used even while the concrete was being poured to form the barrel vault above.

Memories long suppressed returned to me in a flash. I'd done all I could to blot them out after my arrest. To remember days of contentment had made my time in the dark prison even more horrific.

"Intriguing," Gallus said, scattering my thoughts. "Then you'll appreciate what a mess this house is." He lifted the plumb line to a corner and grimaced as the bob swung out crookedly. "I am inspecting the place to see what can be done with it."

"Why?" I asked, perplexed.

"Because I was hired to, that's why. If you are going to stand in my way, will you put away your knife and hold a few things? The boy who assists me was ill today."

Gallus bent to a corner and lifted a box that contained tools, a straight edge, and tablets like those Cassia used, and thrust it at me.

"I mean, why are *you* here?" I persisted without moving. "Not your apprentices or workers?" An *architectus* was usually too grand to do the menial work himself.

"Because I like to study a building for myself. See how it hums." Gallus pressed his hand to the wall, his thumb landing next to a lurid painting of two women giving a man fellatio. Gallus didn't appear to notice. "This wall is whimpering a bit. We will have to shore it up if we don't knock it down entirely."

I tucked away my knife and took the box, heavy for its size. "Someone has inherited the house?" I wasn't certain whether Floriana, or her husband in Etruria, had owned the building or if Floriana had rented it, or worked for whoever owned or rented it. So many things I didn't know.

"Purchased it. He's had his eye on the place a long time. A prime area for shops, I suppose. One day I'll be lucky and land a commission for a decent temple. My masterpiece in carved marble."

"I thought you said the brickwork and concrete were more important."

"Ha. Cheeky, aren't you? A man can still wish to make his name, and temples and public buildings are how that is accomplished." He sighed. "I suppose Gnaeus Gallus, designer of shops, will have to do."

"Who purchased the building?" I asked. This was the sort of information Cassia would want.

"Haven't met the fellow, only seen letters brought by his scribe. Chap called Sextus Livius."

I'd never heard of him, but I noted the name in my head.

I followed Gallus as he wandered from room to room, looking over walls, studying cracks in the ceiling, clicking his tongue in disapproval. The silence of the place unnerved me. I was used to the laughter of men and women, squeals of pleasure real or feigned, voices arguing, joking, or simply conversing.

The house was empty, bedding gone, no possessions left behind. Someone had cleared it out quickly. I thought of Lucia, terrified, fleeing the city, carrying little. What had happened to Floriana's things, and her money?

These questions flitted through my head as I followed Gallus about. Toting the box, watching Gallus test the solidness of a door frame or examine cracks in the ceiling, brought back a long-forgotten time. I was a youth again, listening to my master growl, "Hand me that leveler, and be quick about it."

He'd been impatient, brusque, hard, and brilliant. Dead now, buried under one of his own creations, and I'd been sentenced to the games for it.

Gallus finished his tour of Floriana's domain and gazed down the hall from the front door. "Much work to be done, but it can be managed. Livius might want the whole thing pulled down, but I think the walls are sound."

I agreed. If the beams were reinforced, the roof could be saved as well.

"Thank you for your assistance, Leonidas." Gallus retrieved the box from my big hands. "Was I right that you are a gladiator?"

"Was."

"Ah. What will you do now that you no longer bash other gladiators?"

"Bodyguard," I said at once.

"Pity. If you've been trained by a master builder, I might have a place for you, depending on what you learned from him. You've helped me well today, and you know about the business. Consider it."

I could only stare at him. Gallus had no duplicity in his eyes, and he threw out the suggestion offhand. Very few talked to me as he'd done today, about ordinary things, builder's things. We'd fallen easily into conversation when he'd asked my opinion on the straightness of a wall, or cracks in the floor.

He might only want me to fetch and carry for him, but the thought of working once more on a builder's site was mixed. On the one hand, I longed for it. On the other, it terrified me.

Gallus waited for my answer, so I nodded. "I will consider."

"Excellent. Good day, Leonidas. You'll find my shop on the Clivus Pullius."

He waved and breezed out, leaving me alone and troubled.

I PONDERED WHAT TO DO NEXT. I'D INSTRUCTED CELNUS NOT to let Priscus or his son leave his house without summoning me. Celnus did not like me, it was apparent, but he did see that I was useful in protecting his master.

I'd not be protecting him, however, if Regulus whipped up the rumor that I'd murdered Floriana. I needed a way to prove without doubt I did not.

Thoughts spun in my head, and no solutions put themselves forward. Regulus had derided my new life—*So this is freedom?* he'd said.

At the *ludus*, things had been simple. I trained, ate, slept, did what I was told, and was allowed out on a limited basis, and then only after I'd proved my reliability.

Now I had to worry about too many things at once—who had murdered Floriana, and would I be blamed? Who'd endangered Priscus, and would they try again? How could I, one man, keep him safe? If Nero was so worried, why not send a contingent of Praetorians to watch his every move?

Cassia had told me to ask questions, but ask them of whom? I wanted to hunt up the vigile who'd invaded our house and demand he tell me what he knew—he must have hovered near Floriana's that morning for a reason.

I also remembered the Praetorian Guard I'd spoken to on the Palatine—Severus Tullius. He'd been friendly, and he might know details about Floriana's murder, or be able to find out. The Praetorians closely watched all that happened in Rome in order to keep the imperial family safe.

After this inner debate, which came to no conclusion, I decided to walk through the rain to the Aventine, taking streets that skirted the Oppian and Caelian hills, past the great valley of the Circus Maximus, and to the narrow streets at the bottom of the Aventine Hill. I regretted not bringing the cloak now as I constantly wiped rain out of my eyes.

When I reached a fountain where three bronze fish shot water into a broad pool, I turned to a tiny lane and found the sign of twining snakes, indicating Nonus Marcianus, physician.

Marcianus had turned his back on a soft life to treat gladiators, which he said was much more interesting, and set up a small office on the Aventine, where most of his patients couldn't give him coin for his help. Aemil paid him, but not as much as Marcianus would have made treating the ailments and digestive complaints of people in his own class.

I had no way of knowing whether Marcianus was home or at Aemil's *ludus* but the shop was open so I walked inside, ducking under an awning.

Marcia, carrying a basin of water, dropped it when she saw me, and the basin shattered, sending a wave of water over my boots.

"Look what you made me do." Marcia, who'd always been timid, planted fists on hips and glared up at me. "You're a lout, Leonidas."

"Never mind." Nonus emerged from a cubbyhole in the back, his expression welcoming. "I have another basin ... somewhere."

"I know where it is." Marcia shot me a scowl and started up a narrow staircase in the corner.

"She's been a great help to me," Marcianus said. I wasn't certain if he meant the words as an apology or a defense of her.

"I came to see Marcia, in fact," I said.

Marcianus's good humor faded. "Why? She's my assistant now, not a bed slave."

"Not for that." Not since I'd woken the day of Floriana's illness had I taken much interest in sating my needs. Even in my dreams I'd not found use for it. "To ask her about Floriana."

"Oh." Marcianus contemplated me with less belligerence. "Why?"

"So I won't be accused of her death."

"I see." Marcianus rubbed his thin hair. "But you fetched me when Floriana was ill."

"I could have timed it so you would have arrived too late. I was unlucky that I calculated wrong."

The corners of his mouth twitched. "Cassia thought of that, did she?"

Regulus had said it, but I didn't want to talk about Regulus. I offered him a little shrug.

"Cassia has much intelligence, especially for one so young," Marcianus said. "Treat her gently, Leonidas."

I had no reason not to, but I was too unnerved to argue. "If others believe this, or try to prove I killed Floriana before I left for Ostia ..." I firmed my mouth. "I'm not going back to the games."

Marcianus gave me a conceding nod. "I understand. You are a good fighter, my friend, but I know your heart wasn't in it."

Aemil had expected me to kill men I'd helped train, fighters

I'd grown to like and respect. Occasionally I'd faced a hated rival, but mostly my opponents were men I'd drunk with in companionship only days before.

I was unable to put such thoughts into words. "I won't go back."

Marcianus called up the stairs. "Marcia!"

She clattered back down after a moment, clean basin in hand. I'd never taken Marcia to bed, as my tastes did not run to women who were barely more than girls. The stolla she wore today covered her more than the gauzy piece hanging from one shoulder she'd donned when she'd worked at the *lupinarius*. This stolla was thick linen and covered her from neck to ankles.

She'd caught her thick brown hair in a tail at the back of her neck, exposing a fine-boned, pretty face, devoid of cosmetics. Marcia now looked like the daughter of a lower-class but respectable household instead of the youngest offering in a brothel.

"Leonidas wishes to speak to you," Marcianus said.

Marcia set the basin on a table, her earlier hostility gone. She'd taken her change of circumstance easily, I could see, and regarded me serenely.

"Did anyone come to Floriana the day she was killed?" I asked her. "Why did she go out? Did you go with her?"

Marcia considered the questions without fear, though I sensed Marcianus hovering, ready to intercede if I upset her.

"No one came, not that day," Marcia said. "Floriana rose as usual. She felt better after recovering from the poison but she was in a foul temper. I think someone visited her the night before. I was with customers, so I didn't see who, but I heard her arguing. She can be hard on the regulars, especially if they don't pay, but this was different from her egging someone to give what they owed. She was yelling, and she sounded furious."

"Or afraid?" Marcianus suggested. "Sometimes when people are scared, they're more aggressive."

Marcia pursed her lips. "Possibly. Floriana was going on about something she was supposed to do, but didn't because she'd been sick. But like I say, I didn't see who she was with. I did hear snatches of what she yelled though. *I told you, it's off*." Marcia imitated Floriana's reedy screech well. "*It's too late. We missed him.*"

"Him?" Marcianus asked. "That's interesting."

"Did you hear anything else?" Without a name or knowing who Floriana argued with, I did not see how the information helped much.

"I'm afraid not. By the time I was finished, she was alone and moving the customers through."

Floriana's often had a rapid turnover—men indulged in quick pleasure and were gone. I was unusual in that I stayed most of a night, and with the same woman. Aemil had paid extra for that. I wondered if Floriana's heirs, whoever they might be, would try to collect what I owed for my last two nights with Lucia. I owed it fairly, and it would be unusual for them not to try to gather in all debts.

"The morning of Floriana's death," I went on. "What did she do?"

"She got up and went out, saying she had errands," Marcia answered calmly. "Lucia went with her."

"Did she?" I hadn't heard this from Lucia. "Then she must have seen ..." No wonder she'd been terrified and wanted to flee.

Marcia shook her head. "Lucia came back home alone. She'd gone her own way to do some shopping and separated from Floriana. Later, a vigile brought us the news that Floriana had been found when the fog lifted."

Her serenity faded. Floriana had been a hard woman, but she'd been the only family Marcia had known.

Marcianus put a comforting hand on her shoulder. "Never mind. You're safe here."

"Everyone's gone now," Marcia said sadly. "Lucia started screaming when the vigile announced Floriana's death. She said we were all in danger, and we had to run. The others scattered. I didn't know where to go, so I fled here."

"You are very welcome," Marcianus said. "You're a smart young woman and a good deal of help."

Marcia relaxed a little, but a former slave, used as she had been, would never be completely free of fear.

"I will keep Marcia on as my assistant," Marcianus said, sounding proud. "I can't pay much, but at least I can give the poor girl bread and a place to sleep."

"Enough for me," Marcia said, sanguine.

"You won't take her to the *ludus* when you treat the gladiators, will you?" The men there would recognize her from Floriana's and be happy to drag her aside whether she willed it or not.

"Of course I won't," Marcianus said, offended. "She'll stay here and mix medicines and look at patients who come in my absence. I've needed an assistant for some time."

Marcia said nothing, but I sensed the relief in her.

"Do you know where Floriana was struck down?" I asked Marcia.

"No, but I think she parted with Lucia because she wanted to meet someone. Not in her usual places. The vigiles who brought her body home didn't tell us much."

I thought again about the young vigile who'd invaded our house, claiming he was checking for fires. He'd come to us deliberately, and he'd admitted he skulked about Floriana's the morning she'd been poisoned. I would hunt him up and shake him a little, find out what he knew, if anything.

"What about Lucia?" I watched Marcia, gauging her reaction. "She thought she was in danger by the same killer, that all of you were. That's why you came here."

"I came here because I had nowhere to go," Marcia answered without a pause. "I'd liked helping Marcianus, so I wanted to see if he'd teach me."

Marcianus's face pinched in worry. "Marcia is in danger? From whom?"

I shifted in frustration. "That is what I am trying to find out.

Marcia, do you know any reason why someone would want to kill Floriana?"

Marcia shrugged. "I thought perhaps she owed someone money or she didn't do what someone paid her to. She took side jobs to make more money—Floriana was a hard businesswoman. She made sure we had plenty to eat and rest times, but that was only so we'd be fresh and strong for her customers."

Marcia spoke without rancor, but Marcianus's disgust was obvious. "Well, you have no more fear of that, my dear. That life is behind you now."

I could tell Marcia didn't quite believe him. I'd been on my own on the streets as a lad, and I knew exactly what she had faced. I'd known the mistrust of every man I met, including the builder who'd finally employed me. It had been a long time before I'd been able to let down my guard around him.

"Marcianus is a good man," I told her. "You will do well here."

"Leonidas is flattering." Marcianus folded his arms, his smile slanted. "And wiser than he knows."

I wasn't certain how to answer, so I took my leave of them both and went on with my pursuits.

IT WAS THE FOURTH HOUR, BREAKFAST FINISHED. SHOPS WERE doing flourishing business, Rome as vigorous as ever, despite the rain.

Saturnalia was over, and the new year had begun. Janus, the two-faced god, looking both forward and backward, ushered in a new month. I remembered Marcianus telling me that the senate had once proposed naming December as the first month of the year, since it held Nero's birthday, but Nero had refused the honor.

I thought of the haughty young man who'd delighted in Cassia's applause. Many believed Nero didn't care about the running of Rome, only his own preoccupation with music and drama. Rumor went that he'd instructed for his mother, Agrippina, to be killed because she'd interfered with his pursuit of music. Others speculated that his new wife, Poppaea, had simply encouraged him to get rid of Agrippina so the two could marry.

The quirks of the *princeps* didn't concern me at the moment, beyond his admonishment to protect Priscus. I wasn't foolish enough to involve myself in the affairs of those on the Palatine. Everyday life was challenging enough.

I made my way past the Circus Maximus, where the thump of hoofbeats told me teams of horses were being trained. Nero favored chariot racing, which made him liked by most Romans. He defied the stuffy senators and gave the rest of Rome games and races.

The house where the vigiles of the Subura slept during the day and brought in miscreants at night was near the Clivus Pullius as it went up the Oppian Hill.

I did not know the name of the man I sought, but I had no fear of plunging into the house and searching through beds until I found him. The vigile had plunged into mine.

I didn't need to look for him, as it turned out. The young vigile walked out of the house as I approached it, saw me, and tore off in the opposite direction.

CHAPTER 13

I chased my quarry through the rain, splashing over stones, bumping through crowds and around shouting vendors. The vigile fled past the fountain of Orpheus, tearing around clumps of people, and toward the Porta Esquilina. I pounded after him.

Plenty of people streamed in and out of the triple-arched Esquiline gate, moving to and from Rome's main markets. A litter born by thick-bodied men shoved its way along—the vigile deftly slid around it and ducked into a grove that lined the road up the Esquiline Hill.

Priscus lived not far from here, and my heart jumped. Did this vigile have something to do with whoever hunted Priscus?

The grove of trees I dashed into surrounded a shrine to Venus-Libitina, sacred to undertakers, whose businesses filled the area. I shivered inwardly, having no wish to encounter merchants who dealt with death.

I emerged into a small clearing, in the midst of which stood a square temple, very old, with columns rising into the rain. My vigile was nowhere in sight.

I slowed my steps, my breath fogging in the cold mists. The temple appeared to be empty this morning, no rituals performed on the front steps, no priests sweeping the entrance. Venus-Libitina was being ignored today.

I heard nothing, nor did I see a flash of tunic among the bare-branched trees. The grove held sudden peace after the teeming roads, a place to catch the breath and contemplate.

The only place the vigile could be hiding was inside the temple—however no one but priests of the goddess were allowed in there. To defile a temple held penalties that ranged from a mere thrashing to horrific death, depending on the rules of the place. No one would risk such a thing.

I pretended to turn and walk away, as though I'd given up. I strode under the trees back to the road, but at the last moment slipped into shadows and waited for my prey.

The rain came down harder. Water dripped from branches and darkened the arches of the aqueduct that soared on the side of the hill. Romans drank perpetually fresh spring water, untainted by waste.

I waited in vain. The vigile never appeared, though I stood there until the fifth hour was called by a crier in the street beyond. Either the vigile had sought sanctuary in the temple, or he'd known another way out I hadn't seen.

In disgust I quit the place. I'd find him later. He'd have to return to his watch house eventually.

I decided to continue up the Esquiline and visit Priscus, and after a short walk, reached his home. The benches outside his front door held three visitors, sheltered by a roof over the vestibule. They were his clients—men who'd come to petition Priscus to help them do whatever they needed done. In return, they'd support him with services or votes, or would simply be loyal to him when he needed it. It was midmorning, and a *paterfamilias* usually saw clients first thing, so they must have been waiting for some time. Priscus, I'd noticed however, followed his own rules.

I seated myself after giving my name to the doorman, pretending I too was a new client.

Two of the waiting men were freedmen, and the third wore a toga of the middle, or Equestrian, class. The Equestrian spoke to no one, and looked on disdainfully as the other two began to tell me about matches they'd seen me fight, remembering each blow better than I did.

The middle-class man's face grew more sour when the doorman emerged and asked for me first. The two freedmen thought it my due and cheerfully waved me on.

Priscus had retreated to his garden, in spite of the rain. He wandered the paths among the shrubs, snipping branches here and there. The gardener lounged under shelter of the arched walkway, dozing.

"Decimus has made a full recovery," Priscus told me before I could greet him. "He is resilient, that boy."

"Does *he* know who kidnapped him?" The servants had told Cassia no, but I wanted to hear information unfiltered through servants' stories.

"Hired ruffians, so he says." Priscus snipped another branch and tossed it into the wide basket on the bench. He'd put on a hat against the rain, and water dripped from its brim. "Decimus told me he was walking from his rented house in Antioch to our new warehouse there, and was snatched. He fought, but was dragged off, a bag over his head so he couldn't see. The next thing he knew, he was in a ship. He saw the sailors who brought him food but no one else through the voyage. Twenty-five days he was at sea on a bulk cargo ship. A courier on a faster ship brought me their demand—he knew nothing, did the courier. Only paid to deliver a message."

"Do you think the kidnappers came from an enemy you made?" I asked. "Someone you owed money to—or your wife's business owed?"

"No, no." Priscus was quick with the denial. "My wife had an excellent head for business. She owed no one. Her accounts were impeccable, and all expenses settled when she died. As for enemies ..." He spread his hands. "One always has them, of course. Patricians, especially those from very old families, can be prickly. However, I have fewer enemies than most." He gave me a thin smile. "I do so very little, which is to my taste. When I was a general, I was considered fair if not brilliant. I brought my men home and got them paid."

I understood Cassia's frustration with the man. He was determined that no one hated him enough to threaten his son, even though Nero had hinted he was in great danger. It must be about money, I reasoned. People would risk much for that.

"The sailors were all killed," I reminded him. "Executed on the dock. Who would do that?"

Priscus studied the twig of a brightly flowering bush and made a deliberate snip. Dead leaves fluttered to the ground. "I hesitate to tell you this, Leonidas, because I am a practical man without much use for magic or mystical things." His cheeks went pink. "But I believe the gods watch out for me. I have more than once escaped certain death, either by side-stepping at the right moment, or a guard stopping an assassin, or a guest drinking poison meant for me." His expression turned sad. "The poor fellow."

"Did this man die of the poison?" I asked.

"Hm? Oh, no, indeed. Was quite ill for a time, but recovered. Thank the gods ... again. You might have seen him outside. Square face, looks as though he's sucked a lemon. I feel obligated to take care of him now. He did save my life."

I thought of the irritated middle-class man, and I understood his annoyance that I'd been called in before him. Taking poison meant for another would make a person feel he had certain privileges.

"You believe he was saved by the gods as well," I said.

"I truly do, Leonidas. I am not the most pious of men—I saw too much in the battlefield to believe that supplication to the gods is helpful. While we believe Mars or Jupiter to be on our side, those we fight think the same gods are helping *them*. Both can't be true. But what besides the gods can explain my good fortune?"

"Your son was kidnapped," I pointed out. "Hardly good fortune."

"But he was not murdered, or even much hurt. Whoever was after my money obtained none of it. The second casket was delivered to this house yesterday."

I blinked. "Someone returned it?"

"Yes. Which reinforces my belief in intervention by the divine. Why else would the casket have been found by an honest person willing to send it back to me anonymously, asking no reward? I must conclude that Fortuna favors me."

It seemed she did. I was no stranger to luck—a misstep or a change in wind could mean the difference between me winning a fight or falling—but I also knew that months and years of training beat luck every time.

"I was there to make sure you weren't hurt and your son was returned," I said. "Another stroke of luck?"

"It seems so. I thought of you as soon as Celnus and Kephalos insisted I be guarded. How fortunate, was it not, that you'd been freed the day before? Kephalos went to the Forum and found Cassia right away."

Cassia had told me she'd heard via servants' gossip that Priscus wanted to hire me, and had gone searching for Kephalos. Good fortune again?

Or was there another hand? Someone had decided to free me and sponsor me while keeping their identity secret. Was that person also watching out for Priscus? And why?

My head was beginning to ache.

"At this moment, I can only be grateful. Decimus is home and safe." Priscus's smile lit the gray day.

"Should you stay in Rome?" I thought of Cassia wondering why Priscus did not retreat to the countryside. "Those wishing to harm you or your son might try again."

Priscus returned to his plants, scissors poised. "We seem to be protected no matter where we live, so it makes no difference. Of course, I am keeping my son close to home." He shot me a wry glance. "Which is difficult, as he is robust. Decimus already speaks of returning to Antioch and continuing expanding our business there. I might accompany him when he does. This is a big house, and lonely." He trailed off, the last word quiet.

He missed his wife acutely, I could see. Before I could offer sympathy, he brightened, and handed his basket and shears to the now-awake gardener.

"Come. I want to reward you for your help, yours and Cassia's."

He headed across the garden, and I followed. "You've already paid us," I said.

"I know, but I want to give you something special." Priscus led me to the tablinium, his office, which we reached by stepping up from the garden and inside.

A cabinet filled with small items, some of which flashed gold in the dim light, held seniority on the longest wall. I saw ivory vessels, figures carved in bright blue stone, thin gold bracelets, Greek pots with red and black paintings, a bronze sculpture of a young man plucking a thorn from his foot, and strange pair of flat hands made of bronze, studded with tiny gold ingots.

"Etruscan," Priscus said when I bent to gaze at them. "Quite ancient, I've been told. As ancient as the Egyptians, though I am not certain I believe it."

He reached in and brought out a pair of gold loops, thin and exquisitely made. "These are Egyptian. Give them to Cassia. They will look pretty on her."

I stared at him in bafflement. Cassia was a slave, and most men didn't reward slaves with earrings of beaten gold.

"And for you." He brought out one of the bronze hands. "Why don't you take this? You are as intrigued by it as I am. I'll always have the second one."

His generosity was astonishing. For a moment, I couldn't

speak, the skeptical side of me wondering what he'd want from me in return.

Priscus simply waited, no guile in his eyes. I realized he'd be offended if I refused, so I accepted and thanked him. Priscus sent for Celnus and told him to wrap the gifts carefully and arrange their delivery to our apartment. Safer than me walking home with them.

Celnus wasn't pleased, but he bowed and obediently took the things away.

Priscus saw me to the atrium himself, waving me off, then squaring his shoulders as the doorman went out and returned with the middle-class man. I sent Priscus a sympathetic look as I continued into the vestibule.

Before I left, I asked the door lad to tell Celnus I wished to speak to him. When the majordomo emerged, I repeated my request to encourage Priscus to remain inside and send for me if he wished to go anywhere. Celnus again was torn between irritation and agreement, but promised to do what I asked.

I stepped outside into the rain. The two freedmen I'd conversed with gave me a hearty farewell, and I started down the hill.

As I walked home, I kept an eye out for the elusive vigile, but I never saw him. I was not surprised—a man who patrolled the streets every night would know the back ways through Rome better than I.

It was a bit early for a bath—the most popular hours for them were after the midday meal—but I went in any case, wanting to wash away the sleep, sweat, and grit from the city I'd picked up as I chased after the vigile. The bathhouse was mostly empty, only a few men sitting naked on a bench in the caldarium.

I took time to go through the bodily exercises I'd performed every day at the *ludus* before the lone attendant swiped off my sweat and dirt with a strigil. I was use to exercising more often, and the last few days of inactivity had made me edgy.

The heat of the bathhouse did nothing to soothe me, and I

soon plunged into the pool in the empty frigidarium, swimming to relieve my tension.

That also did not help, because someone came upon me while I glided through the water and tried to hold my head under.

CHAPTER 14

The greatest lesson Aemil had taught me was not to panic in a dangerous situation. Trying to raise my head from the water against the strength of the man's hands would do me no good.

Lungs burning, I dove farther down into the pool, swimming away with a powerful pump of arms. His hold broke, and I was free. I surfaced at the far end of the small pool, gasping for breath.

I made sure to come up with my back to a tiled wall, so he couldn't get behind me. A large bronze fish poked out of the wall beside me, spilling clear water from its gaping mouth.

The room was empty. The waves I'd created sloshed over the pool's sides to wet floor mosaics depicting fish, seaweed, and Neptune's chariot.

I saw no one, heard no one, the sound of the fountain beside me loud in the stillness. The baths didn't fill up until afternoon, and my assailant had caught me alone. Which meant the man, whoever he was, had been following me.

The vigile? No, the hands that had held me were thick and strong, and the vigile was spindly. My attacker was a professional, though, knowing exactly where and how hard to push to keep me under.

I scrambled from the pool, cascading more water over the floor, and snatched up my towel, which I'd left high on a shelf, drying off quickly. Even the frigidarium's attendant had vanished, and I wondered if he'd been bribed.

I changed my mind about the attendant when I saw him asleep on a stool just outside the room. He had big hands, like my attacker, but they hung limply on either side of him as he snored hard.

I retrieved my clothes in the changing room and dressed, keeping a wary eye around me. I shared the room with an aging patrician, surrounded by his servants, none of whom paid the slightest attention to me.

Avoiding the deepest crowds, I walked quickly home. An assassin's knife could find my back in a throng, with no one being the wiser, including me.

This was the second time in a short while that someone had tried to kill me. I'd been attacked the night before I'd escorted Priscus to Ostia. Who wanted me dead?

Regulus, of course. He'd vowed to kill me. But I knew Regulus's fighting grip, and the man who'd tried to drown me today hadn't had it. Nor had the assailant on the street possessed Regulus's tread and movement. Also, Regulus would want to face me, to jeer at me when he drove his blade home.

Baffling and unnerving.

Cassia was in the apartment when I entered. I liked that.

I halted in the doorway, startled by the feeling. It was an ease, a relief almost, to find her puttering about, making her notes, sorting out food and utensils, or whatever else she did.

Today she busily decorated a new table under the shelf that held the *rudis*. She'd set out a spray of flowers, a few candles, and a sketch on a thin board of an older man with a small, wise face.

Cassia didn't turn when she heard my step. "We had no shrine," she said, as though feeling the need to explain. "We ought to honor our ancestors as much as any great family does. This is my father." She touched the picture. "I had a better one of him, but I wasn't allowed to bring anything with me, so I sketched another. Do you mind?"

She glanced over her shoulder, eyes holding trepidation.

I drew near the small table. "The ancestors can make life hard for us if we don't appease them. I think it's the cause of all my misfortune."

I joked, but only partly. I'd never known my father and barely remembered my mother. However, they could reach from Elysium, or wherever they'd ended up, to torment me if they wished.

"I'll add your parents," Cassia said. "What were their names?" She returned to the eating table and took up her ever-present pen, opened her ink jar, and rolled out a bit of papyrus.

"I don't know." I edged closer. "Will you add Xerxes instead?"

Cassia's pen scratched, she not questioning my choice. "You told me about him—close as a brother, you said. What was his full name?"

"Who knows? We took our names when we entered the *ludus*, and that's who we became. He was Xerxes. I was Leonidas."

She looked up at me, the tip of her pen touching her chin. "What was your name before?"

I shrugged. "I don't remember any other now."

Cassia cocked her head as she sometimes did when contemplating. "The one thing all of us never forget, deep inside, is our own name."

That was true. But it was a part of me no one knew, one I'd keep to myself for now.

Courtesans and matrons had teased me trying to learn my name, or they'd demand I tell them. I'd started to claim I didn't remember, until I almost believed it.

Cassia regarded me for a moment or two longer, then she smiled and let me be.

She took the papyrus slip and set it on the shrine, weighting down one corner of it with a small bronze statuette in the form of a tiny god. A household god, one of the dozens of lesser gods who guided us from day to day. It was good to honor them too.

She returned to her stool and tablets. "What did you learn about Floriana?" she asked, poised to write. "Did you see Priscus?"

I plunked myself down on a stool and I told her all I'd done since leaving this morning—meeting Gallus at Floriana's, visiting Marcianus, chasing the vigile, what Priscus and I had discussed, and my encounter at the baths. Cassia noted it all down, but she looked up with a gasp as I described being held under the water in the frigidarium.

"Was it Regulus?" she asked immediately.

"No, the hands weren't right. He'd also find it a cowardly way to settle his anger."

"Or the vigile?"

"Not right for him either."

Cassia pondered this. "Unlikely that a complete stranger would try to drown you in a place he could so easily be caught. It must be connected either to you helping Priscus or to Floriana's death. Perhaps whoever poisoned her believes you know who did it. You were there on the day."

"Asleep," I reminded her. "I'm hard to wake."

"Is that commonly known? They might be terrified that you'd seen them. It was definitely a man who attacked you today?"

"The hands were a man's, large and hard."

"Hmm." Cassia tapped her lip with her stylus. "We have not yet discovered where Floriana was struck down. We should do so." She closed her tablets, setting them in a neat line, and rose to fetch her palla.

"Now?" I asked in surprise. "Where do you think we need to go?"

"As I said before, we ask questions. Someone must know where it happened. If a man is out to kill you, and if Regulus grows rash enough to denounce you, then we must find the murderer, and quickly."

I was on my feet. "I agree, but if killers are stalking me in the streets, you are in danger with me."

"Not necessarily." She was maddeningly calm. "As I say, no one notices a slave. Besides, I can keep a lookout in case he tries again."

I knew, as I took up a cloak against the continuing rain, that I would not be a master who rigidly controlled his servants. The chances of Cassia listening to me and obeying were less than a raw new gladiator winning his first bout against a *primus palus*.

I PUT INTO ACTION MY SECOND IDEA OF A PERSON TO ASK about Floriana's murder. I led Cassia across the Forum Romana, less crowded now that afternoon had come, and to the Palatine.

A man didn't simply walk up the Palatine Hill and demand access to the *domus* of Nero, but I had no intention of going inside today. I halted outside the gate and asked the men on guard if Severus Tullius was on duty.

Cassia proved correct that no one noticed a slave, particularly a female who kept herself covered with her head bowed. The guards' eyes were on me, as was that of the boy sent running to inquire.

I was in luck and Tullius was there. He emerged cheerfully from the palace, brushing past the guards with a nod, and out the gate to meet us.

Tullius and I strolled together among the hill's greenery in the gently falling rain. Cassia walked several paces behind us, a fold of her palla over her nose and mouth to shut out the damp.

I asked my question. Tullius's face creased in confusion, and he took ten or so strides in silence.

"Why are you interested in the death of a freedwoman?" he asked. "A whore at that?"

"Because I don't want to be accused of her murder."

Tullius became still more puzzled. "Why should *you* be? No one would listen. You are a hero—you survived the games with your courage and skill. No Roman will let you fall."

"They might if enemies accuse me personally of the crime," I said.

Tullius's face smoothed with understanding. "Too true, my friend. Every man has enemies, even me. A few of my fellow guards would gladly push me from the edge of this hill if it meant they were promoted ahead of me. As would a few of my cousins, to get to the money my mother left me. She was more well off than she let on, probably to keep the family from touching her for coin." Tullius grinned briefly, then rubbed his nose, scattering droplets of rain. "I heard of the murder you speak of, but I don't know much about it. Let me inquire, and then I will take you to the very spot. A magistrate will have written it down, embellished it into a loquacious report, and sent it to the *princeps* in hope he will be noticed."

I held up a hand. "Don't if it will bring you trouble."

"I cannot fathom how it would. I'll nose into boring documents no one wants to read and send you word. I might come myself, when I'm off duty." Tullius sketched me a salute. "I'll be the toast of my barracks, to say I'm friends with Leonidas the Spartan."

TULLIUS ARRIVED AT OUR APARTMENT THAT EVENING, LATE IN the eleventh hour, before the sun set. He could take us, he said, to where Floriana had been struck down.

We walked quickly, Cassia behind us. I would rather she stay indoors, as the darkening streets were dangerous even for a Praetorian Guard and a former gladiator, but I hadn't bothered to give her the order. I knew she'd only follow, and I'd rather have her next to me, where I could protect her, than hurrying after us in the twilight.

I assumed Tullius would take us to a place in the Subura, near Floriana's house, but he led us north and west and around the Capitoline and the Theatre of Marcellus to the Porticus of Octavia.

The porticus, a memorial to Augustus's sister, was a columned place offering shelter from the heat, rain, or Rome's crowds. Tullius continued around the porticus to a path that ran alongside the Tiber and the bridge to the Insula. I'd taken this route when I'd run to fetch Marcianus from my *ludus* the day Floriana had been poisoned. The stench of the river grew stronger as we approached, carried by a breeze that scuttled the rain clouds.

Tullius halted in a spot where the path was overgrown, hidden from both the bridge and the buildings by a clump of trees and scrub.

"Here." Tullius pointed dramatically. "This is where the body of Floriana was found, stabbed to death."

Cassia came forward, tablet in hand. She made a quick sketch of the path and river, marking notes alongside the diagram.

"What's she doing?" Tullius asked. "The vigiles already have their records ... that's how I found out about this place."

Cassia opened her mouth to explain, but I cut in. "I told her to."

Tullius looked curious, but shrugged and said no more.

There wasn't much to see. The bushes where Floriana had fallen were broken. A few footprints marked the mud, but the rain had washed most of them away. The marks of sandals would tell us nothing—all of Rome wore such shoes. Cassia sketched them anyway, and I did not stop her.

Any blood had been washed away as well, either by the rain or a city worker. This spot was near public buildings, where important people might stroll on a sunny winter day, and the consuls would not want to upset their colleagues and clients with the reminder of a violent death.

I gazed along the river to the arched bridge where people hurried to or from the island in the Tiber, wanting to be indoors before it was fully dark. I also wanted to be indoors, not liking that someone in Rome wanted me dead. What was to say they wouldn't strike down my companions with me?

"None would have seen the murder." I turned from the river and studied the back of the theatre and the Porticus Octaviae. "The fog would obscure what happened, and that early, it still would have been dark." A cold finger traced down my spine. This was the perfect place for an assassination.

"Why did Floriana come *here*?" Cassia asked, her stylus busy. "She must have been summoned to meet her killer, or she asked him to meet her."

Tullius considered this. "She knew him, you mean? I thought it was done by a robber—they'd be thick in the dark and the fog, happy to find a victim in their snare."

"Odd weather for a morning stroll," Cassia said. "And this spot is far from Floriana's home. I would guess she had an assignation of some sort."

"With a lover?" Tullius offered.

"She could bring a lover to her house," I said. "Or meet him at his."

"A *secret* lover, then." Tullius nodded with confidence. "One she didn't want her women talking about."

"Possibly." Cassia's tone said she did not believe this, but she made another note.

Tullius moved to my side. "We should go back."

The sun was sinking behind the river, silhouetting the arches of an aqueduct on the hills beyond. Clouds that had lowered on the city all day broke, and a streak of golden light glittered on the river and the stones of the aqueduct.

The natural beauty did not negate our danger. This area would soon come alive with thieves, along with the desperate who trolled the river collecting flotsam or simply hunkered down on the Campus Martius to wait for stray wanderers. Floriana must have sorely wanted to meet with whoever killed her—she'd be canny enough to understand the peril of this lonely place.

I gestured for Tullius to lead the way back to the main road. Cassia lingered, still jotting notes, until I took her by the arm and steered her after Tullius.

A shadow flitted after us, or so I thought. I swung around, my knife at the ready, but I saw nothing, no one. The river rushed on, the breeze bringing only silence.

Tullius decided to stop at a wine bar and steady his nerves before heading back to his barracks. He invited me to drink with him, but I declined, and said good night.

"We stay in," I told Cassia once we reached our house. I firmly shut the door to our apartment and drew the bolt across it.

"Wise." Cassia negated my suggestion by opening the balcony and stepping onto it to shake out our cloaks.

I joined her and peered over the edge. "I thought I saw someone following us."

"So did I." Cassia finished and moved calmly back into the apartment, folding our cloaks as she went. "It was Lucia."

CHAPTER 15

I shot a startled gaze over the balcony again before I strode inside. "Lucia? Are you certain? How could it be?"

Cassia turned from hanging the cloaks, unworried. "Her hair is an odd and noticeable shade of red. I might be mistaken, but the shape of the face I saw under the cloak was the same. If not Lucia, it was a woman who looked much like her."

I remembered how fearful Lucia had been when she'd parted from me, bundled in the nondescript clothes Cassia had given her. "Why would she return to Rome? She was terrified."

Cassia set out her tablets—she had a dozen of them now, arranged in rows. "To kill you?" she suggested. "Perhaps when the other attempts on your life failed."

"Why should she want to kill *me*?" Lucia's fear had been real, I was certain. "We helped her flee. You sent her to a place of safety ... if she went there."

"I do not know why. I only know that an attempt was made on your life today, and a woman who resembles Lucia appeared and followed us."

My bafflement grew. "Lucia has no reason to kill me. Even if she did, she could have done so any time I slept in her bed."

I didn't like the qualm I had as I spoke. Of course Lucia wouldn't wish me dead. Why would she? I had paid Floriana well for her—at least Aemil had—and I wasn't brutish with her as some of Floriana's clients could be.

I'd also thought Lucia and I were friends, as far as such a friendship could be. But in truth, I realized Lucia had no reason to be loyal to me, no matter what I wanted from her. A woman hadn't held me under in the bath, a man had, but men could be hired, or manipulated.

Cassia offered no more explanations. I moved to the balcony again and peered down at the street, then went back into the apartment and closed the wooden shutters.

In the gloom, I crossed to the front door and left without a word. Cassia didn't try to follow—this time I would have sent her back, and she seemed to understand this.

At the bottom of the stairs, I eased open the door and scanned the dark street. The wine merchant's was shut now, only a tiny flicker of light behind the wooden slats that closed off the shop showing someone was awake.

I slipped outside and moved down the lane. At this hour, few people were about. Most would be inside, doors bolted, dining and sleeping, huddled with their families.

Footsteps sounded on the cross street. I walked to it quietly, not hurrying, my boots making almost no noise. I reached the main street and took a quick glance around the corner. No one.

In no rush, I waited. Anyone following me would wait also, to see what I would do.

It could be a while. I folded my arms against the cold and remained in the side street, out of the wind.

A clump of men passed. The few in togas were surrounded by lackeys with lanterns, trying to light the way through inky blackness.

A darker shape detached itself from a doorway a little down the street and followed them.

A robber hoping for a good take? Or a man seeking the safety of the group? Or Lucia, trying to escape me? The cloaked figure was slender enough to be her.

I stepped out and quickened my pace. The men's guards heard me and turned, lanterns high. Their pursuer sought a doorway, hiding. I went right after her.

The men and their lantern bearers hurried on, voices hushed in fear.

I laid my hands on the follower and yanked her out of hiding. I realized in an instant that it wasn't Lucia, though the man's build was as slim as a woman's.

I stared down at my vigile, his face pale in the darkness. He struggled, but I held him firmly and took his knife away from him as soon as he pulled it. He found its point at his own throat.

"Why are you following me?" I demanded.

His dark eyes were bulbous. "You are following *me*. You chased me a long time this morning."

"Because I wanted to ask you a question. Why are you in this part of Rome?"

"I'm doing my job—what did you think? I'm supposed to patrol the streets at night. Searching for fires or disturbances."

"You were spying on me and trying to sneak away with the group of patricians. I ask again, why?"

"Because you probably killed that woman." The vigile tried to draw himself up, but with me crushing his ribs and holding a knife to his throat, he failed. "I only have to prove it to the magistrates."

"The last time I was accused of murder, no one went to the trouble of making sure they could prove it before dragging me to prison."

The vigile's eyes took on new fear. "They say it's hard to touch you, since you're so protected."

"Protected by who?" I asked before I could stop the words.

His brows rose in confusion. "Don't you know?"

No, I didn't. I had no idea who my benefactor was, which was maddening. I shook him again. "Who is accusing me?"

"How should I know? I do what my watch master tells me. Find out if Leonidas killed Floriana and bring proof, he says."

He was lying. I'd lived with men who lied about every detail in their pasts until I could siphon truth from a good story. His watch master had given him no such orders. The vigile was after me himself, or perhaps he was Floriana's murderer and was trying to cover that fact by using me as a convenient scapegoat.

"I didn't kill her, and you won't find proof I did," I said in a hard voice. "I was traveling out of Rome the morning she was killed, surrounded by witnesses. I had no reason to go to that point of the river so early."

"Eh?" The vigile shot me a triumphant look. "How do *you* know where she was killed?"

"I asked. I was chasing you this morning to ask the same question of you."

His expression told me he was certain I lied. We'd get nowhere while neither of us believed the other.

"Who are you?" I asked. "What is your name?"

"Avitus." His eyes flickered.

"I doubt you work in this quarter," I stated. "It would be a large swath to patrol from your watch house near the Esquiline."

He did not try to deny this. "You were there when Floriana was poisoned. What's to say you didn't do *that*?"

I'd had this same argument with Regulus. "Why should I send for the best physician in Rome if I didn't want to save her?"

Avitus shrugged. "You might have wanted her to be sick. As a warning."

"A warning for what?"

"For what she'd get if she crossed you. She didn't like you coming there, and everyone knew it."

I gazed at him in amazement. "What are you talking about? I'd been going for years, and Floriana never complained."

Avitus glared defiantly. "She wanted you out. Floriana hoped that when you were freed and had to pay your own way, you'd cease coming, but you didn't. Did she threaten you?"

"No." Floriana had told me I needed to pay, but in her straightforward, businesslike way. "How do you know so much about what Floriana wanted?"

Avitus struggled anew. His face was a pale smudge in the darkness but I saw the flood of outrage in his eyes. "Never you mind!"

"Were you a customer?" I studied him dubiously. "I doubt you could have afforded it."

He started to thrash so furiously that I nearly cut him by accident. "You are filth. Gladiator. *Infamis*." Avitus spit on me.

More surprised than angry I pressed the knife to his throat. He gulped and went still.

I opened my mouth to ask why he'd be stupid enough to throw insults at a man who could kill him in the space of a breath, but the clattering of footsteps behind me stilled my words.

"Avitus!" a man called. A lantern glimmered at the head of the street. "Where in Hades are you?"

I clapped my hand over Avitus's parted lips before he could reply. He tried to bite me, so I held him harder. At the same time, I turned him around and pushed him from the curb and into the street.

He stepped hard on my foot with his solid boot. I tossed his knife into the street, and he scrambled after it, stumbling and going down on the stones. While he gained his feet, I took to mine.

I was well away, running into the blackness of the nearest lane before Avitus or his fellow vigiles could start after me.

They didn't follow. I hovered in the darkness, waiting to run or fight, but after a low-voiced conversation, the half dozen of them turned and tramped back the way they'd come. I knew then that Avitus's watch captain truly hadn't sent him after me, because the lot of them would have pursued me until they arrested me. Avitus wanted me for his own reasons.

I heard a soft sound in the dark, and I turned abruptly, my knife out.

Behind me, huddled on the stones, was an entire family—man and woman with three children, one a babe in arms. I guessed they'd been turned out of their insula at the beginning of the month, when rents were due, and hadn't yet found another place to go.

They stared at me in terror, even the babe round-eyed. I was large and hulking, and if I wanted to take all they had, including the wife and the small girl, they knew they couldn't stop me.

I took a step toward them. The lot of them cowered back, the man trying to put himself in front of his wife and children. I quickly tucked away my knife and opened the pouch of coins I wore tied to my rope belt.

I emptied the pouch, setting the coins—about three sestertii's worth in all—a few feet in front of the man. Without waiting for him to collect them, I turned and marched away.

I heard a soft, "Thank you," from the woman, and then I rounded the corner and faded into the night.

WHEN I REACHED THE APARTMENT, THE DOOR AT THE FOOT OF the stairs was wrenched open as soon as I reached for the handle. Cassia waited for me, her eyes wide, her stolla askew. This was the first time I'd seen her anything but pristine.

"What happened?" she asked me.

I merely gave her a tired grunt and moved past her and up the stairs. I was shaking when I reached the top. Cassia slipped in behind me and shut and bolted the door as I went straight to my pallet and sat heavily upon it.

"Will you tell me before you sleep?" Cassia asked. "Please?"

As always, slumber rushed at me in response to strain, but I propped myself up and described my encounter with Avitus. Cassia listened, troubled, then gave a decided shake of her head.

"I will have to find out more about Avitus."

I untied and dropped my belt then pulled my tunic off over my head. "I will. In the morning."

"No, *I* will." Her voice was firm. "You will either frighten him away or be arrested if you threaten him too much. I can find out without anyone noticing. I believe you should discover who purchased Floriana's building. It is not unusual for speculators to hover about waiting for an occupant or an owner to die to snatch up a property. Perhaps someone did not want to wait—Floriana was a healthy woman from what you tell me, not a sickly crone."

I heard the words but sleep came at me, and I ceased fighting it. I struggled with the blankets as I lay down.

"I have no more coins," I mumbled. "Gave them to a family sleeping on the street. I know you'll want to make a note."

"Oh." Her voice went soft, and then I surrendered to oblivion. The last thing I remember was the blankets being straightened around me, and Cassia's quiet words.

"That was good of you, Leonidas."

CASSIA WAS CHEERFUL THE NEXT MORNING WHILE I GROGGILY ate bread and drank watered-down wine, my head muzzy from sleep. She'd gone out to fetch water and our breakfast before I'd awakened, though I'd never heard her depart.

"If you wish to learn what goes on in Rome, go to the fountains," she said as she finished her last bite of bread. "The women who draw water know everything about everyone in the city, from the slums to the villas. They already knew I work for you, and how you were freed, and that you now have a benefactor. The questions they asked were unnerving."

I imagined the women's salty language as they prodded Cassia about living with a gladiator. They likely didn't believe her when she told them we slept in separate beds. Cassia was a comely young woman, but even if I'd wanted to use her as a courtesan, my body had decided recently that it was uninterested in activities of the bed other than sleep.

"They know Avitus," Cassia continued. "He's a common sight on the streets of the Subura, especially after dark. He's not above flirting with any woman as he escorts her home, for her own safety, of course."

I thought of the terrified young man in my grip last night and could not picture him flirtatious.

"He knew much about Floriana and things she said, or at least he claimed to," I said. "I wondered if he worked for her as a lad." Floriana had stocked lovers to please any taste.

"Possibly." Cassia brushed crumbs into a cloth and folded it. "A boy growing up in a *lupinarius* might decide to take his vengeance on Floriana. If those in the house knew him, he'd be let in and out without a second thought."

"But I didn't see him the night Floriana was poisoned. I've never seen him there at all. The first time I set eyes on Avitus was on the street outside the morning I fetched Marcianus."

"Perhaps you simply didn't notice him before."

I shook my head. "I noted every person at Floriana's each time I went there. I made certain no enemy was within—I couldn't be sure someone wouldn't try to siphon my blood as I slept."

Her brows went up. "Siphon your blood?"

"The blood of a gladiator cures many ills. Did you not know this?"

"I have heard such a thing, but it's absurd." Cassia carried the cloth to the balcony and shook the crumbs from it. She returned to the table and sat down, folding the fabric with precise creases. "I've read every treatise in Greek and Latin I've been able to find on disease and medicine, including Hippocrates, and there is no evidence that your blood carries magical healing powers."

I too had my doubts—if my blood were so magical, why didn't *I* heal more quickly? I'd taken a bad blow early in my career that had laid me up for a month. I'd survived only because of Marcianus's skill.

"In any case, I never saw Avitus before that day," I stated firmly.

Cassia rummaged in the box beside the table and pulled out her inevitable tablet, opening it and carefully marking the wax with her stylus.

"Why do you do that?" I asked irritably.

Cassia glanced up at me, dark eyes framed with black lashes. "Do what?"

"Write everything." I waved my hand over the tablet. "Keep your records. What good are they? Did they save you from being sold at the slave market? From having to work for a gladiator and be needled by the women at the fountains?"

Her stylus froze, and her face tensed. "My father taught me to do so. It helps me make sense of the world."

But her father had died, leaving his daughter alone and unprotected.

"Why were you sold?" I asked abruptly. "You could have carried on your father's work at your mistress's villa. Even if they didn't trust a woman in their scribe's position, you could have assisted the next one. You are obviously skilled in reading and writing. And organizing," I added. Our apartment had been orderly from the day we moved in.

Cassia's color rose. "The mistress decided I should go."

"Why?" I asked again, but I thought I knew.

I had observed not a few moments ago that Cassia was a comely young woman. When her father had been alive, he'd have protected her, holding a high enough position in the household to have some influence over its master, or at least to earn his respect.

Once her father had gone, Cassia, a slave because she was the daughter of a slave, would have been alone and vulnerable.

"Which was it?" I gentled my voice. "The *paterfamilias*? Or his son?"

CHAPTER 16

Cassia kept her head bowed for a long time after my question. When she raised it, her gaze remained on the table.

"The master," she whispered.

Sudden rage gripped me. I did not need to ask her for the details. The master of the house could have anyone he liked to slake his needs, and his wife could do nothing. As long as a man had affairs with those of a lower station, woman or man, he would not be censured.

I would not ask whether the master had simply made known he wanted her or if he'd acted on it. By the haunted look in Cassia's eyes, plus the deep fear she'd had of me when I'd first met her, I suspected he'd acted on it.

While a wife could not stop her husband chasing his pleasure, she could at least make certain her rival was out of the house.

"So the mistress sold you," I finished.

"It happened very fast. She never even spoke to me. The majordomo of our household put me in a cart, and one of the master's guards drove me to Rome and to the market. I was not even allowed to bring any of my things." Silent tears welled from her eyes to spill down her cheeks.

I wanted to press her hand in comfort, but did not think my touch would be welcome. I knew what it was to be used, to be fondled and stroked without assent, because I was there for other people's entertainment. That was why I was *infamis*, made for nothing but spectacle. I might be hailed as a hero of the games, followed about in admiration, and have drawings of myself on everything imaginable, but in the end, I could be discarded, like a vase with my visage on it, when it was no longer wanted.

I curled my fingers on the table. "You have things now. I won't take them from you."

Cassia looked up at me, one wisp of hair straggling from her perfect coif. "If Regulus has you arrested for murdering Floriana, they will be taken. I might be arrested with you, as your accomplice."

She spoke the truth. Though Cassia had nothing to do with the murder, she might be killed simply because she belonged to me. Even if she was spared, she'd have no one to protect her if I was executed.

I tore another hunk of bread from the round loaf. "Then we had better prove I didn't do it."

Cassia wiped her eyes and nodded. She took up her stylus again, making shaky marks in the wax, and we said nothing more about it.

I FINISHED BREAKFAST AND WENT OUT. I BROUGHT A CLOAK this time, as the January air was cold, coming hard on the heels of the rain. The streets were wet, glistening under the morning sun.

Neither Cassia nor I had heard word from Celnus that Priscus or his son had moved from his house, though I would check on him today. Nero's adamance unnerved and puzzled both of us.

I left Cassia going over the sketches she'd made of the place Floriana had been killed. I could see nothing in them, but I had already discovered that Cassia's thoughts worked differently from mine.

Men were tearing apart Floriana's house when I reached it, hammers bashing holes in walls, flakes of the paintings on the outside falling to the pavement. The painted buttocks of a man drifted away on the wind.

The *architectus* I'd met here, Gnaeus Gallus, had not come today. The foreman watching the workers, who were stripped to loincloths for the heavy work despite the cold, faced me impatiently as I asked about him.

Gallus had told me his shop was on the Clivus Pullius, and the overseer now told me exactly where.

The Clivus Pullius was a winding path that led up the Oppian Hill. On its first curve, near the spot where it intersected with the Clivus Suburanus and the Vicus Patricius, I found Gallus's shop.

The architect's small office did not open to the street like the others around it, but I saw the painting of a *libella* on the wall—an A-shaped frame from which hung a plumb line. I peered in through the open door and saw Gallus standing over a tall table, drawings spread before him.

"Ah," he said when he spied me. "My gladiator friend who is a builder at heart. Have you decided to lend your assistance?"

I wished I could. The small room brought back memories. I'd done much manual labor, as the builder utilized my strong back and arms, but I also remembered the scattered tools, the drawings, the scent of marble dust and travertine, the muddy smell of concrete.

The man I'd worked for hadn't held the lofty title of *architectus*, but essentially he had been that, working in a small provincial town near Rome, building homes for the plebs but assisting with a few villas as well. I'd followed him in wonder, silently absorbing all.

"I want to ask you about Floriana's house," I said to Gallus. "The *lupinarius*."

Gallus was surprised but nodded. "Ah, yes. The new owner has decided to pull it down, though I told him the walls and roof could be saved. He wishes to put in a row of shops and apartments above it, another insula in a city full of them. Well, at least I can make sure the thing is stable."

Insulae falling down around their inhabitants, killing many, was unfortunately not rare. Landlords wanted the buildings constructed as cheaply as possible and didn't bother with maintenance afterward.

"Who is the new owner? You said his name was ... Livius?"

"Sextus Livius." Gallus scratched his forehead, leaving a streak of charcoal from his marking stick. "He owns an insula on the Aventine and shops in the Carinae. Known for buying up derelict properties and imposing his will on them."

"Who did he buy it from?" I asked. "Floriana?"

"No, I do not believe the lady of the house owned it. Let me see ..." Gallus rummaged through a haphazard stack of tablets and rolls of papyrus, opening scrolls and tossing them aside. Cassia would be appalled at his careless system.

"Ah, here we are. This is a copy of the contract. Livius bought the building from one—let me see—a lady, Porcia Caelius, wife of a senator called Decimus Laelius Priscus."

I stilled, my blood growing cool. "Priscus."

"Yes." Gallus perused the document, not noticing my sudden tension. "Purchased from her widower, rather. She had owned the building, but it passed to her husband upon her death."

"Her husband." My mouth was dry around the words.

"Indeed." Gallus glanced at me over the open scroll. "Do you know the fellow?"

"I've met him," I said grimly.

There was no reason Priscus would have told me his wife had

owned the building where Floriana ran her house. I was a bodyguard, a nobody. Priscus had only imparted information about himself on the road to Ostia because he'd wanted to converse to assuage his worry.

Cassia had mentioned that those who wished to acquire property sometimes did so by ruthless means. Had Livius wanted the building and kindhearted Priscus wouldn't turn out the tenants, and so Livius had killed Floriana? Or had Priscus been restricted on selling the building with tenants in it, even prostitutes?

Something tightened in my stomach. I'd hoped I could simply run Floriana's killer to earth and make him take the blame. An easy solution. Untwisting property ownership and motives for acquiring or selling it made my eyes itch.

"Thank you," I told Gallus, and turned to leave.

"Now where are you off to?" he called behind me.

To see Priscus, but I did not tell him that. "Errands. Good day to you."

"You seem quite interested in that house, Leonidas. Is there anything I can do to help?"

Gallus sounded genuinely willing to assist, but I had to wonder about his motives as well. He longed to make his name as an architect—he could have found an opportunity with a house in a cheap district occupied only by women who sold sex.

"No." I glanced around his shop, liking it and hoping I was wrong.

"Do come and see me if you decide to return to building," Gallus said as I stepped out the door. "I need another assistant."

I nodded and took myself away, heading in a steady stride toward the Esquiline and Priscus's luxurious *domus*.

TWO CLIENTS WAITED OUTSIDE PRISCUS'S DOOR. HE DID NOT have many compared to his neighbors—on my way, I passed houses where the clients filled the benches and spilled into the street, men waiting patiently for their turn with the *paterfamilias*.

The middle-class man, the one who'd saved Priscus's life by drinking poison meant for him, was again in the vestibule. His face screwed up in annoyance when I appeared. The second man I'd not seen there before, but that client kept his eyes on his boots as he slumped on the bench.

The lad at the door ran inside when he saw me. Soon he reappeared and beckoned me in, earning me a snort of distaste from the Equestrian.

Celnus met me and disdainfully led me, not to the garden, but to Priscus's tablinium.

"He is very busy," Celnus snapped before he pulled back the curtain of the tablinium and announced me.

"Leonidas." Priscus, in spite of Celnus's insistence, sounded glad to see me. "How are you, dear boy? How is Cassia?"

A man who asked after a slave was unusual, but then, Cassia was an unusual slave.

"She is well." I said nothing more, and Priscus glanced at the majordomo, who hovered.

"I'll speak with Leonidas for a time, Celnus. I'll call you when we are finished."

Celnus sent his master a cool look but turned and stalked away. He left the curtain drawn back.

"He belonged to my wife's family," Priscus said apologetically. "Freed upon her father's death, but he wished to continue working for her. To keep an eye on *me*, you see." His smile was thin. "Dear Porcia married beneath her."

"You are a patrician." Rich or poor, patricians had lineage stretching back to the old Republic.

"Yes, and Porcia's was of the Equestrian class. But my family never had much power, in spite of our name, and never any money to speak of. In Celnus's opinion, my wife shouldn't have glanced at me twice. But I am very glad she did."

The sorrow in his eyes struck me anew. Priscus had loved her well.

"She owned property," I said abruptly. I glanced behind me to see if Celnus listened, but he'd retreated to the atrium, where he and Kephalos conducted a discussion in low but heated voices.

Priscus blinked. "She did. Rather, her father did. All over Rome and around the Bay of Naples. I'm not sure of all of it. Celnus looks after that part of the business."

"One building was sold recently. A house in the Subura. It was used as a brothel."

Priscus's brows went up. "Was it? Well, that old devil. I had no idea. I wager my wife did not either."

"Did you know about the sale?"

Priscus shook his head, the very picture of innocence. "I told you, I don't delve into the business much. I help my clients and those of my late wife's father—she was his only child. She had married before, but she kept all the properties she'd inherited from her father, and kindly passed them to me and to Decimus. But the accounts are beyond me. I'm a soldier, not a merchant. Celnus and Kephalos take care of all of it." Priscus gestured to where Celnus and Kephalos continued to whisper together.

The two men did not like each other, I could see. They held themselves stiffly, though they bent close to converse.

"Do you trust them?" I asked.

"They have never given me reason not to." Priscus's answer was stiff. "My wife trusted them."

Yet, he claimed to know nothing about the properties his wife owned and let the two servants, one a freedman, one a slave, handle all his accounts. They could be selling houses and siphoning off the money for themselves, and Priscus would never be the wiser. I wondered what Cassia would make of their accounts.

"The man who bought the house is a speculator," I said. "Buys up empty properties and turns them into insulae or shops."

"Many in Rome do," Priscus said. "So I'm told. My wife's father did the same."

"Do you know the man who bought this particular house? Sextus Livius."

Priscus studied the ceiling in thought. "Can't say I do. My acquaintances tend to be old campaigners, like myself. We reminisce about battles, making them far more glorious than they truly were. We rarely talk about property or speculators."

I read no duplicity in him. Priscus appeared to be what he claimed, a former general who'd found happiness with a wife who'd happened to be wealthy. Now he had little left of her but his memories. *And all her money,* I reminded myself.

"Why do you want to know this, Leonidas?"

I saw no reason not to tell him the truth. "A woman was killed, and I do not wish to be blamed for it. She lived in the building you sold. She died the morning we rode out to Ostia."

"I see." Priscus rocked on his heels. "I will be happy to tell the magistrates you were with me that morning. You were right beside me, and you couldn't have done it. Unless you committed the deed beforehand, of course."

Exactly what a magistrate would say. Priscus could only know about the time he was with me.

"The building was sold very quickly after that," I said.

"Yes, so it seems." Priscus's face darkened. "Celnus," he called into the atrium. "Attend me, please."

Celnus broke from Kephalos and moved to us, not hurrying. His slow stride said he obeyed only because he was obligated to.

"Sir." He bowed when he reached Priscus.

"Leonidas tells me you sold one of my properties, soon after the woman who lived there was killed."

Celnus did not appear startled, shocked, or guilty in any way. He gave Priscus a smooth nod. "As the house was now empty, and it was a ... brothel, I am sorry to say ... I felt you no longer had need of it. A man was willing to purchase, so I took the liberty of selling it."

"There's nothing wrong with a brothel," Priscus said. "A man must tend to his needs, and that is what they are for. As long as he doesn't become a fixture there or behave without honor."

Celnus gazed down his nose. "The buyer offered a very good price."

Priscus waved a hand at him. "You see, Leonidas? A straightforward business transaction. Though I'd have been pleased if you or Kephalos had told me of this," he said sternly to Celnus.

"Kephalos was preparing to inform you, in his monthly report on your finances."

"I'm certain he was." Priscus softened his tone. "Never mind, Celnus. I simply wanted to know. But please do not sell any more properties without speaking to me first."

"Of course, sir." Celnus was good at being unctuous. He bowed again to Priscus, sent me a veiled look, and glided away.

"It never does any good to shout at him," Priscus said once Celnus had vanished beyond the atrium. "He only gives me that heavy-lidded stare."

"Did Kephalos belong to your wife as well?"

"No, no. I picked him up on a campaign years ago. He's brilliant, if a bit close-mouthed. He and Celnus loathe each other, but they both know a soft place when they find one." Priscus chuckled, self-deprecating. "Thank you for trying to help me."

I'd wanted him to help *me*. "Would you mind if Cassia examined your accounts? As a favor to you," I added when Priscus frowned. "She's very good at accounts."

"You mean with Kephalos being none the wiser?" Priscus again thought, then looked crestfallen. "No, he'd never let her near. Never mind, Leonidas. Even if he is cheating me a little, I don't feel it."

He might not feel it *now*, but in future it could trouble him. I recalled a senator's wife who'd once had an affair with Regulus. She'd believed her husband's finances healthy and untouchable, until the senator discovered one of his clients had been embezzling from him for years. Their riches disappeared overnight, and the senator and his wife had moved to a remote province to make ends meet. Regulus had regretted the loss—she'd been generous with gifts.

"All has been well here?" I asked. "No more attempts on your life?"

"None." Priscus gave me his beneficent smile. "As I say, Leonidas, the gods look after me."

No, *people* looked after him, and he didn't realize. I wished I could question Nero closely—he must know exactly who wanted Priscus harmed. But I knew I would not be able to speak to the *princeps* merely because I wished it.

Cassia and I were left to find out for ourselves.

I said none of this to Priscus as I bowed and took my leave of him.

ON MY WAY HOME, I WAS FOLLOWED AGAIN. I KNEW IT WITH every step. Before I turned to the Vicus Longinus, which led toward our apartment, I ducked into a tiny lane, startling an elderly woman who sat on the pavement, weaving dried grass into a basket. I leaned against the wall, waiting.

My patience was rewarded when I heard rushing feet along the main street, and then a person in a cloak darted past, a male figure this time.

I stepped out right behind him. The man did not notice me but strode on past another few shops, before he halted in frustration, scanning the crowd ahead.

I leapt forward and seized him before he could react, dragging him into another side lane, my arm looped around his throat.

The cloak fell from a shaved head, and enraged eyes glared at me. It was Regulus.

CHAPTER 17

Regulus twisted from my hold, and I quickly stepped out of his reach. If he had a knife, he'd use it. We eyed each other uneasily.

People widened space around us, some moving on as rapidly as they could, others halting to stare. Two gladiators facing each other on the street was something to watch, or a danger to avoid.

An older man with half his teeth gone asked excitedly, "Are you going to fight? A denarius on Leonidas."

Regulus beamed the man a huge, false smile and flung his arm around my shoulder. "Never. I'm thanking Leonidas for sparing my life. All hail the champion of the games."

His hold on me tightened as those around us cheered. Some looked relieved there wouldn't be a bloodbath on the cobbles today, some disappointed.

"Another time," Regulus said into my ear. "Be waiting for me, Leonidas."

"Why don't you want to live?" I asked him. "Save your winnings, buy yourself free."

"I *do* want it ... now. But that moment when I asked you, old friend, you denied me. I could have gone out a hero. Now you're the gods-damned hero."

"No." I broke from him but without force, as the people around us continued to watch. "Now I'm no one."

I turned on my heel and strode away.

I FOUND CASSIA HUNCHED OVER THE TABLE AT HOME, studying the markings she'd etched onto her wax tablets at the site of Floriana's murder. She'd unrolled a piece of papyrus, already covered with writing, and had drawn in curving lines, labeling them with marks that looked Greek. I knew only one Greek letter, theta. A theta next to a gladiator in a mosaic or other picture meant he was dead.

Cassia did not look up when I entered, her focus entirely on her notes. Her dark hair made a precise curve over her cheek to the nape of her neck, where it was caught in a small knot. She'd claimed to know nothing of hairdressing, but not one lock of hers was out of place.

"Priscus's wife owned Floriana's building," I announced as I discarded my cloak. "It was bought by a man named Sextus Livius. Priscus claims he's never heard of him."

Cassia raised her head. She touched her finger to the papyrus as though marking her place.

"His wife?" Her surprise melted, and her gaze went remote. "That is very interesting."

I sat down heavily on my stool and rested my arms on the table. "Priscus knew nothing of the sale. His majordomo and scribe did it for him. I want you to look over his accounts."

The surprise returned. "What is your idea? That Celnus and Kephalos killed Floriana in order to sell the building to a speculator? Perhaps because the speculator offered a large amount of money?"

I nodded. "And the two of them—or maybe only one—pocketed much of it. I wonder what the price was, and what Priscus actually got."

"Mmm." Cassia touched her stylus to her chin as she liked to do when thinking. "Yes, I can imagine Kephalos building up a fortune for himself, one sestertius at a time. He strikes me as a resourceful man, and tight-fisted. He certainly tried to wriggle out of paying us our full share for the Ostia trip."

I noted she always said "we" and "us" when she talked about my bodyguard post and the payment for it. As though we were a unit.

And perhaps we were. I'd never have found the job if Cassia hadn't hunted for it. I'd have remained in bed, asleep.

"Would their accounts tell you? I asked Priscus if you could have a look at them, but he claims Kephalos would never allow it."

"I see." Cassia continued to tap the stylus, leaving a pale streak on her chin. "Kephalos is clever. If he is embezzling, he'll have hidden his crime well. He might not let me see the books, but I can converse with him and perhaps make him say more than he intends. Kephalos is a bit more forthcoming to me, because I speak Greek."

"I wonder if Priscus speaks it."

"No." Cassia's lips twitched. "He does not. A source of contempt for Kephalos. Yes, I will speak to him and Celnus, and see what I can find out."

She gazed dreamily into the distance, as though enjoying thoughts of interrogating the arrogant scribe.

"What does all this mean?" I waved at the sketches.

Cassia straightened the papyrus page. "Diagrams of the place Floriana was killed. Here is the Porticus Octaviae." She touched her stylus to a straight line labeled with letters. The river, a wavy line, was obvious, but she'd written words there too.

"What are the round things?" Small oval shapes and smaller, rounder ones dotted the drawing.

"Impressions of boots and sandals. I drew what I saw there."

"There was so much mud and rain—everything was smeared."

"I know. They may mean nothing." The stylus moved. "This is the path between the Porticus Octaviae and the bridge, which many people use, but it's interesting all the same."

"Every man in Rome wears boots or sandals. Most made by the same leather workers."

"That is true." Cassia tapped the paper. "These small round marks are from cleats on the bottoms of boots, the kind soldiers wear."

Cleats. I suddenly remembered the man who'd tried to attack me the night before we'd left Rome. I'd heard, as he'd run off, the click of iron hobnails on stone. My skin prickled, but I tried to make myself be practical.

"Soldiers train on the Campus Martius, not far away," I said, more to myself than to Cassia. "Probably cross the bridges in and out of town via this path all the time."

"Yes." Cassia did not seem worried that every person in Rome could have tramped through the mud that day and left their boot prints. "I will consider everything."

My unease was making me hungry, as had my travels through the streets. "Let us visit the *popina* and eat. We can look at diagrams later."

"I agree." Cassia rolled up the scrolls and closed the tablets. "I have not sat here all morning writing, however. I did discover more about Avitus."

I had started to rise, but I sat back down, intent. "What did you find?"

"I went to the house where he lodges. He wasn't there when I visited, but I spoke to the woman who draws the water and scrubs the floors. You had the idea that Avitus grew up at Floriana's, was perhaps a boy for use, but no. He is from Rome... the Aventine. He spent a few years in the army, in Hispania. When he returned to Rome, he joined the vigiles."

"Then he must have been her customer," I said. "He claimed

to know much about Floriana, though I never saw him at her house."

"Puzzling. When you find him again, you must not let him go until he has a better explanation for himself."

I intended to squeeze every bit of truth out of Avitus, even if he had nothing to do with Floriana or the attacks on me.

"Shall we have a repast?" Cassia reached for her cloak. "We can think better when we are not hungry."

She'd said "we" again. I decided, as I wrapped my cloak around me and ushered her out, that I did not mind this. I'd always been alone. Now I was part of "us."

FOR THE NEXT TWO DAYS, I SEARCHED FOR AVITUS WITH NO luck. Even positioning myself outside the house where his squad lodged did not help. He seemed to have taken some leave.

Likewise, I hunted for Lucia, or at least the woman we thought was Lucia. Why she'd returned to Rome when she could have been safe in Capua, I didn't know. Then again, the woman might not be Lucia at all. Whoever she was, she kept her distance.

I also saw no sign of Regulus. Aemil had a rigid training schedule that even the *primus palus* had to follow. From early morning to late afternoon most days, Regulus would be locked in practice or helping to train other fighters.

In the meantime, a man came from Priscus's house, delivering the gifts he'd generously bestowed on us. The messenger obviously thought his master mad, but he left us the box and departed quickly. I wondered why the things had taken days to reach us, but of course, we were not important people in Priscus's life. Perhaps Celnus had delayed the delivery, maybe trying to dissuade Priscus into giving the things to us at all.

Cassia expressed no such doubts. She delighted in the

earrings, and we set the gold-studded bronze hand on the shelf alongside my *rudis*.

Using the excuse of thanking Priscus for the gifts, Cassia decided to visit his *domus* and have her talk with Kephalos. She returned home that afternoon, a smile on her wind-chilled face.

"Kephalos is a snake," she said as she patted her already neat hair into place. "He and Celnus have been taking money from poor Priscus for years, even before his wife passed away."

"How do you know this? Did you see the ledgers?"

"Unfortunately, no. Kephalos keeps them hidden, and I knew within moments that he would never show them to me. But I learned much by flattering his intelligence, and he revealed things without meaning to. Celnus is a harder nut, but even he let down his guard. Priscus's wife trusted both of them too much, although they were more careful when she was alive and overseeing the accounts. Priscus does not bother, the foolish man."

None of this surprised me much, though I admired how Cassia had pried the information out of the two disdainful servants. "Priscus likes to remind people he is a soldier with no head for finance," I said. "An easy man to take advantage of."

"He is kind as well." Cassia settled herself at the table and opened her tablets. Their number had grown, and I suspected she spent plenty of our earnings on them. "Kephalos told me that long ago, Priscus set a boy in the household free and placed him with a family to raise. Said he saw great potential in him."

"What happened to this boy?" I asked with interest. Sometimes a kind deed could go wrong, the recipient nursing resentment for years. Or those jealous of the recipient might harbor ill will, maybe enough to pay pirates to kidnap a man's son or make attempts on that man's life.

"Kephalos doesn't know. Apparently Priscus doesn't know what happened to the boy either. Whether he lived or died is a mystery. Priscus doesn't even know the name of the family who took him, according to Kephalos. He did everything through an intermediary."

I thought it might be worth finding out why Priscus had done such a great act of kindness, though it wasn't unusual for a patrician. They would free a slave or adopt a son of another family simply to show their benevolence. The slave or son would become a client or heir, obligated to the patrician for life. The most unusual thing about this boy was that Priscus hadn't boasted about it.

"Did you tell Priscus that Kephalos was stealing from him?"

"Not today. I spoke only to Kephalos and Celnus. You said Priscus suspected it, and he does nothing. As I say, he's kind."

"To the point of madness."

"Perhaps."

I leaned on my hand against the cool stone wall. "Why did Kephalos tell you so much? Was he not suspicious of your questions?"

Cassia sent me a quick smile. "I pretended to commiserate with him—a scribe and accountant of his talent forced to work for a rather feckless gentleman. Priscus is highborn yes, but will never amount to much." Cassia lost her smile and flushed. "I'm afraid I told him I knew what it felt like, to have to work for a man of no scholarship."

She peered at me anxiously, but I felt a well of mirth stirring inside me. Whoever had paired us had a strange sense of humor.

"That was wise of you," I said. "Kephalos looks at me like a turd stuck to his sandal."

"I rather played on his pity," Cassia said in a small voice.

I barked a laugh, loud in the small room. "You were clever."

Cassia relaxed as though she'd feared my anger. "My father taught me how to assess a person and discover what will appeal to them. They will tell you much more than when they are hostile to you, he said."

"Kephalos *was* hostile to you, I thought."

"He was annoyed he couldn't cheat us of our fee. I explained that my adamance to collect the entire amount was so you would not be brutal to me. He believed me."

She said the words lightly, but I heard the slight tremor in them. Cassia had lost much of her worry about me, but still, she could not be certain.

I sat down, as I'd grown accustomed to doing, and regarded her across the table.

"I learned as a boy that I was very strong. Aemil's training made me stronger still. I understand how easy it is to hurt and kill. I would only be brutal to you if you were a gladiator attacking me in an amphitheatre. Then I'd fight for my life."

The rambling explanation appeared to puzzle Cassia more than reassure her. I drew a breath and went on.

"I know I can kill anyone I have a mind to, or at least hurt them badly. I decided long ago that I wanted to have more friends than enemies, so I fight only in the arena—or when I'm attacked on the street. But not with people I take care of."

Cassia ran her fingers along a tablet, tracing its square wooden cover. "I was sent to take care of *you*."

I shrugged. "We must take care of each other. Neither of us knows how to cook."

That won a tiny smile. "That is so." Cassia stilled her fingers. "We must hurry and make certain you are not accused of this crime. Priscus's fee will last only so long."

"I should take another job, you mean."

"Indeed. I will search for another generous man in need of protection. Perhaps heading to a finer destination than Ostia."

"We can't expect to always be paid highly," I pointed out. "I've done plenty of guarding, and some don't pay much at all."

"True." Cassia's trepidation fled, and the businesslike gleam returned to her eye. She'd called Kephalos a snake, but Cassia resembled a hawk regarding prey when she turned her attention to our funds. "What we will do is make you a very special guard —men will pay handsomely to say they had Leonidas watch over their steps. Yes—let me think on this ..."

I left her to it. I had already learned never to stand between Cassia and her interest in accounts.

THE NEXT MORNING, CASSIA ASKED ME TO TAKE HER TO SEE Marcianus. She wanted to speak to him about the poison that had been given to Floriana, she said—how strong it was, how long it took to work, what it was comparable to, and so forth.

I ceased understanding her after about the fifth word and agreed to walk with her to the Aventine.

When we reached Marcianus's shop, he was not there. At the *ludus*, Marcia told us. She wore a palla even more plain than the one I'd seen her in on my last visit, and had bundled her hair into a simple style. She looked young and uncomplicated.

"Can you tell me about the salad Floriana ate that night?" Cassia asked after we'd exchanged greetings and spoke of Marcianus. "Who prepared it for her?"

Marcia's eyes widened into frightened ovals then she flung herself past me and tried to flee into the street.

CHAPTER 18

I caught Marcia around the waist and pulled her back into the shop. She struggled, but I held her fast, her feet off the ground.

"What about Floriana's meal makes you want to run?" I demanded.

Marcia pushed at the iron bar of my arm and glared at me. "Nothing. I don't know anything about it."

Cassia regarded her with cool interest. "When Marcianus questioned you the morning he treated Floriana, you said there had been only lentils and bread taken in the house. You knew of no salad."

"That's what I'm saying now." Marcia lifted her chin, but her belligerence couldn't quite hide her fear.

"Before, you were only puzzled," Cassia went on relentlessly. "Now you are afraid. What happened to change your mind?"

"I don't care what *she* says." Marcia's voice rose. "I didn't know anything, and I won't be taken to a magistrate for it."

"What who says?" I asked.

Marcia pedaled her feet, kicking me, but it was like being kicked by a fly.

For a moment, I thought Marcia might answer me, but a male voice cut through the crowd who'd gathered outside the door to watch the show. "Leonidas, what are you doing? Put her down at once."

Only Nonus Marcianus could chivvy a gladiator into obeying his every command. I gently set Marcia on her feet, and she wrenched herself from me and hurried to Marcianus.

"Do you mean Lucia?" Cassia asked her.

"No," Marcia said loudly. "I don't mean her at all."

I knew she did, as did Cassia, and by his expression, Marcianus.

"Lucia came to speak to you, didn't she?" Cassia asked. "Did she tell you what to say if you were questioned?"

Marcia closed her lips tightly and folded her arms. Marcianus put himself between her and me.

"Leave her be, Leonidas. She has suffered enough."

I thumped the doorframe in frustration, sending a flake of red paint from the lintel drifting down to rest on my tunic.

"Whatever Lucia told you, tell Marcianus," I said to Marcia. "He can decide whether I need to know."

Marcianus scowled at me. "She is an innocent girl, and helped me save Floriana's life. She'd not have done that if she'd put Floriana into that state in the first place."

"We don't believe she did," Cassia said. "She is being loyal to Lucia." She switched her gaze to Marcia. "It is important we speak to her. Do you know where she is?"

"No." The answer held a ring of triumph. "I have no idea where Lucia ran off to."

Cassia pinned Marcia with her scrutinizing stare, then nodded and adjusted her cloak. "Thank you. We will leave you alone now."

She strode past me out the door, as though expecting that I'd follow. If Marcianus hadn't been so angry with me for frightening Marcia, I suspect he might have laughed.

"I BELIEVE SHE TOLD THE TRUTH." CASSIA SPOKE WITH conviction as we made our way along the crowded street toward the Circus Maximus. "About not knowing where Lucia is, I mean."

"Marcia saw her, though," I growled.

"If she confesses to Nonus Marcianus, he might tell us."

"Possibly not. He's protective of her." I admired him for that, but at the moment, his loyalty exasperated me.

"Yes, but Marcianus likes you. If he wants to keep you from being arrested, he will tell us. In the meantime, it would be best if you found Lucia yourself."

I studied the streams of people walking down the hill to the valley of the Circus Maximus. We passed a bathhouse with a continuous flow of men and women entering, ready to spend their afternoon washing and relaxing.

"How do I search for one woman in all this?" I swept my arm across the view. "Especially a woman who does not want to be found."

"You have known her for some years, haven't you?" Cassia asked in a reasonable tone. "Where would she hide?"

I had no idea. I tramped along, my large body breaking a path in the crowd, Cassia following in the wake I created.

Or, perhaps I did know. Lucia had rarely left Floriana's, but she'd spoken of walking in the gardens of the Baths of Agrippa. There, she'd wrap herself in her palla and stroll anonymously among the pruned trees and shrubbery.

"There is one place," I admitted. "She spoke about it to me."

"It is a start. Shall we go there now?"

I doubted Lucia would be in the gardens simply because I wanted her to be. She'd need to eat and find a place to sleep every night—attendants herded people out of the bath complex at the end of the day, so she would not be camping there.

But, as Cassia indicated, it would be a place to begin instead of walking up and down the streets of the city, checking every cloaked woman until I found her.

I took a street that skirted the long side of the Circus and emerged near the river in the shadow of the Palatine Hill. From there we took the path that followed the Tiber past the place Floriana had been struck down, and northward through the Campus Flaminius.

It was a lengthy walk, and Cassia flagged by the time we reached the baths. A wind had sprung up, cold with winter, smoke and steam from the huge bath complex thick in the air.

Agrippa, the close friend of Augustus, had set up these massive public baths, which I'd used many times in my life. The *ludus* lay a short distance across the river and Aemil had paid the small fee, so I often retreated here after a tiring day of training.

We strolled in past a tall marble statue of a man set high on a pedestal. Cassia gazed at the statue in amazement and then, when she could tear her attention from it, peered eagerly through the rotunda to the library full of scrolls.

"I've heard of this place." Her whisper echoed in the cavernous hall. "I've always wanted to come. The statue at the entrance is by Lysippus. A true Lysippus, not a copy."

I didn't know who Lysippus was, but Cassia's awe told me he was a famed artist.

The vaulted halls were filled with people talking, arguing, debating, laughing. Men and women diverged into the changing rooms, but they would merge again in the baths. Floors of marble and terra cotta led to bathing rooms and the gymnasium. We took the route to the gardens.

"I understand why Lucia made this her retreat," Cassia said in admiration as we emerged into the green space. The garden held colonnaded walks, with benches in niches, trees and greenery, and statues peeking out here and there. "Marcus Agrippa had great vision, was very keen on civic works."

I didn't know much about the man beyond the buildings he'd left. Gallus, the *architectus*, would have loved to work on a project like these baths or this garden—he'd said wistfully that he wanted to build something all admired. Perhaps one day he would.

Cassia and I walked the garden's paths, which were quiet. With the winter cold, most people had retreated indoors to the warm baths.

Nowhere did I see Lucia skulking, or even the cloaked figure of a woman. If Lucia had sought sanctuary in these gardens, she wasn't here now.

"She might have taken rooms in the area," Cassia suggested. "To be near a place she liked."

Finding out would take a massive search, though admittedly less so than looking for her in the heart of the city. The Campus Martius, where the baths lay, was on the outskirts of Rome. It held training grounds for the legions and was not as heavily populated.

We left the quiet oasis of the gardens and returned to the streets. Not many insulae lined the area, as for a long time, none had been built on the Campus Martius. But after more prominent men had started erecting buildings, such as the Theatre of Pompey, Agrippa's baths, and the nearby Pantheon, shops had appeared, and over them, rooms for the shop owners, which were sometimes rented out to other tenants.

Cassia fearlessly approached shopkeepers who were closing up for the afternoon, and asked about their lodgers. She knocked on doors if they were already shut. Lucia would recognize me too quickly, so I skulked a block away, pretending interest in a tavern, while Cassia questioned the inhabitants around the Saepta Julia, where I'd fought in gladiatorial combat, and the Vicus Pallacinae.

I realized as I watched Cassia follow one worker ruthlessly until he turned in exasperation to answer her, that slaves would more readily speak to other slaves. I was wise to let her get on with it. In the world of slaves, Cassia, as a learned scribe, even if a woman, outranked many. She had a fine sense of her own place, and used it.

Cassia returned to me, ordered stew and wine from the *popina*, and handed me the jars to carry home.

"No one has seen her," she said, deflating. "I'd hoped this would be easier. Lucia is a distinctive woman."

"She might have dyed her hair a different color," I suggested. "If you were asking about a red-haired woman that might be the only thing they would remember."

"I described her in more detail than that." Cassia frowned as we navigated the increasing foot traffic toward the Quirinal. The Vicus Laci Fundani led us east and north, away from the crowds of the imperial fora. We passed a crossroads shrine and took the Vicus Salutis, which returned us to the Vicus Longinus and our tiny street off it.

When we reached our apartment, I sat glumly down to the soup, lukewarm now, and the leftover bread from breakfast. I could not see that we'd made any headway in our tedious search.

"I suppose we at least learned that Marcia knows something," I said after a time. "And that Marcianus won't let us shake it out of her."

"He will tell us if it's important, as I said." Cassia ate serenely, spilling not a drop.

"You believe in him."

"So do you," she countered.

I could not argue. Marcianus had kept me alive when I'd been a raw recruit, full of bravado and energy but lacking in skill. I studied a scar on my upper arm, where a sword had sliced it to the bone. I still had the arm, with only the scar cutting across it to attest to the injury, because of Marcianus.

"I trust him, yes."

But I wished I *knew* exactly what had happened to Floriana instead of having to rely on trust. I'd trained hard as a fighter so that I could compensate for the uncertainty of the arena. It was better to be over-prepared and never use half the moves I knew than not prepared enough—which could spell certain death. Knowing was better than guessing.

A thought struck me. I dropped my spoon into my bowl, sending dregs of soup fountaining to the table. Ignoring Cassia's look of dismay, I jumped to my feet.

"I know where she is."

Before Cassia could form the word, *Where?* I was out the door, my passage fluttering the cloaks on their pegs.

CHAPTER 19

We'd been so close. I cursed under my breath as I tramped back the entire way we'd come after leaving the gardens.

The Saepta Julia loomed, glittering under the afternoon sky, its colonnades dwarfing the line of shops where Cassia had hounded landlords and their servants.

Beyond that and Agrippa's baths, I passed the stables that held the chariot racing teams, and crossed the bridge to the far side of the Tiber. From there I charged to the wall and the gate that closed off Aemil's *ludus*.

I hammered on the gate. The guard opened it, but when he recognized me, he tried to block my way with the gate and his body.

I shoved both aside and stormed into the *ludus*.

The open training area within was lined with wooden posts on which gladiators practiced stabbing and hacking. The practice swords were wooden—the real weapons were safely locked away until the games.

Men who were stripped to loincloths, their skin ruddy from the wind even as they sweated, battered at the posts. When I barreled inside, they ceased, straightening up and wiping brows to watch this new drama.

Aemil, who'd been scrutinizing a clumsy recruit, jerked upright and started for me. I outpaced him as I made for the sleeping quarters and strode unerringly to my old cell. I yanked open the cell door even as Aemil caught up to me.

Lucia rose from the bunk inside, her bright red hair tumbling down her back, her eyes wide with fear. Regulus was nowhere in sight.

"Leonidas—"

The word was cut off by a roar behind me, and then Regulus had me by the neck. He dragged me backward out of the cell and into the practice area, and I let him, wanting to face him out of close quarters. Winter wind struck us as we emerged, Regulus's hands hot on my skin.

I was glad I'd rushed out without grabbing a cloak. Regulus would have strangled me with it by now. I slammed an elbow at his windpipe, and spun from him when he jumped from the blow.

"She's mine now." Regulus glared at me, breathing hard. "Get out, Leonidas."

"Lucia is a freedwoman. She can go wherever she wants."

Regulus's answer was to come at me again. I caught him by the arms, mine straining to hold him off.

Aemil sprang into us and jerked us apart.

Aemil was smaller than either of us, but he'd been training gladiators for many years, and knew exactly how to control them. Not that Regulus calmed. He snarled, baring his teeth like an animal.

"Praxus!" Aemil shouted at one of the gladiators who had gathered to watch the spectacle. "Bring two swords." He had us in his grip, which was as strong as I remembered from my green youth. "You two are settling this, now."

Regulus transferred his glare to Aemil. "I want to kill him, not dance with him."

"Your obsession is dulling your edge," Aemil snapped. "End it. Leonidas wins, you concede he's better than you and did you a favor letting you live. You win, he never comes back here. He'll be dead to you."

"Can I break his limbs?" Regulus asked eagerly.

"Whatever you want. But *I* decide the victor."

Aemil released us. We broke apart, my heart hammering. Though I'd sworn off death, the impending fight ramped up my excitement, letting blood burn through me as it hadn't since I'd left the Circus of Gaius a free man.

Praxus, so new to the *ludus* that I'd never met him, rushed forward with two wooden practice swords. He shook with nervousness as he handed them to Aemil, who inspected them and tested their balance.

"Evenly matched." He gave a nod of approval to Praxus, who looked as though he'd melt under it.

Aemil handed a sword to Regulus who nearly ripped it from his grasp. I took the other more quietly, my mind already focused on the coming fight.

Lucia, the murder, Priscus, my new life ... faded. Nothing mattered at the moment but battling a fully trained gladiator.

This time, I was ready to win.

The sword might not be metal, but it was heavy, the tip whittled to a point. Aemil believed we'd learn to avoid being stabbed if the swords truly cut. Regulus could kill me with the wooden blade if he tried hard enough.

I shucked my boots and tunic, facing Regulus in my loincloth. He did the same. I flipped the sword, its leather-wrapped hilt familiar against my palm.

Regulus tossed his sword from hand to hand. The look in his eyes told me he'd do his best to kill me this day.

Aemil instructed us to stand ten paces apart, and then he stepped back to referee. He'd done this so many times in my life that I had the sensation I'd never left this place. Regulus and I were sparring, demonstrating to the newer fighters what to expect in the arena.

"Fight!" Aemil yelled. He balanced on the balls of his feet, ready to watch and follow us. We might fight to the death, but only within the rules.

We circled silently, eyeing each other, two predators waiting to strike.

Regulus kicked dust with his bare right foot, as he liked to, a ploy to distract his opponent. In the arena the action swept sand upward to sting though the eyeholes of the helmet. We had no helmets today, but the dust headed for my face before I turned sharply to avoid it.

Regulus had expected this move to slow me down and give him a few seconds to find his opening. So I attacked him.

A shout rose from the watching gladiators. I rammed Regulus with the side of my sword, my body following to harden the blow. I'd timed it to get under his reach, and felt him smack my naked back with his wooden blade.

Before he could do more than scratch me, I shoved him away, resuming a fighting stance to wait for my next opportunity.

Regulus immediately launched himself at me, but I'd seen him coming. He'd given himself away with the tiniest shuffle to his back foot, which most would not have seen. He'd made the same mistake on the day of our last bout.

I met him, smacking my sword hard into his chest. Regulus had raised his arms to stab down at me, and I caught him with my powerful shoulder, lifting him and sending him backward and to the ground.

A gladiator of lesser skill than Regulus would have been finished, my sword at his throat. But Regulus was up again, legs flashing as he sprang to his feet.

His breath was ragged, but so was mine. Sweat trickled into my eyes, and I gave myself a slice of time to step back and wipe it away.

Regulus followed me and struck again. I met him blow for

blow, our bare arms used as shields. Aemil hadn't given either of us any defenses except our own adeptness.

We slammed together then burst apart, and I hammered him mercilessly. In my final fight, I'd gone easy on Regulus, wanting to defeat but not hurt him beyond Marcianus's skill.

Today, I decided to end this. He would realize why I'd been *primus palus* and that he'd never have taken the title if my benefactor hadn't chosen to free me.

I heard the roar emerge from my throat as I drove Regulus across the yard. He parried my strikes well but could not get his sword past my precisely moving arm. Aemil skimmed beside us and the other gladiators followed, the scent of their sweat-soaked bodies cloying the air.

Regulus suddenly rushed me, trying to duck under my reach. I let him think he had then caught him in a headlock, spinning him around and pulling him off his feet. I kicked his legs out from under him, and he had to let go of his sword to grab my arm, hoisting himself on it to keep from being strangled.

In an instant, I had him on his knees, my arm tight against his neck while he struggled for air. I jerked his head back and jammed my blade to the hollow of his throat.

I heard around me the tumult of the crowd, the chant of my name, and I again wanted to lean into the sound. I smelled blood, the hot sand, the metallic tang of the inside of my helmet. The small practice yard became an amphitheatre or the floor of the Circus Maximus, with all of Rome come to watch Leonidas the Spartan triumph.

"*Practicum est*!" Aemil yelled. *A killing stroke*. "Regulus is down. Leonidas is the victor."

Regulus thrashed, trying to fight his way to his feet. I tightened my arm around his throat, cutting off his air. His exertions slowed, and a gurgle crossed his lips. Finally, his eyes rolled back in his head, and Regulus slumped to the ground.

I waited—he'd feigned unconsciousness before and then leapt up to strike at me the moment I'd let down my guard.

This time, Regulus was well and truly out. I loosened my arm from his neck, and he fell to the dirt in a sprawl of limbs.

I dragged in a breath. The arena drained away and became the practice yard lined with arched openings to the cells. The screaming crowd faded to the admiring shouts of the gladiators of the school.

Aemil pried the wooden sword out of my hand. I flexed my fingers, sinews cramped.

"You are the best, Leonidas." Aemil clapped me on the shoulder. "None can touch you. Stay and help me train this rabble. I'll pay you coin. I heard your benefactor is only so generous."

"No." I wanted nothing more to do with the *ludus*. This fight had been personal.

Aemil released me, eyeing me with confidence. "You'll come back to me one day. Though you'd better go now. When Regulus comes to, he's going to be furious. Your friendship is over, I think."

I knew this. I also knew I'd hoped my camaraderie with Regulus would turn into the bond I'd shared with Xerxes. It never had, as much I'd pretended. Xerxes had been large-hearted, but Regulus loved himself above all else.

Without a word to Aemil, I resumed my tunic and boots. I made for the gate in time to see Lucia, who'd emerged wrapped in her cloak from Regulus's cell, try to slip out of it.

I ran after her, the energy from the fight still with me. I caught up to her, seized her by the arm, and hauled her from the *ludus* and down the street.

I PULLED LUCIA ALL THE WAY ACROSS THE CAMPUS MARTIUS to the Vicus Longinus and so to our apartment and the waiting Cassia. Lucia fought me every step. She even appealed to passers-by, but most recognized me, and none wanted to interfere with Leonidas the freedman if he wanted to drag a woman home.

Cassia hurried in from the balcony as I towed Lucia inside. Lucia tried to grab the doorframe, but I pried her grip from it and slammed the door.

"What were you doing with Regulus?" My words came out a croak, barely discernible.

Cassia poured wine from an amphora, added water from a pitcher, and thrust the cup into my hand. I drank, the sour liquid burning my throat.

"He wouldn't let me go," Lucia said. Her cloak fell away to show her stolla torn at one shoulder, her arms goose-bumped with cold. "He didn't want you to find me."

"Why did you fight me then?" My voice was clearer but retained its harsh note.

"Because I can't trust you any more than I can him." Lucia's words clogged with tears that filmed her dusty eyelashes.

"Why not? We sent you to safety. Why did you come back?"

"To warn you." Lucia sniffled, wiping her nose with the back of her hand. "But I don't want you to know everything I've done."

I restrained myself from shaking her. "Warn me about what? What have you done?"

"She poisoned Floriana," Cassia said clearly and calmly. She stood with her hands folded, her neat appearance a stark contrast to Lucia's mud-splashed dress and wild hair.

"She gave Floriana the salad that poisoned her," Cassia went on as I gaped. "As I have suspected. What Marcianus told me this afternoon confirmed it."

CHAPTER 20

"*You* fed Floriana the poison?" I roared as Lucia cringed in my grip. "*Why?*"

Lucia's panic dissolved as her face crumpled, and she went slack. I released her. No more fight in her, she buried her head in her hands and sobbed.

I looked across her to Cassia. "Marcianus came here?"

"Not long after you departed. He told me what Lucia had gone to see Marcia about—to order her to change her story that the only food served had been lentils and bread. Marcia was to tell everyone she remembers now that they all had salad and that only Floriana was sick, eating rhubarb leaves by mistake."

I bent my glare on Lucia again. "I could be fitted up for her murder, Lucia. Why by all the gods would you poison her? What had she done to you? You could have come to me if she'd threatened you—I'd have protected you."

Lucia raised a face streaked with tears and mucus. "She did nothing to *me*. Floriana was planning to kill *you*."

Both Cassia and I went mute with shock, Cassia as amazed as I.

"Kill Leonidas?" Cassia asked. "Are you certain?"

"Oh, yes." Lucia nodded fervently. "She told me. I was to keep him sated, make certain he slept soundly that night. Then Floriana would come in and ..." Her face screwed up and more tears wet her face. "But I couldn't. Leonidas has always been kind to me. I didn't want him to die." She collapsed against the wall, her body wracked with sobs.

I moved my jaw until the words in my head emerged. "Then, after Marcianus saved her, you stabbed her to death?"

Lucia's head jerked up. "What? No! I didn't wish to *kill* Floriana, only make her sick so you could get away. No, *he* killed her."

"*He* who?" Cassia demanded.

"I don't know." Lucia turned to Cassia in appeal. "You must believe me—I don't know. Floriana met with a man, but I don't know who he was. He wanted her to kill Leonidas, and after he'd gone, Floriana told me I had to help her."

Marcia too had mentioned a man meeting with Floriana. My heart sped. I needed to put my hands on him.

"What did this man look like?" Cassia moved swiftly to the table, opening a tablet and snatching up her stylus.

"I never saw him. Only a shadow. He'd visited her a few times, but when I asked about him, Floriana shut me up quickly. Once she even struck me. I asked why she wanted *you* of all people dead, Leonidas, and she said because you had agreed to guard a patrician on the road to Ostia. She only told me that because I would not cease my questions until I had an answer."

Cassia paused in her quick writing to meet my gaze. "Because he'd be escorting Priscus?" She frowned. "No, that can't be true. I met with Kephalos about the job the evening before Floriana took sick. Priscus hadn't hired Leonidas officially yet."

"I only know that Floriana told me of it that night, after Leonidas arrived and was asleep." Lucia wiped her face. "Perhaps the man heard that you and whoever this Kephalos is had met, and was certain Leonidas would be hired—everyone wants him as a guard."

"Hmm." Cassia made more notes. "Are you certain you have

no idea who the man was? What he looked like? Anything can help."

Cassia's no-nonsense demeanor calmed Lucia somewhat. Lucia, I was growing to realize, was ever a woman who needed someone to guide her.

"He wasn't a highborn man, as far as I know. He didn't wear a toga. A tunic. And boots."

Cassia stilled, her focus sharp. "What sort of boots?"

Lucia went blank. "Boots. The ordinary kind. With hobnails—he clicked when he walked."

"Caligae?" Cassia asked.

"I suppose. I don't think he was a soldier, though—the legionnaires don't come to us." Lucia drew shaky breaths. "He might have been an urban cohort, or—"

"A vigile?" I asked abruptly.

"Possibly. I'm sorry, Leonidas. This is why I am so afraid. He knows I knew Floriana's plan, that I know he killed her, but I won't recognize who to run from."

This stranger also knew about Priscus and had wanted to prevent me protecting him. Nero himself had admonished me to make certain Priscus was unharmed.

"Why?" I directed the question at Cassia. "What great power does Priscus possess that makes the *princeps* himself want to keep him safe? And a vigile want him unprotected?"

Lucia shook her head. Cassia switched her gaze to her. "Is there more? Priscus is not an important man, by all accounts, but he is very wealthy. Does someone want his fortune?"

Lucia's face became more ashen. "I don't know this Priscus, but I dare say nothing more. Even the words could bring death to all of us."

My skin prickled, my blood still hot from my battle with Regulus. "What words? Did you tell Regulus any of this?"

"No. I promise you. He tried to make me tell him, but I refused. He wants you to fall, Leonidas."

"I know. I will deal with Regulus. Tell us."

"You should flee," Lucia said, eyes wide. "We'll all go to Mount Albanus, to the sanctuary you sent me to. I slipped away, but I want to go back."

"You *should* return," Cassia said. "They will keep you safe. Leonidas and I have no choice—our benefactor requires us to live in Rome."

"Then I will say nothing." Lucia let out a breath. "And you will be safe."

"I am certain it is too late for that." Cassia's crisp tones made Lucia jump. "Leonidas will have been seen bringing you here. The man who killed Floriana knows of your connection to him, and probably already believes we know everything. So, please ..." Cassia threw out her hands, inviting Lucia to trust her.

Lucia swallowed and lowered her voice to a whisper. "I think the man wants to kill the *princeps*."

Cassia shot a fearful glance out the open balcony. Below, customers were arguing with the wine shop owner in the waning afternoon, their voices loud. The rush of Rome went on beyond them.

Lucia was not wrong—even uttering that sentence could send us all to execution. Death continued to chase me, no matter how I tried to elude it.

Cassia squared her shoulders, as though forcing herself to be sensible. "Why on earth would this man tell Floriana something so dangerous? He must have been lying, to goad her into helping him. I think the target is Priscus, not the *princeps*." She lowered her voice a long way before she pronounced Nero's title.

"I don't know." Lucia opened and closed her fingers, which were chapped from the wind and cold. "I heard Floriana and the man speaking of it. I have no idea what this patrician you guarded has to do with anything." Her voice broke. "I don't know anything at all."

Cassia had moved back to her table during Lucia's speech, sorting her tablets, working backward through the stack. She paused at one, opening it to study the words inside.

"When you were here before, asking for Leonidas's help, you said *they* would want to kill you," Cassia reminded her. "Now you speak of only one man."

Lucia blinked. "Did I? I wasn't sure—he could have hired someone to help, or have a partner ..."

"Today you are certain it is one?"

"I only saw one man at Floriana's. But she was strong, and crafty. It would have taken more than one to strike her down."

"You mentioned a husband—in Etruria. Do you think he wanted her dead, or was he part of this conspiracy?"

Lucia clearly did not know this either. "I've met her husband—he wasn't the same as the man I saw that night with Floriana. Different build, different voice."

Cassia made a note. "It might help to locate this husband anyway. What is his name?"

"Gaius Martinus," Lucia choked out.

"He might have had a hand in it. I will try to discover if he was in Rome at the time. He'd want to come for Floriana's things or any money she'd left. For now ..." Cassia wrote the name then closed the tablet and laid it and her stylus on the table. "You should return to the *Domus* Ceres. And do not get caught."

Lucia glanced at me, worried. "Alone?"

"I can't escort you," I said. "Cassia is right that I bring much attention. You'd not be safe with me. Do you know of anyone else you can trust?"

Lucia studied her toes in her shabby sandals. "No," she had to conclude.

"When it is safe to return to Rome, we will send word." Cassia rummaged in her box and brought out another handful of copper coins. "This should help."

Lucia stared at Cassia in surprise, but she was quick to take the money. "Thank you," she said softly.

I walked her downstairs, Lucia wrapping herself in her threadbare cloak. We moved past the wine shop, where the customers seemed to be reconciled and now spoke with the wine merchant in more congenial tones.

At the corner, I halted and put kind hands on Lucia's shoulders. "Why did you come back to Rome, if you were safe elsewhere?"

"To warn you." Fresh tears formed in the corners of Lucia's eyes. "The more I thought things through, the more frightened I became. I tried to speak to you alone, but *she* is always there." Lucia jerked her chin in the direction of our lodgings.

"Cassia works for me. Of course she's there."

"When I waited for you to come out alone, Regulus found me. He dragged me to the *ludus* and told me I was his now. I think he meant to hurt you by that, but I don't think you were hurt." Her voice went quiet and she touched my chest with regret.

"You are my friend," I said. "Regulus doesn't understand that."

"He understands that you are a better man than he, and he does not like that. He called you some terrible names." Lucia looked briefly amused, as though some of those names had been quite funny. She stepped closer to me, her touch sensual, practiced. "That woman will dig her claws into you and not let go. When you have wrested yourself free of her, come and find me. We will revel in old times."

I didn't believe Lucia was correct about Cassia, but I cupped her cheek. "The gods go with you."

"And you, Leonidas."

She studied me a moment longer then turned and faded into the shadows. The crowd in the Vicus Longinus swallowed her up, and she was gone.

When I returned to our apartment, Cassia was already bundling herself in her palla.

"You should stay here," I told her. "I will find Avitus and take him to a magistrate myself. He'll fight me, and he could hurt you."

Cassia blinked at me. "I was not rushing to hunt Avitus. We should get word to the Palatine that the *princeps* is in danger."

"He is always in danger," I said irritably. "And Avitus might have nothing to do with this—Lucia might have seen another vigile. We won't know until we question him." I did not trust Avitus, but I wanted to be certain. I full well knew what it was like to be accused of a crime I did not commit.

"If we tell someone all we know—perhaps that Praetorian Guard who likes you—then *he* can search for Avitus. We can never seem to put our hands on the wretched lad."

"And Avitus would be executed, even if he's innocent."

Cassia paused. "Do you believe he's innocent?"

"No," I had to say. "He was outside Floriana's the morning after her poisoning, very interested in the proceedings. He claims he knew her, but he'd never been a customer or worked there. He broke in here trying to find out what *we* knew." I still needed to have the door bolts replaced with better ones. "You believe the round markings you found where Floriana died are from the cleats on Avitus's boots, don't you?"

"Yes."

I growled. "It is probably true we should report this—but what if Avitus *is* innocent? He being at Floriana's by chance?"

Cassia contemplated this, touching her lip. "What if you speak to the Praetorian, and ask his opinion? We do not have to name Avitus. Only that you think Floriana might have been involved in a plot, and she has been killed. The plot might still be on, or it might not. But if we do not warn anyone, and Nero is killed, and conversations are traced back to us ..."

"We are dead." I let out an angry sigh. "It is dangerous knowledge either way."

"If we pass it on, perhaps it will become less dangerous for us."

"Until we are brought in and interrogated," I grumbled.

"The word of a slave is worthless," Cassia said. "They might interrogate *you*, but now they have to do it following the law."

I remembered the stink of the Tullianum prison, the rats, the groaning of men, the fear. My sentence, though it was supposed to have broken and killed me, had been far less horrific than what others had faced.

"Or I could find Avitus and carry him to the guards," I growled.

"Which will take much time. He knows the city and is slippery."

I had to agree. I did not like Cassia's solution, but she was right. Any delay in reporting the knowledge would look as though we were part of the conspiracy. I took up my cloak and ushered her out into the bright Roman afternoon.

WE HAD TO TRAVERSE SEVERAL GROUPS OF GUARDS WHEN WE reached the top of the Palatine, who were more interested in asking me about previous matches than what my business was. When I finally conveyed what I wanted, I found that Severus Tullius was not in.

"He's at the camp," the guard who took my request said. "What do you want him for?"

I hesitated, trying to think of a plausible excuse. Cassia had become a mute bundle of cloth behind me, not venturing to help.

Before I decided what to say, a man in a toga with a shaved head strode from the courtyard, ignoring the guards. "You." He pointed at me. "Follow. Now."

The guard, with an annoyed grimace behind the other man's back, let us in.

We crossed the courtyard, which contained a film of dust from the masonry work being done on the other side of it. A long arcade was under construction, and I would have liked to linger to watch the work.

Our guide had not indicated Cassia was to stay behind. He strode ahead of us in a bad temper, his toga dragging from his arm through the dust.

We went not to the peristyle garden as before, but into a smaller chamber with walls decorated with scenes from chariot races. A man in a racing tunic and gloves—a charioteer—stood before the paintings, absorbed in them. I saw no guards in the room with us, but I sensed them lurking out of sight.

The man in the toga cleared his throat, then abruptly pivoted and left us.

The charioteer turned around, Nero himself.

"My friends." He gave us a nod, as though he'd invited us for the sole purpose of admiring the paintings—and maybe he had. They were very well done, the horses lifelike as they leapt, nostrils flaring, chariots pounding down the long stretch of the Circus Maximus.

I bowed low—Cassia had already abased herself on the floor. Nero waited a moment, then bade us rise.

"I have so few friends that I wish to call you thus. The young lady is a true musician." He sounded admiring.

I had heard it was not unusual for a *princeps* to have slaves and freedmen in his most intimate circle. Claudius had been surrounded by them, and a favorite concubine of Nero's, Acte, had been a slave. I supposed it was easier for the *princeps* to trust those who had no actual political power.

"I saw you approach, and assumed the guard would fuss about letting you in," Nero continued. "I sent my majordomo to fetch you, because I knew it would annoy him."

Cassia glanced at me, worried. I went over phrases in my head, trying to find ones that would warn Nero without having the two of us arrested and tortured until we coughed out the entire story, including the names of Lucia and Avitus.

Nero forestalled me by launching into a speech. "I want to

tell you everything, Leonidas. You deserve to know. I will tell you why I chided you to protect Decimus Laelius Priscus from all harm, though you must not share this secret on pain of death." He held us with a stern gaze, the same that had ordered soldiers to go after his mother shipwrecked on an island, and murder her.

He threw out his hand in a dramatic gesture. "If Priscus dies," he announced. "Then I am doomed to die with him."

CHAPTER 21

Cassia stared in amazement. I must have had the same expression, because Nero suddenly burst out laughing.

"You look like fishes, your mouths agape." Nero barked a laugh. "But alas, it is true. If Priscus is harmed, I will be assassinated. I know this every day when I rise, and every night that I retire."

Cassia stirred next to me. She wanted to ask questions, but talking without leave invited punishment. I had to speak and hope I satisfied her curiosity.

"Who would do this? Why do you not arrest that person?"

Nero's smile was patient. "Because I have no idea who is making the threats. I've received letters, outlining exactly what will happen to me if Priscus is harmed. They are not nice letters. They are left in the *domus* in secret, and no one knows who delivers them or writes them."

That spoke of someone who knew the buildings well, or had help from inside them.

I shifted my weight uneasily. "Why Priscus? He seems a harmless man."

Nero spread his fingers. Behind him on the wall, a charioteer snarled across at another driver, ruthless determination in his eyes.

"Priscus was liked by my uncle, trusted. One of the few senators to be. I suppose it was feared that I'd destroy Priscus simply because my uncle favored him. I have explained that I don't care about him one way or another—he is rather dull, isn't he? Stays at home tending his garden. His son runs his mother's business from Halicarnassus, and the lad cares about numbers. Not drama or music, not even politics." The disgust Nero exuded was acute.

"You have no idea who threatens you about him?" I asked. "It is not his son?"

"I have just said the son has no interest in politics," Nero snapped. "He is weak. I have him watched. See how easily he was captured?" He shuddered. "I want that *never* to happen again. Priscus came too close to being killed in that adventure, and he'd have been grieved to lose his son. Perhaps to the point of taking his own life, which would not help me. Thanks to you, both father and son are well."

I thought of how the pirates who'd ransomed Priscus's son had been found slain to the man. "Did you have his captors put to death?"

Nero looked uncomfortable. "Did you expect them to be allowed to live? I had them put to the question first, of course, but none knew the name of the person who hired them. They communicated by letter, and would receive a cut of the ransom. So you see, there is someone in the shadows, a powerful man—or a woman, perhaps. Never trust a woman, Leonidas. They can appear weak, while at the same time they are cunning, knowing how to goad men into doing terrible deeds for them."

Nero's mother, Agrippina, had been a woman of great ambition. She was now dead. Nero's first wife was likewise dead, and a new one had slid into her place.

He swept his eagle gaze to Cassia. "What do *you* think? Who should I hunt for? Man or woman?"

I did not understand how Nero expected Cassia to have an answer for him, but she replied with confidence.

"It is not a woman."

"Oh?" Nero's haughty anger faded into curiosity. "Why not?"

"A woman can command men, yes, but often the men in her power fall out over rivalry for the woman's attention. If it were a woman, you'd likely have found out who by now—one of those jealous rivals would have told you. A careful man, however, if he keeps to himself, might not be discovered."

Nero studied her thoughtfully. "I had not considered it that way, but I believe you are right. Men can conjure jealousy as well, of course." He flicked his attention to me. "I am certain Leonidas has had men coming to blows over him."

"But Leonidas is a fighter, a simple man," Cassia said. "Not a commander."

"Our servants always see so clearly," Nero said to me. "She is right, of course. Very well, then it is a man I need to find." He let out a breath. "Which is unfortunately proving most difficult. This fellow must have loyalty and wealth. The only reason I don't haul in every man of that description and have them beaten until they confess is that this person seems fixated on Priscus. They care not what *I* do, not how much money I spend on sandals or wall paintings, as long as that bloody Priscus is well." Nero's derision returned. "That is why you must protect him with your life, Leonidas. If he is hurt, I will make sure you die before I do."

I believed him. I thought over what Lucia had told us, that Floriana had wanted to kill me so I would not guard Priscus on his way to Ostia.

That information, coupled with Nero's story, made me decide to keep silent on Lucia's assertion that there was a plot to kill Nero. Whoever had killed Floriana did want Nero dead, but in a roundabout way that Nero was already aware of. If I saved Priscus, Nero lived.

I bowed low. "I will see that Priscus is well, and serve you." I didn't have much choice.

FOR THE REST OF THE VISIT, NERO CHANGED THE SUBJECT entirely and asked my opinion of the painting of the charioteers, and which team I supported. "Greens," I said. I knew that Nero favored them.

My answer pleased him. Even gladiators, especially seasoned ones, were allowed to watch the chariot races, and so Nero took pleasure in recounting meets we'd seen, including the all-day races he sponsored. Cassia stood in silent patience—I wondered if she'd ever attended a race in her life.

Eventually, Nero decided to dismiss us. I do not think he'd tired of the subject, which I heard he could discuss for hours, but the novelty of speaking to a gladiator and his slave had probably worn off. Nero shouted for a servant—the door opened instantly—and Cassia and I were escorted out of the palace.

We said nothing to each other while we walked down the steep slope from the Palatine to the Forum Romanum and joined the throng of people there. Cassia broke off from me to pause at shops and fill her basket with a pot of oil, a box of spice, and other sundries. She led me to a bakery where she purchased hard rolls, at half price because they were left over from the morning rush.

I helped her carry it all home, where she prepared a meal from lunch's leftovers plus what she'd bought this afternoon.

"We need to speak to Priscus," she said once she was settled.

"That is obvious." I slumped to my stool and drank deeply of the wine she poured. "The man who recruited Floriana did not want me protecting Priscus—he must know that someone out there will have Nero killed if Priscus dies, no matter how it's done." I paused, letting the wine warm me. "Unless both killers are one and the same."

"I don't think so." Cassia took up her spoon. "I will read through my notes, but the attempt to have Floriana kill you so you could not protect Priscus seems clumsy. Any man who has the power to threaten Nero and not be caught is more careful. Clever. Ruthless."

"A clumsy attempt makes me think of Avitus. He never could get close to Nero, and would have to try to assassinate him in a roundabout method."

"What we have is two crimes." Cassia used the handle of her spoon to draw imaginary vertical lines on the table. "First—a man who finds Priscus important to him hopes to keep him alive by placing Nero under a threat that if Priscus is killed, Nero will be as well." She frowned as she pondered. "Priscus is very wealthy. A client might want him alive and unharmed for as long as possible, to keep that wealth trickling to him."

I recalled the clients I'd seen waiting for Priscus, particularly the sour-looking middle-class man. "Such a person would have to have his hands on many reins."

Cassia sent me a little smile. "You are still caught up in the chariot-racing talk. Though I agree." She drew a horizontal line with her spoon. "Second—a man wishes to kill Nero but knows he never can get close to him or trust anyone close to him. He hears of this strange bargain that Nero keeps Priscus alive to preserve his own life, and decides to use that as his assassination attempt. All he has to do is kill Priscus—I suggest Priscus was supposed to have been murdered when he delivered the ransom—why else would a dozen pirates be sent to meet him and insist on Priscus coming alone? If you had not been there, both Priscus and Decimus would be dead."

I agreed. I remembered how I had to insist on coming along to the final ransom delivery, and the pirates had finally agreed to allow only me to accompany Priscus. They must have believed they could easily dispose of me as well.

Cassia went on. "The pirates are instructed to attack, Priscus and his son will be killed, and the incident put down to a ransoming gone wrong. The pirates flee with the money, never to be seen again. Presumably to meet with whomever hired them, or perhaps they were to keep the full ransom as their payment. The assassin wants Nero dead—the money is immaterial."

A very wealthy man could let go two caskets of gold if it achieved his goal. Usually those who planned to assassinate Caesars were rich and powerful. They did not kill for money but out of ambition or fear of what that *princeps* would do to Rome. Of course, that description did not fit Avitus.

"But Priscus lets Celnus talk him into hiring a bodyguard," I said slowly. "He asks for me."

"And the assassin realizes that you can thwart his plans. You are the best fighter in Rome. Even a group of pirates would have trouble against you—which proved to be the case. So our assassin goes to Floriana, knowing you frequent her house, and gets her to agree to kill you in your sleep. Perhaps he offered her a fortune, as he did the pirates. Or he had some sort of hold over her. She might have been terrified into helping. Only Lucia's loyalty to you kept you alive. She put rhubarb leaves in Floriana's salad, which made Floriana sick enough to take to her bed and spare you. When you fetched Marcianus to save Floriana's life, Floriana might have experienced remorse for trying to harm you. She meets with the killer behind the Porticus Octaviae, possibly to explain what went wrong, or to tell him that she wants no more part in this, and he kills her."

Cassia made an abrupt line below the last then turned her spoon around and went back to eating her stew.

"The man Lucia and Marcia saw must have been Avitus," I said. "The description fits him. Would he have the connections to arrange a kidnapping in Antioch? And an exchange in Ostia? And money to pay Floriana to help him? Or perhaps he was only a go-between."

"Either is possible." Cassia chewed thoughtfully. "The vigiles are made up of freedmen who devote themselves to keeping the peace and watching for fires. Freedmen can become quite rich if they are clever. Perhaps Avitus took the job as vigile in order to further his plan to assassinate the *princeps*. Vigiles roam the streets at will, day and night, and enter any house they like, as Avitus did with us."

I broke my roll into pieces and dropped them in the stew. "Maybe we should wait for Avitus to try to kill me again, and grab him. I'll turn him upside down until he confesses."

"Set a trap, you mean?" This idea did not seem to alarm Cassia in the slightest. "Hmm. We could do that, without simply waiting for him to turn up."

"How?" I asked.

"Leave that to me. Now, let's finish our meal and visit Priscus, before it grows too dark."

"Celnus won't allow us see him in the evening," I warned. "Visits are only in the morning, unless Priscus invites us to dine."

"Leave that to me as well. I would like to question the team of Celnus and Kephalos again. They know much, those two."

I'd learned enough about Cassia to pity them. She'd pry information from them whether they liked it or not.

We both turned our attention to finishing our meal, then made ready to trudge to the Esquiline.

As expected, Celnus did not want to admit us. The master was dining, Celnus said with his usual contempt. Priscus was with guests and would not be disturbed. Cassia told Celnus cheerfully that we'd wait.

Celnus began to argue, but Priscus's son, Decimus, who'd emerged from the inner recesses of the house, spied us and bade Celnus to let us into the atrium.

"Father will want to see you." Decimus spoke to me, not Cassia, who did her best to fade against the wall. I left her to interrogate Celnus and Kephalos, and followed Decimus toward the triclinium.

Priscus was hosting a supper for five. Reclining couches surrounded a table laden with dishes. Priscus was draped in a toga, which he wrestled with as he reached for grapes, cheese, and his cup of wine.

Three guests, all men, surrounded him—the fifth place was for Decimus.

"I've brought you a gift, Father," Decimus said as we entered.

Priscus brightened, shoved aside the folds of his toga, and climbed to his feet. "My friend and guardian, Leonidas. Please, join us. We'll make room."

I assessed the faces of the three guests, one of which was the middle-class client who'd once saved Priscus's life. The expressions on each ranged from surprise, to distaste, to downright disgust from the middle-class man.

I knew that if Priscus let a gladiator, even a former one, perch on a dining couch with his distinguished visitors, the gossip would be all over Rome tomorrow, and Priscus ridiculed. *He* saw no shame in speaking to those he wished, but he would not be praised for it.

"I am humbled by your kindness." I spoke awkwardly, but no one expected a gladiator to be smooth-tongued. "I will not sully your table with my presence. The fact that you admitted me to your house is enough."

"Come, come, you must be hungry." Priscus waved at the table. "There is plenty."

"I dined already, at home," I said, seizing on the excuse.

Priscus looked puzzled at my refusal, but he did not pursue it, to the relief of his guests.

Decimus seated himself, sharing the couch with the middle-class man. His friendly greeting and deference to the man softened that gentleman a touch. Decimus had a youthful charm about him, and a quick-wittedness that his father lacked. I assumed he took after his mother.

"Is he here to perform?" one of the other men asked. The bright whiteness of his toga with a purple stripe told me he held high office and had the money to keep his garments pristine. "Here to show us some of his winning moves? I have seen you fight, Leonidas the Spartan. You are quite skilled. My son admires you greatly."

"He's no Spartan," the middle-class man said in disparagement.

Priscus moved to my side. "Gladiators take grandiose names, or are given them. I will speak to him, as I know he'd not have come if it weren't important."

He ushered me out of the triclinium and to the peristyle garden. I saw, through the opening to the atrium, that Cassia was deep in conversation with Kephalos—he regarded her with a frustrated frown.

Light from the rising moon filtered through the open roof of the peristyle, turning the trees' leaves silver. The trickling fountain lent a peaceful note.

Priscus settled a fold of his toga on his shoulder and wiped his brow. "Truth to tell, my friend, I am happy you came along. Tedious fellows. But one must play host every so often, or be lambasted. What can I do for you?"

"Who is the Equestrian?" I gestured behind us, as though he could see the middle-class man in the dining room. "You said he saved your life by drinking poison meant for you."

Priscus glanced heavenward. "Calls himself Gaius Drusus Aquilinus. 'The eagle-eyed one,' he says. More like the eagle-nosed one." Priscus chuckled. "He was a client of my father-in-law's, and I, the dutiful son-in-law, continue to see him. He's a plebeian who bought his way into the Equestrian class, with the help of my wife's father." Priscus dropped his voice. "He wanted to marry my wife, at one time—thought her father should have her divorce me and take him. My father-in-law disabused him of that notion quickly enough. I might not be all my father-in-law had dreamed of, but I am patrician born, and he was a snob. My wife wouldn't hear of it either, because she detested dear Aquilinus." He smiled in fond memory.

"I wonder if he'd have the wish to kill you," I said.

Priscus raised his brows. "You believe he wants me dead? I'm not certain why he would. He'd lose my patronage—he likes that, even if he dislikes me."

"He could become your son's client if you were gone, couldn't he?"

"Possibly. But Decimus is his own man. No, I can't believe it of Aquilinus. He's rather a coward."

"We have discovered that someone indeed is trying to kill you," I said. "A threat you should take seriously. They hope your death will cause that of the *princeps*."

In brief sentences, I explained what we'd discovered from Nero. Priscus listened in disbelief, his skepticism growing as I finished.

"That is the most absurd thing I've ever heard," Priscus said, scoffing. "You must learn that our *princeps* enjoys drama, the more the better. Depend upon it, Leonidas, his entire tale is a parcel of lies."

CHAPTER 22

Priscus stated the words loudly, determinedly. He began to fold his arms, but the toga prevented him, and he tugged at the fabric in annoyance.

"You once told me the gods looked out for you," I said. "Could it be a person instead?"

Priscus ceased pulling at the toga and folded his hands. "I have friends, Leonidas, but I doubt very much that any love me enough to threaten the *princeps* to keep me alive. What man would?"

I glanced at the dining room, to see Decimus emerging. "A son, perhaps?"

Whatever comment Priscus had opened his mouth to make died on his lips. "Decimus?" Amazement then worry flared and dimmed. "He honors his father, yes, but that is taking it a bit far. But ..."

Decimus entered the garden, the wind that swept it ruffling his dark curls. "They're becoming restless, Father. They want the *paterfamilias*, not the heir."

"They'd do well to cultivate your friendship," Priscus growled, then he sighed. "I do despair of all this bootlicking.

Decimus, Leonidas has proposed that you keep a running threat to Nero that he will die if anything happens to me."

Decimus began to laugh, thinking it a jest, then his laughter faded.

"I?" He pressed his fingers to his chest. Decimus also wore a toga, but it draped his frame elegantly and remained in place. "I doubt Nero—or any man—would be afraid of *me*. I have little power. I'm good with figures, and those in Halicarnassus have learned to fear my accounting skills. That is all." He came forward until the three of us made a small group in the middle of the peristyle. "But this is amazing. Are you certain someone could hold the *princeps* hostage for my father's life?"

"I only know what Nero told us," I said.

"Us?" Decimus's brows climbed.

"Cassia and me."

"Oh, your slave, who so kindly saved the ransom money. Do you know she refused to take one *as* more than the fee she'd agreed upon? Kephalos tried to short her, but she wouldn't have that either."

"Cassia is very precise," I said.

Decimus chuckled. "She is indeed. I promise you, Father, I am committing no conspiracy to keep you alive. If someone is, though, I'd like to meet him. And thank him."

Priscus flushed. "You are kind, my son."

"A son can love his father," Decimus said cheerily. "Even an adopted father."

I broke in. "The trouble is, a person out there *is* trying to finish off Nero by finishing off you. He succeeded in having Decimus captured, and nearly killing you when you went to pay the ransom."

Decimus tucked in his lips and nodded. "That is true, Father. I was abducted as I walked home late at night and taken on board a ship. Rather unusual pirates, I thought—though some do raid the shorelines. But how would they know my family had the money to pay? I dress rather plainly and draw little attention to myself. I concluded they'd followed me for some time and discovered who I was, but still it is strange. But if it was part of a plan to attack my father and through him, Nero ..." He rubbed his chin, lost in thought.

Priscus snorted. "Farfetched."

"Not necessarily." Decimus turned to me. "I thank you for telling us, Leonidas. I will certainly put more guards on my father, and on myself, if they are using me to reach him." He gestured toward the house. "I will walk out with you, Leonidas. You, Father, need to go back in before Aquilinus infuriates the senator and ends up in prison. He'll expect you to pay his way out."

Priscus made an exasperated noise, bade me a polite good night, and made for the dining room at the other end of the peristyle. I watched him square his shoulders before he shoved open the door and marched inside.

"I adore my father, but he can be hard-headed," Decimus said.

"He's a soldier. He keeps telling me that."

Decimus looked amused. "He uses it as an excuse to avoid the social graces. Not that I blame him. I find the social graces tedious as well, and prefer to spend my time among books. I inherited that from my mother, may the gods cradle her."

He made a reverent gesture to the shrine of his ancestors as we entered the atrium. Cassia emerged from the shadows, hugging her cloak around her. Kephalos and Celnus were nowhere in sight.

Decimus softened his voice. "I will take care of my father. Thank you. May I call on your services if I need more might to protect him?"

"Yes," I said simply. Even if Nero hadn't ordered me to look after Priscus, I'd agree. I found that I liked the unworldly Priscus.

"Godspeed on your way home. Wait—take a lantern."

Decimus moved to a table where lit lanterns had been set, presumably to light the guests' ways home.

Decimus handed me a glowing grill dangling from an iron stick. I accepted it with thanks, though I thought smacking a thief with it would be more effective than scaring him off with the light.

Cassia said nothing at all as I bade Decimus a final farewell and we stepped into the street. A litter surrounded by nervous slaves swept by, moving swiftly through the darkness, and then the road was quiet.

I hefted the lantern, which threw a feeble spangle onto the cobbles. By this I saw Cassia's face, and her smug expression.

"What did you discover?" I asked. More than I had, I wagered.

"Something very important." She adjusted a fold of her palla over her mouth, but not before I saw the smile. "It will explain much, I think."

I wanted to demand she tell me everything, but I knew that wasn't wise in the middle of the road winding down the Esquiline.

We hadn't gone far before running footsteps sounded behind us. I and Cassia stepped aside to let whoever it was pass, but a sudden rush of movement had me pushing Cassia into the doorway of a closed shop. I whirled with my lantern, ready to strike.

The pursuer charged straight at me. I slammed the lantern into him, with a quick, hard smack, pushing him into an alley. He stumbled but was quickly up again, lithe and agile. The light of the lantern, before it fell and flickered out, showed me the face of Avitus.

He tried to get around me, but I blocked the way. Avitus knew the city well, and the way he danced from foot to foot, trying to move past me, told me that this tiny lane had only one outlet.

I caught Avitus and threw him into the wall. I crowded him, grabbing his hands before he could go for a knife.

"Leave off," Avitus cried. He struggled mightily, trying to kick me, but he was slow, and I anticipated and stopped every move. "Let me go."

"Not until you cease trying to kill me," I growled.

"I'm not trying to kill you." Avitus's breath smelled of garum, which did not improve my temper. "You're trying to kill *me*."

"You paid Floriana to send me to the gods while I slept." I pressed my hand around his throat when he started to protest. "Don't deny you were there—Lucia saw you. Which is why you're after her too."

Avitus's bulging eyes shone in the moonlight. "Never. I'd never ..."

Cassia's voice came from behind me. "Did you meet Floriana at the river, and murder her because she'd failed? And knew your plans?"

"No!" The choked word was adamant. "I'd never hurt her."

"The mud near where her body was found was marked with the imprints of hobnails, like those on your caligae," Cassia said.

Avitus stopped struggling and glared at both of us. "Well, they weren't mine."

I ground his head against the wall. "You knew Floriana, but you weren't a customer. You never worked for her either. So why were you there the morning she was poisoned?"

"Of course I'd go when she took sick." Avitus grunted for breath. "She was my mum."

In my surprise, I loosened my hold. In the arena, that would have been fatal, but Avitus only hung in my slackened grip, terrified and angry.

"Floriana was your mother?" Cassia asked in surprise. "Is there a record of this we can check?"

"I dunno. Suppose."

I pictured Floriana, with her angular body and too sharp face.

Did I see the same features on Avitus? I couldn't be certain in the darkness.

"If she was your mother, why did none of her ladies know?" Cassia asked. "Lucia would have told us if she'd known you were her son there to visit."

"It was a secret." Avitus's face was streaked with the sweat of fear. "You can't tell anyone—please, by all the gods, tell no one. I can't be a vigile if it got out I'm a slave."

"Floriana was a freedwoman," Cassia pointed out.

"Not when she had me. But she gave me to my father, who was a legionnaire, and he pretended I was his son by another woman, a free citizen. He invented her. I didn't know until a few years ago that Floriana was my true mum. My father finally told me when I wanted to join the vigiles. It was never exactly clear whether or not I was a freedman." He trailed off into a mumble.

"A legionnaire took you in and raised you?" I asked, incredulous. "By himself?"

"He wanted a son." Avitus glowered in defiance. "He looked after me. He married when I was about ten summers, and *she* became my mother. She was wonderful. She's gone to Elysium now."

His sadness tugged at me. I remembered the boy I'd been, when the only mother I'd known had slipped away in the night. They'd had to pry my hand from hers, and then I was alone.

"So you went to find Floriana," I prompted.

"Yes, I did. She was happy, once she believed my story. But I never went near the night she was sick, and I never, ever killed her. I wouldn't. She was my *mum*."

His adamance rang of truth. When Avitus had lost his beloved stepmother, he might have tried to find his real mother to help fill the hole the stepmother had left.

Then again, Avitus might have gone to see Floriana to make certain she never told anyone he'd been slave born and possibly never freed by law. His father probably hadn't filed official documents if he'd simply told everyone Avitus was his freeborn son.

My idea that Avitus had murdered Floriana hadn't quite fizzled away—he still had a motive. But if he wasn't a killer, he might be a witness.

I carefully lowered Avitus to his feet and released him, positioning myself to seize him if he tried to run. He drew a few ragged breaths but remained in place.

"Lucia described a man visiting Floriana," I said. "He wore a tunic with boots like yours. A vigile, she thought. If not you, then who? What other vigile would visit her?"

Avitus wrinkled his brow in confusion. "None. The men in my house went to a different *lupinarius*. I'd never let them near Floriana's."

"One of them must have gone." Cassia's tone had gentled. "Perhaps you could find out for us."

"Find out who killed her?" Avitus's eyes took on a fanatic light. "I'd like to know that, yes. But I don't know how."

"Ask," Cassia said. "Ask everyone in your house, and in the other houses. Who was on watch the night she was poisoned?"

"I already know *that*. I read the log. But I know all the patrollers well—none would try to convince Floriana to kill a gladiator—why should they? Especially a gladiator who's won them a lot of money on wagers."

"Where were these men on the morning Floriana died?" I persisted. "Who went to meet her behind the Porticus Octaviae?"

"I don't know. No one."

"Or did *you*?" I pressed him to the wall again. "So she wouldn't betray that you weren't qualified to be a vigile?"

"No." Avitus's eyes widened. "In any case, I don't care anymore. They could have slung me out if they wanted—I'd rather have looked after Floriana even if it meant I had to quit the watch. I don't care about being promoted through the ranks—I'll never be an officer, anyway. They come from the legions. Some even rise to be Praetorian Guards, like Severus Tullius, but that has no interest for me. I'm happy with what I have."

I stilled, and Cassia went very quiet.

Then I grabbed the front of Avitus's tunic. "Severus Tullius was a vigile?"

Avitus's alarm warred with perplexity. "A vigile captain—my captain. Went up to the Palatine about a year back. Why?"

CHAPTER 23

At Avitus's announcement, I abruptly dropped him, turned on my heel, and marched back to the road.

"Where are you going?" Avitus bleated behind us.

Cassia answered him. "To the Palatine. Come with us. We might need your help."

Avitus said nothing, and I imagined him staring, open-mouthed. Then I heard rapid footsteps as he scrambled away in the opposite direction.

"Never mind him." I strode rapidly, and Cassia had to run to catch up. "You go home. I'll find Tullius."

"No, indeed." Cassia trotted beside me. "You will need me to explain things."

That was true. If I could think clearly, I'd have decided we needed more authority, and perhaps run for Marcianus or even Priscus. But rage burned through my blood at the man who'd pretended to be a friend, who'd flattered and praised, offering to help, while he lied about everything. He'd showed us where Floriana died, yes, but he'd known there would be nothing to see there.

Rome was vastly dark, and I'd lost the lantern Decimus had

given us. We passed another party with a litter, this one surrounded by five guards with torches. The guards tensed as I approached, the slaves shuffling the litter aside, ready to lower it and fight if they had to—or perhaps run and abandon their master to his fate.

I took Cassia by the hand and pressed past them. They muttered in relief once we'd gone.

The Subura was one of the most dangerous places in the city at night. Even I had remained indoors at Floriana's when I stayed there and left again in daylight. Aemil had always known where I was and that I'd return in the morning.

Desperate men who would slay another for the fabric of his tunic roamed the gloom. I sensed them, heard the click of pebble on stone, the whisper of footsteps. Cassia's clothing alone would bring a good price, not to mention her person.

I kept tight hold of Cassia, pulling her against my side. We tripped on each other's feet, but I refused to let go.

"Let me fetch my notes," she whispered to me.

I agreed we'd need proof to sway our argument. Magistrates and lawyers valued records, and I'd have to convince them I wasn't wrong, or mad.

We cut to the street that led to our apartment, where all was dark but marginally safer. The wine shop had shut hours ago, boards fitted into grooves to cover its opening.

"Leonidas?" An amazed voice came out of the gloom. "Thank Vesta. I'm lost."

Gnaeus Gallus the architect materialized from the corner. Moonlight that had shimmered on Priscus's garden sliced a white gleam on Gallus's high forehead. His eyes were wide, full of fear.

"What are you doing here?" I demanded.

He was another person connected to Floriana's. I'd first found him walking through her house to study its walls, deciding whether it could be saved. I'd reflected that it was unusual for a lofty *architectus* to do an assistant's job.

Perhaps he'd been there for another reason—to destroy

anything that could connect him with Floriana. I'd noted that all her belongings had been cleared out—I'd assumed the women had taken what they could before they fled, or perhaps Floriana's husband had sent people to empty the place. But I hadn't seen who'd done it, and Gallus had been there ...

"I worked late on a job," Gallus said quickly. "Tried to get back home. Took a wrong turn. I don't know this part of the city. Would you walk me there? For pay, of course. I wouldn't presume—"

"No." I cut him off, and he flinched. "No time."

Cassia had already started up the stairs and banged open the door above.

"Why?" Gallus asked in perplexity. "Where can you be going this late?"

I hesitated. If Gallus told the truth, and he was simply lost, he could wait safely in our rooms until we returned—if we did. If we did not make it back, he could navigate his way home in daylight.

But if he was involved in this conspiracy ...

"The Palatine. Come with us."

Gallus blinked. "The Palatine? Now? Why ...?"

I regarded him stubbornly. "Come with us, and I will see you safely home. Otherwise ..." I made a gesture that said I'd leave him to the Fates.

Cassia clattered down the stairs, a leather bag over her shoulder and a small lantern in her hand. "Let us be quick."

Gallus's brows rose as I took the lantern and immediately fell into step with her. He waited a few heartbeats, then pattered after us. "I admit, you have me curious. And us keeping together will be safer than me blundering about in the dark."

I scarcely listened as I led the way down the hill, again holding Cassia close. A pair of vigiles nervously patrolling headed for us, but I growled at them, and they faded into the shadows.

Our lantern made only a feeble light in the darkness as we

moved around the quiet Forum Romanum and began the climb to the Palatine. Gallus puffed behind us up the hill, tripping on loose rocks.

Guards met us before we reached the top, demanding our business. One who'd been on duty when I'd visited previously recognized me and escorted us to the gate. Nero must have given the word that we were to be admitted at any time, because the gate guard led us in without hesitation. He raised his brows at Gallus, but I indicated the man was with me, and we were at last ushered into the courtyard.

The man with the shaved head and toga—I never learned his name—forestalled us there. Before I could tell him I sought Severus Tullius, not Nero, the man barked, "He is dining. You will wait."

He bent a hard-eyed stare on Gallus, who'd opened his mouth as though to explain who he was. Gallus snapped his mouth shut and remained silent.

The shaved-headed man led us across the courtyard with its huge fountain into an anteroom with walls of Egyptian marble and a floor mosaic depicting galloping horses. A small table graced the room, which was otherwise empty.

Our guide deserted us without a word. Two lamps lit our surroundings, allowing Gallus to study the walls with professional interest.

Cassia went to the table, which was a slab of marble supported by a gilded pillar in the form of a buxom nymph. She removed scrolls and tablets from her bag and began sorting them into piles.

A slave brought a tray bearing three cups of wine and left it wordlessly on the table. Cassia gave him a nod of thanks. He studied us curiously as he went out, no doubt wondering what sort of odd people Nero was welcoming to his presence this late.

I ignored the wine, and Gallus didn't notice, too absorbed in running his hands over the walls. Cassia took a polite sip or two as she continued to sift through her notes.

At one point I stood behind her, wishing I could make sense of her writing. "What did you learn at Priscus's house?" I asked. "You were about to tell me."

"Hmm?" Cassia jerked around, as though having forgotten my presence. "Oh, nothing about this. At least, not directly." She cast a surreptitious glance at Gallus. "It will keep."

She returned to her scrolls. Her expression became one of rapt concentration, and I left her alone.

We waited for nearly an hour by my calculation. I'd grown bored enough to lift a wine cup when the shaved-headed man returned. I set the untasted wine down, both relieved and annoyed as the man beckoned for us to follow.

Nero met us in a wide, vaulted room with windows set high under the arched roof. The cavernous darkness was broken by a line of oil lamps hanging from one wall, illuminating a beautiful chamber full of multi-colored marble.

The *princeps* stood in full splendor in a tunic trimmed with gold, a purple toga, and a crown of beaten gold leaves on his curled hair. His sandals were filmed with gold, and he wore golden rings and armlets as well as a gold pectoral studded with rubies.

"You are fortunate that my dining companions are tedious this night." Nero's eyes narrowed in displeasure. "Senators and their toadies currying favor. Stale old men. Who is this?" He pointed at Gallus, who'd bowed low.

"An *architectus*," I answered quickly.

Gallus straightened his body but kept his head bowed. "I am honored to be allowed into this astonishing abode." He risked raising his eyes to the glittering porphyry that wound through the columns that lined the room.

Nero made a dismissive gesture. "It was cobbled together by my forbears. I am building a far grander house than this."

"Ah, yes, the *Domus Transitoria*." Gallus beamed with admiration. "An architectural marvel."

Nero softened a little. "You brought in an *architectus* to study my work?"

"We came to find Severus Tullius," I said.

Nero's brows went up. "And who is he?"

"One of your Praetorian Guards. I wish to speak to him."

Nero continued staring at me like a basilisk. Cassia's whisper came around me.

"It is very important, sir."

Nero flicked his gaze to her, then he snapped his fingers.

Three servants materialized out of the darkness behind him. "Fetch a Praetorian Guard called Severus Tullius. Tell him to come alone. Be quick."

The servants faded. Nero spoked to Cassia directly. "What is this about?"

Cassia lifted her bag and withdrew a handful of scrolls. "I have evidence here of crimes committed against a murdered freedwoman called Floriana."

Interest flickered in Nero's dark eyes. "Why not take this evidence to the captain of the urban cohorts?"

"Because it involves an assassination plot against you," Cassia said, her voice unwavering. "One that involves an attempt against the life of Decimus Laelius Priscus and his household, including arranging his son to be kidnapped for a large ransom. The freedwoman was killed for knowing the plot and for a failed attempt to murder Leonidas."

Nero listened, a twitch pulling at his lower lip. "What has this to do with one of my guards?"

Before Cassia could answer, the servants returned with Severus Tullius himself, who looked astonished to see us.

"Sir." Tullius, in a tunic and toga, bowed then gazed in wonder at me. He glanced at Gallus and became more baffled.

Gallus, on the other hand, regarded Tullius with startled recognition. "I know you, don't I?"

Tullius studied him more closely. "No—who are you?"

s—I did see you. At the house I was hired to evaluate. ura. You were there when I first arrived, going through and taking things out. Very thorough, you were."

Tullius's jaw went slack. He clearly did not remember Gallus, had likely dismissed the man as no threat and forgot about him.

"I suggest you were there taking away things that would incriminate you," Cassia said. "Perhaps a note sent to Floriana, or money paid to her."

Tullius focused on Cassia, while Nero looked on, his ennui changing to fascination.

Then Tullius turned a deep shade of red. He produced a sword from the folds of his toga, and ran at Cassia, a killing rage in his eyes.

As soon as the blade flashed, guards appeared from the corners. Nero held up a hand. "No."

I leapt after Tullius and grabbed him by his toga, using the smothering folds to throw him off balance. Cassia scrambled aside, gathering her scrolls to her, wasting a precious moment to snatch up one that had fallen to the floor.

Tullius fought free of me and again went after Cassia.

I tackled him from behind. As we struggled, Cassia skittered aside, and Gallus, finally coming out of his stupefied stance, pulled her to safety.

Tullius twisted out of my grip and spun to face me, the toga falling. Tullius stepped quickly free of it, and whipped the cloth around my feet.

As a *secutor*, I often fought the *retiarius*, who went at his opponent with a trident and weighted net. I easily kicked aside the tangling folds, Tullius's eyes widening as I came at him.

My intention was to knock Tullius down, take his sword from him, and deliver a blow that would stun him senseless. His fellow guardsmen would take him away and lock him up, and Cassia could hand over her evidence. Tullius would be Nero's problem, and I could go home and sleep.

Tullius evaded me, and I heard Nero laugh as I chased him

across the floor. Guards filled the entrances to the room, blocking Tullius's way out.

He turned and faced me, sword held loosely in a practiced hand. Only the best of the legionnaires became Praetorian Guards, and they trained daily. Tullius moved lightly on the balls of his feet. He might not be able to escape, but he could kill me and Cassia and shut our mouths..

"Continue," Nero said as I assessed Tullius. "Fight him, Leonidas. Here and now. My own gladiatorial game." He smiled, entertained.

"No more killing," I said quietly. "I'm not a gladiator anymore."

Nero skewered me with an impatient stare then switched it to Cassia. "Are you certain your records, or whatever you have in that sack, will prove that this guard conspired against me?"

"Yes." Cassia hugged the bag to her, fear on her face, but her answer rang with conviction.

"Good." Nero returned to me. "To the death, Leonidas. If he lives I might pardon him. If he loses, you will be his executioner."

I met Nero's gaze before I quickly averted mine. I regarded the guards at the door, three on each, then Tullius, and finally Cassia, alone and protected only by Gallus. If Tullius won free, he'd kill her—I saw that in his eyes.

I flattened my lips, making my choice. "I'll need a weapon."

CHAPTER 24

Nero made an abrupt gesture to one of the guards. The guard came forward, grim-faced, unsheathed his sword, and handed it to me. His look at Tullius as he stepped away was one of unhidden disgust. Tullius could count on no help from him.

I closed my hand around the hilt, hefting the sword. It was different from the blade I carried in the games, the *secutor*, a short, stabbing sword. This was longer and heavier, with an edge that would slice.

I'd trained with many different weapons, though I preferred something more compact than what I held. I also was used to fighting in loincloth only, which though it made me more vulnerable, let me move freely. I'd have no arm or shin guards either, and no shield.

But even in tunic and boots, standing on cold marble instead of hot sand, I knew I could win.

The walls fell away. The sunshine of a warm Roman day fell upon me, and I heard the spectators begin to chant.

In the next instant, the games were gone, and I was in the

dirt of Aemil's *ludus*, jabbing my wooden sword at the posts alongside Xerxes while Aemil bellowed commands at us.

I saw Xerxes's grin spread across his face before he turned on Aemil in a mock attack. That attack had him thrown to the ground, Aemil kicking him, Xerxes laughing all the way.

I thought I heard Xerxes now, his good-natured drawl behind me. *You can take this feeble son of a whore, Leonidas.*

I heard Aemil as well, his Gallic accent conspicuous. *Watch him—he's tricky. Even if he is a pretty Praetorian.*

Xerxes again. *He nearly killed you, murdered Floriana, and tried to attack Cassia. Don't let him win, Leonidas. I'd be so ashamed.*

Then the voice of Regulus, *No more death? Stupid bastard. You're a gladiator. You embody death. You'll never leave it behind.*

The voices faded, and the walls of the Circus Gai returned, along with the noise. Nero sat in his box in purple and gold, his jewels glittering in the sunlight.

I saw Tullius, his affability gone, a trained killer in his place. He raised his sword.

I ran at him, sidestepping at the last minute when he braced for my attack. While he readjusted to keep me in sight, I whirled, aiming the sword for his unprotected back.

Tullius ducked in time, using his momentum to spin in a circle away from my descending sword. Lithe and fast, he countered with his own sword, poised to thrust it upward into my heart.

I deflected the blow, and our blades rang. I hated having no shield, but Tullius didn't have one either. He was right-handed, his left side open and exposed.

Praetorians were military elite, often having campaigned as legionnaires in Gaul or Britain or the East before taking up a position in Rome. Tullius had captained a vigile troop, who were also trained military men.

I saw that training in Tullius's moves, which were tight, practiced, deadly. If he planned well, he could escape this room and probably the palace, but the rage in his eyes told me he'd rather remain and slay me, the man who'd betrayed his plans.

We circled each other warily. The chamber was silent, our watchers riveted on our every move. I saw Cassia's eyes fix on me as she rested one hand on a marble pillar, the glittering stones inside it catching the light.

Tullius attacked me with sudden and rapid blows, pushing me across the floor as I deflected. He got a lucky blow to my sword arm when I reached the far wall, sending a gush of blood over my skin.

"Coward," Tullius snarled. "Face me."

I'd survived forty bouts. Thirty wins, eight draws, and two losses. It would be carved on my tomb.

The losses had been my first fights, and I'd been spared because the crowd liked how well I'd fought. After the second time, I'd vowed never to be at anyone's mercy again.

Tullius's insult flew past me and evaporated to nothing. I growled in my throat, Leonidas the Gladiator finished with hiding in his cell.

The sound of the crowd returned, infusing my strength. *LEE-O-NI-DAS. LEE-O-NI-DAS.*

I joined the shouts with a wordless one of my own. I pushed from the wall, smearing the marble with scarlet, and slammed myself at Tullius, using my bulk to shove aside his sword arm.

He danced out of the way, coming back to slash at me viciously. Blood splashed as I spun aside, the sting of the cut barely noticeable.

I smashed my sword at him. Tullius parried. The fight turned furious, each of us raining blows onto the other, aiming for arms, stomach, neck, head. Tullius grunted and cursed while I retreated to deadly silence.

We went around and around, me using my strength and experience, he his quickness and skills. We were evenly matched. He bled from shallow cuts, as I did. If he broke any of my bones, he'd move in for the kill—this bout would not end in *stans missus*, a draw.

Tullius danced around me, light on his feet. He pretended to go for my exposed side then drove his sword at my face. I quickly turned my head, but not fast enough. I braced for the blade to slide into my unprotected skull.

The blow never reached me. Tullius jerked at the last minute, the sword sweeping wildly askew. I blinked and wiped sweat from my eyes to see Cassia tugging her heavy bag by its strap back to her feet. Whether she'd lost hold of it on purpose or by accident, I couldn't say, but the bag had tripped Tullius and ruined his aim. I wanted to laugh.

Gallus quickly pulled her back to the wall as Tullius, in his fury, swung on her. I rammed myself into him, forcing his attention to our fight once more.

I realized I'd been letting him score hits on me because I felt sorry for him. Tullius had committed treason, and in spite of Nero's claim that he might pardon Tullius if he won, I was certain the man would head for a miserable death.

His willingness to attack Cassia sealed his fate. I steadied my sword and went at him. I would be his executioner, as Regulus had begged me to be his.

Tullius met my blows with energy. I hammered at him with strength and precision as much from Aemil's training as the master-builder's when he'd taught me to hone blocks of marble long ago. The crowds in my head urged me on.

I floated on the noise as I stabbed and parried, using my left fist to both punch and fend off blows. Finally I darted forward and seized a handful of Tullius's dark hair, twisting his head to bring him to his knees.

Tullius stabbed upward, going for my heart. I swiftly bent out of the way and struck his sword hand with my knee. His grip slacked, and then my kick sent the sword skittering across the floor.

I had his head bent back, the sword point at his throat.

Tullius glared. "Kill me." His voice rasped in the echoing room. "Do it." With the chanting crowds in my head, I barely heard him. *Iugula! Iugula!* they bellowed, urging me to finish him.

"Do it now," Tullius said furiously.

He'd face torture and execution if I spared him. His name and his family, whoever they were, would be dragged through scandal and shame. Tullius's body would be broken, his death not pretty. As a citizen he'd avoid the more bizarre forms of execution in the arena, but he'd die a traitor. Nero would not be kind.

My sword hesitated. No more death, I'd vowed. And yet, I'd found that death and violence did not stop with the games.

Regulus was right—we were gladiators. Dealers in death. It followed us.

I firmed my grip, ready to strike the killing blow. At the same time, Cassia, who'd dropped her bag again, gave a little cry and fell to her knees.

I jerked my head up as Cassia landed on her hands, gasping for breath. Gallus hurried to her, while Nero took a few steps back, as though fearing she might contaminate him.

Tullius began to laugh. "It seems I miscalculated. My misfortune."

For a moment, I could only frown in confusion. Then I abruptly recalled the wine brought to us by the servant as we waited for Nero to summon us. I'd been too restless to partake, and so had Gallus. Cassia was the only one who'd drunk.

Tullius must have poisoned the wine. He'd tried to kill us before we could reveal his crimes. No wonder he'd been so surprised to see us when he'd entered Nero's chamber.

This rushed through my head as Cassia began to convulse.

She was the one person in all the world who'd steadied me in my uncertainty, who understood we had to survive on our own, and who'd gone at that survival with hard-headed resolution. Without Cassia, I'd have swum in circles and sunk, not even understanding I was drowning. She'd been the rock that had held me up without me realizing it.

Now she would die.

"Why?" I roared.

Tullius abruptly ended his laughter, his fury surging. "Because he killed my father, that's why!" His glare cut to Nero. "*He* decided my father supported Britanicus and tried to block his way to the throne. Brought my father to trial on trumped-up charges, when my father had done *nothing*. A misunderstood conversation, a rival happy to ruin my family. I was already in the legions, a long way from home, in bloody Damascus, and I couldn't get back to stop *any* of it."

Tullius gasped for breath, his eyes fixed in his rage, as though he'd forgotten I gripped him, ready to end his life. "I had a new purpose—work through the ranks and become a Praetorian Guard. I changed my name in case he got any ideas to slay me as well." He pointed a shaking finger at Nero. "The money my mother left me helped me plan. I didn't need it for myself—it all went to my goal. No one pays attention to the guard at the end of the room—I heard him talking one day about Priscus and the strange bargain that Nero dies if Priscus does."

His laughter returned, rasping in his throat. "Terrified him. Easy to take advantage of such a thing—I make certain Priscus dies, and then watch while Nero is assassinated. I wouldn't have to do a thing! A whore and a fool of a patrician and his insipid son are small sacrifices compared to what *he* did to *me*. So is your slave." Tullius shifted his gaze to me, savage triumph in his eyes. "*You* should have died from that poison, Leonidas. Remember that when you weep at her funeral."

Spittle flecked his lips—his rage was complete. So was mine. His lack of remorse about Cassia sealed his fate.

I tightened my grip and plunged the sword into Tullius's throat.

Blood poured over my hand, hot and wet. The wrath left Tullius's expression, replaced by gratitude, even relief. Then his eyes emptied, and he died.

Nero began to speak. I had no idea what he said. I flung

Tullius's body and sword aside and ran to where Gallus held Cassia. She shivered, eyes closed, face waxen.

I lifted Cassia from Gallus and cradled her close. "Fetch that wine," I barked at Gallus. "Hurry."

Gallus, understanding, stumbled from me and rushed to the door. The guards tried to stop him, but a command from Nero made them part.

I turned with Cassia in my arms, looking for a safe place to lay her down.

Nero was clapping his hands, issuing orders to slaves rushing into and out of the room, a few dragging away Tullius's pathetic body. "Take her to a chamber," he ordered one bunch. "Fetch my physician. She'll have the best of care."

"No." My snarl made the *princeps* of the Roman Empire stop and regard me coldly. "Send for Nonus Marcianus, from the Aventine. He's the best physician in the world."

Nero continued to stare at me then he gave me a nod and snapped another order at his slaves.

The shaved-headed man reappeared as more guards surrounded Nero. "You," the man said to me. "Bring her."

He turned and marched out of the room, not bothering to see if I'd follow.

CHAPTER 25

The shaved-headed man took me to a room with a sleeping couch, hangings screening it from the passageway outside it. It was a small chamber with plainer decorations than any I'd seen in this *domus*.

Cassia was limp and gray-cheeked by the time I laid her down, her breathing shallow, lips blue. I knew she'd not last the night.

The wait for Marcianus stretched. Gallus found the wine cups, saving them just as a servant had gone in to clear the table. He'd brought all three, two still brimming, the third half-empty.

The hapless servant, a slave whose job it was to deliver food and drink to whomever in the palace required it, was hauled before the shaved-headed man and beaten. From his sobbed confession, it was clear he'd had no idea the wine had been poisoned.

His story was that Tullius had told him guests awaited Nero in the long antechamber and they should be served wine at once. Tullius had inspected the glasses once they'd been on the tray, turning his back to the servant to sniff them. He'd wanted to make certain the guests had the best wine, not inferior stuff, Tullius had explained.

I believed the slave. Tullius would have given the command in his offhand way, and the servant would have had hurried to obey without question.

"Leave him," I shouted at the shaved-headed man. "No one else should suffer for Tullius. *You* should for not noticing he was an assassin."

The slave was released, and the shaved-headed man made himself scarce.

Cassia should not suffer for Tullius either, or for my slowness. Tullius had been too friendly, too ingratiating. I was used to men excited to meet a famous gladiator, and I'd taken his fawning as truth.

He'd had the height and build of the man who'd attacked me in the street and again in the bath. Avitus had been too spindly—Gallus, Celnus, or Kephalos too feeble. The middle-class man who toadied to Priscus also was too soft to be my attacker.

I'd also suspected the man who'd purchased Floriana's lupinarius, but he was probably an elderly patrician who lived in a villa outside Rome and never bothered to look at his own properties in the city. I'd never thought of Tullius.

Cassia must have known—she'd been adamant about something when we'd left Priscus's house tonight. Our meeting with Avitus had overshadowed it, and she'd assured me it would keep. If I'd made her tell me her thoughts ...

I held her hand, which was too cold. If she died, what would happen to me?

Our benefactor would simply send me another slave, I knew. But never one like Cassia. She was too unique to be discarded and replaced like a broken amphora.

Marcianus arrived at last. I heard his hurried conversation with Gallus and then the *medicus* was beside me, his thin frame and large nose familiarly drab in this grandeur. Marcia had accompanied him, she almost completely shrouded in her plain brown cloak.

Marcianus sniffed the glasses, then dipped his finger into one and delicately tasted a drop of the wine inside.

"Subtle," he said under his breath. "How long between the time she drank and the time she fell?"

I couldn't speak. I didn't know, in any case. The events had blurred, our haste through the city to the palace, our tedious wait for Nero to send for us, ending with my fury as I fought Tullius. His blood still stained my tunic.

"The fourth hour of night had been called," Gallus said. "But not the fifth."

"She didn't drink too much. That is good." Marcianus's thin hand landed on my shoulder. "I'll do what I can, Leonidas."

I understood that Marcianus expected me to leave while he doctored Cassia, but I refused. I remained stubbornly next to the bed, only stepping aside enough to let him work.

He purged Cassia, holding her over a basin in Marcia's hands while Cassia heaved up all she had in her stomach. Marcianus laid her back down and poured a draught of something from one of his flasks into a cup. He tried to feed the draught to Cassia, but she had gone motionless, her lips slack.

Marcianus brought out a long metal tube, which he inserted into Cassia's mouth, much farther than I thought possible, and decanted the liquid into it.

Cassia came to life then, gagging and trying to cough. Marcianus held the tube inside her for a few moments before he carefully slid it out. He supported Cassia upright while she coughed, but she mercifully soon subsided.

I didn't like Marcianus's worried look as he handed the apparatus to Marcia and lowered Cassia to the couch. "Is she dying?" I asked bluntly.

"No need for her to." Marcianus was his usual optimistic self. "I've emptied her stomach and given her something to counteract the poison. Now we must wait."

Cassia's breathing was ragged. Soon her eyes closed and she sank into sleep, her chest barely rising.

The night drifted past, moon setting into blackness. Cassia was so very still that I had to lean to her to feel her breath on my cheek. Marcia bathed her face with scented water and straightened the covers, which were the finest linen.

I barely noticed who came and went in the room besides Marcianus and Marcia. Where Nero had gone, I didn't know, nor did I know what they'd done with Tullius's body. Gallus remained, obviously still not braving the streets to go home, and hovered worriedly at the edge of my vision.

The lamps sputtered out and were relit by silent servants. They were flickering still when the stars outside the high window faded, and dawn touched the sky.

Cassia lay motionless, her face as gray as the light that seeped into the room.

My heart burned as it had done the night I'd learned Xerxes had been slain and carried off before I could bid him farewell. I'd held that pain inside for a long time afterward, and even now, thinking of him brought a dull ache.

I did not want to experience that pain again. Cassia had to live. I didn't understand how to function in ordinary life—she did.

I liked waking to hear her returning from her morning errands, her sandals swishing on the floor, water sloshing into basins and jars, as the scent of the fresh-baked bread she set out for our breakfast wafted to me. I enjoyed watching her hunch over her tablets, one lock of hair trickling down her cheek as she wrote. She loved letters and numbers, not only writing them but reading them. She was so different from any person I'd ever encountered, and I did not want her to go from my life.

I lifted a scalpel from Marcianus's bag, a thin blade of Noricum iron, and cut a crease across my palm before he could stop me. Blood welled up on my skin.

I gently dipped my fingers in it then wiped the blood across Cassia's bared shoulders and her cold face.

"The blood of a gladiator," I told Marcianus and his quizzical gaze. "It can heal."

Marcianus drew a breath to say, *You know that's nonsense,* as he had many times before, but subsided.

I folded my fingers over my palm, and waited.

When sunlight at last trickled through the window and touched Cassia's cheek, she stirred. She murmured in her sleep and turned her head, a frown brushing her face.

I let out a breath, hopeful, but Marcianus continued to look worried.

"She's better, isn't she?" I asked.

"That remains to be seen."

"What did he poison her with?"

"Arsenicum," Marcianus said. "I think."

My fears rose. "You aren't certain?"

"Such a poisoning can resemble other things. But I'm fairly sure. There was a large dose in the cup, but she didn't drink all of it, and much of the poison would have settled into the bottom. Thank the gods you didn't down a cup in one go, or it would have killed you."

My heart gave a stricken beat. "Cassia took only a few sips."

"As I said, that is good. It gives her a chance."

I flexed my hand, which stung from the cut I'd made. I seemed to feel the wooden *rudis* I'd clutched as I'd walked out of the ring for the last time, until my hand had frozen around it. Cassia had gently pried it free, letting me begin my new life.

The beam of sunlight moved to touch her eyes. Cassia made a soft noise and again frowned.

"Must fetch the water," she whispered and started to push at the covers.

"Cassia."

She turned toward my voice and blinked open her eyes, forehead puckering. "I'm sorry, Leonidas. I'll bring the bread." She pushed at the covers again then fell back, letting out a quick breath. "I seem to be so very tired."

I rested my hand on her shoulder, over the dried smear of my blood. "Never mind. Rest, Cassia."

She opened her eyes and smiled at me, then drew a long breath and drifted into a quiet sleep.

Marcianus closed his bag, his cheerfulness returning. "She will be all right. Let her sleep, and take her home." He looked me up and down. "You'd better sleep too. I don't want to have to carry *you* anywhere."

I was too exhausted to respond to his humor. I left the bed to stretch out on the floor beside it. I curled around myself as I'd done many a night in my life, when I'd had nothing but a hard slab and no blankets. Within moments, I was fast asleep.

I woke with a grunt when something poked my side.

"Wake up, Leonidas." Cassia stood over me, in her palla and stolla, a slender piece of gilded wood tapping me. A blanket covered my body, a pillow under my head.

While I stared muzzily up at her, Cassia let out a breath of relief.

"Thank the gods. I've been trying to rouse you for hours. It is long past time for us to go home."

Our apartment was musty and stale from being shut up all morning, and noisy—the wine shop was open, with customers lined up to collect their drink for the day.

Cassia immediately lifted the water jar from its place in the corner and headed for the door, ready to fill it as she did every day. She staggered under the clay pot's weight, and I took it out of her hands.

"You are not well," I declared.

"A bit dizzy, yes." Cassia pressed fingers to her temple. "Marcianus said I would be ill a while yet."

"Rest." I pointed at her bed. "I will fetch the water."

She began to laugh. "You, go to the well? That's a woman's task."

"Then the women will have something to talk about today." I hefted the jar to my shoulder and strode through the door and down the stairs.

"Wait, I must tell you ..."

Cassia's voice drifted behind me. Whatever it was could wait —I'd fetch water and then bread from the bakery. She could talk to me as we ate.

I felt light as I walked, lighter than I had even when I'd been handed my freedom and departed the *ludus*. Then I'd been stunned, uncertain. Today I knew I'd been given a gift.

Marcianus had brought Cassia back to life. He'd done it not by the magic of my blood or his invocation of the gods, but by his expertise. I would have to find some way to repay him.

Tullius was dead, and Nero had heard his confession. Tullius would no longer threaten Priscus, and I would not be accused of Floriana's murder. I would eat my breakfast, see that Cassia was comfortable, and we could both sleep.

The well nearest our house sat the bottom of a *castellum*, a tower that collected water from an aqueduct and sent it via pipes to the public fountains. The basin at the foot of the tower dispensed water through the mouth of a carved-stone Bacchus, stone leaves surrounding his scowling face.

Most people drew water early in the morning, so only one startled woman was there at this hour. She drew back when she saw me, her mouth dropping open, then she jerked her vessel from the spigot and hastened away, water sloshing in her wake.

I set the jar I'd brought beneath Bacchus's mouth and let him spill water into it. The fountain's basin sported a carved groove that allowed the ever-flowing water out into the gutter, where it trickled along the street, seeking escape into the sewers.

"You are Leonidas?"

I rose, lifting the full jar, now heavy and damp.

The man who addressed me was perhaps ten years older than I, with black hair in thick curls. He was tall and broad of shoulder, filling out a tunic of fine linen. He wore no toga, but his boots were well made, and a thick gold wristlet proclaimed his wealth. Three burly men stood behind him—his guards. No man wearing so much gold should walk about alone.

"I am." I suspected he was an admirer of Leonidas the Spartan, and I waited patiently for him to tell me which bouts he remembered.

"I am Sextus Livius."

I couldn't place the name for a moment, then I recalled that Sextus Livius was the speculator who'd bought Floriana's house.

He went on. "I had a message from Gnaeus Gallus, the *architectus,* that you wished to speak to me."

I lifted my brows. "I sent no message."

"I believe your slave conveyed the message through him." Livius reached behind him, and one of his guards slid a thin scroll into his hand. The scroll was tiny, only a few inches long when he opened it. I saw words on it in neat writing. "I thought it best to come to you myself."

"I already know you purchased the house Floriana worked in. That you make many such purchases."

"Yes." Livius regarded me with dark eyes that reminded me of another's I'd seen. I suddenly realized whose.

My expression must have betrayed me, because Livius nodded. "Is there a place we may speak?"

Without a word, I gestured him to follow. I led the way back to our apartment, balancing the water jar on my shoulder.

"The guards will not fit," I said as I opened the door from the street. "I can give you my word you won't be harmed."

"They will come if I shout." Livius indicated I should precede him up the stairs.

I entered the apartment and set the jar in its corner, my tunic damp from the water slopping over. Cassia hurried in from the balcony—she'd obviously not taken to her bed as ordered.

"Oh, good. You found him." She smiled at me, pleased. "I sent a message to Sextus Livius while you slept on the Palatine."

The three guards had remained downstairs. I'd left the doors open in case they wanted to rush in to Livius's defense.

I brushed droplets of water from my tunic and faced him. "Priscus is your father. Isn't he?"

CHAPTER 26

Livius regarded me in surprise. "Your message said you knew this."

Cassia would have written the message, which she'd given Gallus to deliver. How she'd discovered Livius's identity, I did not know, but now it was clear what she'd been trying to whisper to me since we'd left Priscus's *domus*.

I remembered her telling me the story that Priscus had set free one of the boys in his household because he'd seen good in the lad. Priscus had placed him with a family through an intermediary, according to Kephalos and Celnus.

The deed was more understandable if the boy had been Priscus's own son, perhaps by a mistress. Priscus had spoken of his wife with so much love that I suspected the liaison had happened before his marriage.

"He allowed you to be adopted," I said. "So you'd have a chance."

"He was incredibly kind." Livius spoke with reverence. "I was indeed adopted by a man—Julius Livius—who raised me as his own. When he went to his ancestors, I inherited his wealth and his estates throughout the empire, making me one of the richest men in Rome."

Ideas fell together. I wasn't certain I was right, but as Cassia would not speak, I did.

"Powerful enough to threaten the *princeps* if Priscus is touched?"

Livius regarded me quietly with a hint of a smile. "You knew this?"

"I guessed it."

He nodded, the calm with which he acknowledged his complicity showing he was powerful indeed.

"I can call on the assistance of many people from all tiers, plebeian to patrician." Livius's smile was self-deprecating. "I never had ambition for such power when I was younger—it arose as a consequence of my inheritance, and I learned to use opportunities. I have no wish to remove the *princeps* or establish another in his place. I only wish to keep alive the one man who is important to me. A truly good man, who should live out his life in peace."

When Livius finished this speech, he glanced from me to Cassia. "This is secret knowledge, my friends. It can go no further."

If it did, I sensed, Cassia and I would be the first to pay. That was his unspoken promise.

"We will keep your confidence," I said. "I too would like to see Priscus left in peace. He is a good man."

Livius's expression turned wry. "Priscus is a bit ... unworldly. I will do all in my capacity to protect him."

"As will I." I had a thought. "Did you return the money to Priscus? The casket of gold the pirates managed to capture?"

Livius acknowledged this with a nod. "My men were there that day, lurking in watch, ready to intervene if necessary. But there was no need. You were as good as your reputation indicates. My men alerted the Ostian authorities that the men were brigands, and were there to help round them up once they fled you. My head guardsman had the presence of mind to walk away with the casket while soldiers arrested the pirates. I hear the *princeps* ordered the pirates executed immediately. He's being praised for it, for keeping the waters that much safer for the rest of us."

Livius's neutral expression gave me no indication about what he thought of Nero's deed. But I saw satisfaction that he had saved his natural father along with Priscus's coin.

"It was good of you," I said.

"I had no use for the money." Livius brushed his generosity aside. We studied each other a moment, then Livius drew a breath. "I will detain you no more. Good day, Leonidas the Spartan."

I gave him a nod in farewell.

Livius turned to depart but paused at the top of the stairs. "If you need a friend, do call on me. I am indebted to you for saving my father's life, and that of his son."

He glanced at our shrine to the departed as though reflecting on the irony that he'd saved the family he could never acknowledge. Then he squared his shoulders and strode out.

We heard his even tramp on the stairs and his barked order to his guards. I moved to the balcony to watch the four walk away, Livius always surrounded. Crowds parted for them like water from a prow.

Cassia joined me on the balcony, and I sent her an accusing look. "How did you know?"

"Celnus and Kephalos." Cassia kept her voice low, though the shouts and calls of people on the street would prevent any from hearing our conversation. "As I said, they told me about the freed boy. When I spoke to them last evening, they said they knew the boy had been adopted by a very wealthy landholder, though not who. But a wealthy landholder decided to purchase a building that belonged to Priscus, one this landholder likely couldn't sell for much, yet he pays a premium price for it. I thought it was obvious."

She shook her head, her pitying exasperation with her informants clear.

"Do Celnus and Kephalos know Livius is his son?"

"No, indeed. They have all the pieces, but cannot put them together."

Again, the pity. I'd met few men with minds as quick as Cassia's.

I moved inside, out of the sun. "I didn't bring bread. I'll fetch it."

"No." Cassia forestalled me. "I will. The walk will do me good, and you won't know what to ask for. The baker is tricky."

"Tricky?" I yawned, my long night weighing heavily upon me.

"Sly, I should say. It is best I deal with him. I'll return soon. Why don't you nap until I do, and we'll have lunch."

I could barely keep to my feet. I did not like to send Cassia out alone, but I knew she would talk rings around this baker, as she likely did every day. I'd rest and look for her if she remained out too long.

Cassia waited until I'd fallen to my pallet. I felt her lay a blanket over my prone body, and loosen and remove the shoes from my feet. I would doze and be ready for her return. Later, I'd go find a carpenter who could do something about our flimsy door.

I swore I only blinked my eyes before Cassia was removing her palla and straightening her hair. The smell of baked bread filled the small room.

"Excellent. You are awake." Cassia set the bread on the table and poured out wine, as though she and I had slept peacefully all night, no adventures at all. Cassia, I was coming to know, was resilient.

"I spoke to the baker," Cassia said as I rose and shambled to the table. I smelled fusty—I'd make for the baths after this. "He is awaiting some shipments of goods from Ostia, and he would be pleased to pay us to guard them from there to Rome. I told him we would take the job. I managed to win a good price." She sat down, pleased with herself.

"Then I suppose we are to Ostia once more." I broke apart my bread, dunked it in my wine, and shoved it into my mouth. The bread was yeasty and soft—this baker made decent enough loaves. "Will you let me go to the baths first?"

"Of course." Cassia sent me a smile. "We won't leave for a few days. You'll have plenty of time to bathe and rest."

I grunted something and returned to my meal, but a warmth eased through me, relaxing me in a way I'd not felt in a very long time.

Before I'd left Nero's house this morning, Gallus had approached me, his relief at Cassia's recovery evident.

"I am glad the girl is all right." He'd peered at me in curiosity. "You care much for young Cassia. Is she your mistress?"

"No," I'd said sharply, then softened my tone as I caught sight of her, wrapped in her palla, speaking earnestly to Marcianus. "She is my friend."

AUTHOR'S NOTE

Thank you for reading! I'm thrilled to present Book 1 in the Leonidas the Gladiator mystery series.

For years I've been picturing a former gladiator wandering the streets of Rome, becoming involved in other people's troubles while dealing with his own. With him is Cassia, trained as a scribe, assisting him with her book smarts and knowledge of the Roman upper classes.

I was able to get the project partway off the ground with the novella, *Blood Debts*. That story takes place after *Blood of a Gladiator*—I wrote it to insert into an anthology (although it's also available on its own), but preferred a full-length novel to introduce Leonidas and Cassia and their circumstances and launch the series. *Blood Debts* can be considered Book 1.5, and the series continues after that.

I had the great fortune to travel to Rome to research this series. I was overawed by the ruins of the Forum Romanum, and I never wanted to leave! I could easily picture Leonidas walking the stone-paved streets and passing beneath the massive columns of the Temple of Saturn and that of Castor and Pollux.

One reason I went to Rome was to get a sense of the scale of it. Many photographs of the Forum are taken from the balcony of the Capitoline Museum above it (I did this too—the museum is well worth the visit), but while the Capitoline Museum has a great view, it does not give me the same feeling as standing on the Via Sacra with the monuments towering above me. They are huge! The engineering that went into constructing these buildings is amazing.

While many of the ruins we see today did not exist in Leonidas's time (the reign of Nero: AD 54-68), I was still able to get a sense of what he would see, how much energy it takes to climb the Palatine Hill or up to the Capitoline, and what richness had been in the *domii* of the Palatine. Excavations continue to reveal more each year.

Though Leonidas was freed long before the Flavian Amphitheater (Colosseum) was constructed, I of course had to take an extensive tour of it, going to the underground tunnels and cells where the gladiators and animals were kept, as well as to the arena floor. The amphitheater's oval was elongated so that all seats had a great view.

I stood on the Colosseum floor, looking up at the ring of seats, and imagined it filled to capacity, with the roar of the crowd eager to witness violence and blood.

All I could think was, "Not for me!" I'll leave the fighting and the adulation to Leonidas and his colleagues.

I chose to set these books in the reign of Nero because so much happened during that time: the great fire, the building of the Golden House, the Jewish revolt, the revolt of Boadicea, and the revolt of Vindex that led to Nero's downfall.

Many more novels for Leonidas are planned as he adapts to his new life and he and Cassia learn more about each other.

Mystery, murder, mayhem, intrigue, and Roman history await!

If you'd like to be kept informed of when new books are released, please sign up for my email blasts at:

http://eepurl.com/5n7rz

ALSO BY ASHLEY GARDNER

Leonidas the Gladiator Mysteries

Blood of a Gladiator

Blood Debts (novella)

A Gladiator's Tale

Captain Lacey Regency Mystery Series

The Hanover Square Affair

A Regimental Murder

The Glass House

The Sudbury School Murders

The Necklace Affair

A Body in Berkeley Square

A Covent Garden Mystery

A Death in Norfolk

A Disappearance in Drury Lane

Murder in Grosvenor Square

The Thames River Murders

The Alexandria Affair

A Mystery at Carlton House

Murder in St. Giles

Death at Brighton Pavilion

The Custom House Murders

Kat Holloway "Below Stairs" Victorian Mysteries

(writing as Jennifer Ashley)

A Soupçon of Poison

Death Below Stairs

Scandal Above Stairs

Death in Kew Gardens

Murder in the East End

Mystery Anthologies

Past Crimes

ABOUT THE AUTHOR

Award-winning Ashley Gardner is a pseudonym for *New York Times* bestselling author Jennifer Ashley. Under both names—and a third, Allyson James—Ashley has written more than 100 published novels and novellas in mystery, romance, historical fiction, and fantasy. Ashley's books have been translated into more than a dozen different languages and have earned starred reviews *Publisher's Weekly* and *Booklist.* When she isn't writing, she indulges her love for history by researching and building miniature houses and furniture from many periods.

More about her series can be found at the website: www.gardnermysteries.com. Stay up to date on new releases by joining her email alerts here:

http://eepurl.com/5n7rz

Made in the USA
Monee, IL
14 May 2021

68617573R00146